NECROPHOBIA 4
HELL CITY

JACK HAMLYN

NECROLOGUE

By that point, I wasn't even sure how long all of it had been going on. Time seemed to have lost all meaning. I could only remember events.

I remembered my life in Yonkers with my son, Paul, and my wife, Ricki. I remembered that the first zombie I saw was Bill Deforest. He had been dead a week. I found him feeding on one of my neighbors. That's how it had started for me. After that, the dead were everywhere, filling the streets. I remember hiding out in my basement with Ricki and Paul and Diane, Ricki's sister. I remember that first night very well—the dead tore the neighborhood and our house apart and we trembled, waiting for them. The next day we headed out with another neighbor, Jimmy LaRue, and hooked up with my old friend, Tuck. Tuck, an ornery ex-Marine Vietnam War hero, had a survival bunker, a tower, and we did all right there until an air strike destroyed it. I remember the night we fled from it very well because that was the night the zombies got Ricki and there wasn't a damn thing I could do about it.

We hid out at one place after the other. Long story short, we met a woman named Riley who had escaped from a school in the Bronx where she was being held captive by ARM (the American Resistance Movement) in a school that had become a sort of rape camp. We staged a raid on the school and got nearly all the women out of there. We were proud of that. I know I was. It was fights like that that kept me sane.

After that?

Well, one raid after another, always on the move as the dead stalked us and we fought running battles with ARM and countless other survivalist groups. I ended up on my own in NYC—the city of the dead—and fought street by street, house by house, only to be drafted by The Brigade and pressed into a zombie extermination unit. The entire idea was ridiculous, of course. There were millions and millions of zombies in NYC. Exterminating them one by one was an impossible task. Suffice to say I escaped to the Catskills to find my friends, ended up in a helicopter crash, was hunted by survivalists, befriended by a cannibal who fed me human meat (I didn't know it at the time) and escaped again to hook up with Robin. Still trying to find my family, Robin and I fought outlaw bikers and zombies and were imprisoned in an ARM blood farm which was liberated by mutants. I'll skip the maggot entity—it still makes my flesh crawl.

After all that, I found Tuck and the others or they found me and then we were heading back to the Catskills and the Silo. And the truly ugly part was that I had the worst feeling we weren't going to make it.

DEAD ON ARRIVAL

"How long?"

Tuck smiled in the flashlight beam. "About ten more minutes, give or take. These babies have fifty gallon tanks, Steve. You can't fill them in five minutes, you know."

I knew, but I was worried. We were standing in the parking lot of a gas station that was long abandoned like everything else. Our armored vehicles—Guardian ASVs—were pulled up to the back of a big diesel tanker that had been left there probably during the primary Necrophage outbreak. In my mind, I could just about see the driver getting his rig into the lot to unload his tank, but he never did because he was infected. He probably died and rose up to walk amongst the ranks of the living dead.

That was the ugly reality of this brave new world of ours where dead things no longer stayed in their graves, but violated all the rules of tried and true natural science and walked again as flesh-eating zombies. It sounded like the plot of a bad movie or a cheap paperback, but it was true enough. God knew, it was true enough.

Tuck, ever resourceful, had spied the parked tanker when they had passed it the day before and made a mental note of it for refueling the Guardians. He and Jimmy handled it. It was really a matter of popping the locks on the tanker valves, then plugging the hose into the tanks of the Guardians and opening the valve with a wrench. It was strictly gravity feed so we didn't need a pump.

But it took time.

More time, I thought, than we really had to spare.

Four hours before, Robin Arduccio—my teenage sidekick, you might say—and I had hooked up with Tuck and the others by sheer chance after we fled the hellzone of Perryville. We brought another survivor along with us, Sandy, and that brought our number up to eleven. We were spread out across the parking lot on perimeter guard. While the vehicles were refueling, we were very vulnerable and I think we all felt it.

I know I did.

We had put a lot of miles behind us, but we had a long way to go back up to the Catskills to the Silo. I had never been there. It was a situation Tuck and the others fell into during my absence. I was excited about it, though. Not just because of the security of the place and the people there—nice, normal people—and the fresh food and soft beds and hot showers, but because that's where my son was. I had been gone from him for over six weeks by my figuring and maybe as much as two months. There was no way to know exactly. All that time while I was fighting to survive so I could get back to him he had thought I was dead.

To me, that was the greatest horror of all.

Paul had lost his mother to hordes of the walking dead and now he was living with the awful certainty that he had lost me, too. It was something I had been living with for a long time and it was eating me alive. I had already gotten on the radio several times, but even at long range it's only good for about twenty miles and the Catskills, of course, play havoc with communications.

That's why I was itching to get going again.

Every mile brought me closer to the point where I could communicate with the Silo and let him know I was all right. Patience. It was really just a matter of patience, but I was running real low on that. Feeling on edge, I walked over to Robin and bummed a cigarette from her. She and Ginny were talking about something very heatedly, but fell silent as soon as I got within hearing range. That made part of me paranoid, while another part really didn't care.

"Thanks," I said, getting a nice little kick of nicotine that sharpened my mind.

"Well, I'm always happy to be of service," Robin said. "That's what I'm here for."

Ginny sighed.

I smiled. Sarcasm was part and parcel of who and what Robin was and it helped her keep her edge, you just had to learn not to take it too seriously. I scanned the parking lot, not really liking what I saw. Everyone stood around in little groups chatting, not paying much attention to what was going on around them. Scott and Seppy, two of the Silo crew I didn't know real well, were chatting and laughing about something. Carrie and Sandy were leaning up against one of the Guardians. Diane and Sabelia were the only ones that looked vigilant, but both of them seemed more interested in me than any potential threat.

But I was okay. I had been through the ringer in the past six weeks and I looked rough. There was no denying that, but I was far from done in.

The minutes crawled by.

My nerves were getting worse. Something was bothering me. Whether it was the fact that we were on the outskirts of a little town which was always a threat or I just needed some damn sleep, I couldn't be sure.

"Shit!" I heard Scott say. "They're coming!"

We were all alert then and we had weapons in our hands. I saw right away what he was talking about. The dead were coming. And not just three or four of them but dozens coming from the direction of the town. They pushed a wave of hot putrescence before them as they came out of the darkness. We started shooting right away, dropping them as they came on.

"See if you can hold 'em off a few more minutes," Tuck said. "We almost got a full belly here."

Easier said than done.

Diane climbed into the Guardian that was already fueled, turned it over and got the lights on so we could see just what sort of hell was facing us. It was bad, real bad. The zombies were coming in waves like breakers crashing onto a beach. There were hundreds of them and they were coming for us. We were doing a good job of dropping the scattered groups out in front, but there was no way we could hope to repel the bulk of them with nothing but M4 rifles. We needed heavier firepower.

Carrie climbed up into the turret, the remote weapons station, and sighted in on the deadheads with the M2 machinegun. She started firing into their ranks, .50-caliber rounds literally making them explode as she strafed them with short, economical bursts to save on ammo.

Everyone else had drawn back to the vehicles.

"All right, load up, everyone!" I called out. "There's too many of them!"

They needed no further urging, climbing in through the side doors. By then, the zombies were filling the parking lot despite the fact that Carrie was cutting them down like trees. There was always more and more. Jimmy, Scott, Seppy, Ginny, and Carrie hopped into one Guardian and the rest of us climbed into the other.

The Guardians were great.

Make no mistake about it, but they were cramped. They were designed for four people—driver, commander, gunner, and dismount—not six. I remember guys in Iraq that loved them, but hated how tight they were inside, especially when they were outfitted in full battle rattle.

"Got it!" Tuck said.

He climbed in and we shut the doors. There were so damn many zombies that Ginny in the lead Guardian and Sabelia in ours, started blasting away with not only the .50-cals but with the 40mm grenade launchers, cutting us a path. Diane was driving our Guardian and I climbed into the right seat, the commander's chair, and watched the action through the bulletproof windows.

"QUIT FIRING!" Tuck shouted at Sabelia in the turret. He pushed past me and got on the radio and told Jimmy pretty much the same thing, that he wanted no shooting.

"What the hell's up with you?" Diane asked him.

"I'm conserving ammo. We'll need it later."

"So we're just going to sit here and twiddle our thumbs?" Sabelia said.

Tuck turned to me. "Tell your old lady that I don't twiddle."

Sabelia was fuming, her hot Latin blood nearing full boil. I gave her a look that told her to play along. I knew Tuck well enough to know he was up to something. He had a plan, but he would not share it until he was ready.

"We're in no danger," he said. "We're locked in. They can't get at us."

"I don't get it," Robin said.

But I did. I got it real well. Tuck was up to something. He had some kind of master plan in mind, only he wasn't going to share it with us until he was damned good and ready. I only understood one small part of it.

He was using us as bait.

CREMATION

Up in the front, I watched the dead massing.

It was surreal and nightmarish.

In the floodlights of the Guardian, the dead swarmed in with gnashing mouths and hooked fingers. Several approached the front of the vehicle, their faces bloodless and waxen, patched with mildew and grave fungi. More and more moved in, staring into the lights with eyes like boiled eggs, white and oily. For a moment or two, they just stood there like graveyard statues. Then they began to move, trudging through the remains of the others that the machineguns had ripped open. There were gutted torsos and scattered limbs, heads with faces blasted free, bones and blood and excreta…a liquid slopping pool of it like the drainage from a slaughterhouse.

"Oh God," I heard Diane say.

I threw a spotlight out there and saw nothing but the dead crowding in until the lights were filled with what seemed hundreds of corpse faces. It was like the gates of Hell had been thrown open.

"We're going to have to blast our way out," Sabelia said.

"Not a good idea," Tuck told her.

"Why the hell not?" Sabelia asked.

But I already knew.

I could smell it.

The stench of the dead was strong out there, as it came in through the air vents and firing ports. But there was another smell now: diesel fuel. It was pungent and gagging. That was Tuck's plan, of course. The fuel was still running from the tanker out there, gushing from the hose and spreading across the parking lot.

I got on the radio. "Jimmy, no shooting. I don't care what happens. No shooting. We're sitting in a lake of fuel."

"What the hell happened?" came his reply.

"Tuck forgot to shut the valve off on the tanker."

Tuck laughed with a perfectly evil sort of sound.

The radio crackled. *"Funny how he forgets things."*

"Yeah, ain't it?"

Robin giggled. "Good old Tuck," she said. "Using us as fucking bait so he can have a zombie barbecue."

Tuck laughed again.

Meanwhile, the zombies were filling the lot steadily. Several dozen were investigating the Guardians. They knew we were in there and their hunger demanded that they get at us. They kept slapping their hands against the doors, clawing and scraping and pounding their fists. More and more swelled in.

By then, the stink of diesel fuel was making our eyes water.

The girls were coughing and making gagging sounds. I was, too.

"Man, I'm getting a serious head rush here," Diane said, as if she were enjoying it.

"Okay, Tuck, that's enough now," Robin said. "I'm pretty thoroughly asphyxiated here."

He turned to me. "Steve, tell Jimmy to back on out. Tell him to cut around the station and into the field. Get on the road. We'll join him there."

I relayed the message and Jimmy's Guardian revved up and backed away into the darkness. I could hear zombies thudding off of it, the tires rolling over them. Then we were backing away, too, knocking clusters of them aside and rolling over still more. The Guardian lurched as it smashed them beneath its wheels with crunching and pulping sounds. It was sickening. Once we were free of the masses, Diane swung the vehicle around and paused at the edge of the field as Tuck had instructed her.

"All right," he said as wave upon wave of the dead filled the parking lot. "Lob some incendiaries at them, Sabelia. When she lets 'em fly, drive like hell, Diane!"

Sabelia swung the turret around, sighting in on the undead mobs with the roof-mounted night sight and opened up with the 40mm grenade launcher. The MK 19 is technically a grenade machinegun because it puts out something like sixty rounds per minute. We didn't need that kind of firepower, though, so Sabelia just fired off a couple rounds and that was plenty. As soon as they flew, Diane got the Guardian rolling with some haste.

Through one of the gun ports, I saw what happened.

The white phosphorus rounds struck dead center of the zombie army with hissing red-white clouds of fire. The lake of diesel fuel went up instantly. It made a rushing *VAROOOOOM!* sort of sound, engulfing not only the dead in an eruption of flames, but the gas station and the tanker truck, too.

And that went next.

There was a thundering explosion that made the Guardian jump and the lot, the station itself...hell, even the *trees* nearby went up in the mother of all conflagrations, an immense, blinding fireburst as the tanker split open like a peanut shell and released an ocean of burning fuel. I saw a gigantic white-hot mass of rolling fire rise two-hundred feet into the air and then rain back down like napalm. The zombies were incinerated by that point and black clouds of smoke blew across the field, rising high into the sky like the spouts of tornadoes.

Even some distance away inside the Guardian, we felt the heat.

By then, we were rolling down the road and gradually the glowing inferno that painted the sky red disappeared behind us.

"See, Tuck?" Robin said. "That's why little boys shouldn't play with matches."

There was silence for maybe two seconds before we all burst into laughter. If comedy depended on timing, then Robin's was perfect.

KICKED IN THE TEETH

About twenty miles down the road, the shit started flying as we suspected it would. It began when the radio crackled and Jimmy came over the com and said, *"We just seen lights up ahead. Looks like a chopper coming in low...yeah, there it is again."*

By then, Diane had spotted it. "I saw it. It just flew back over the treetops."

"Things are going to get hairy now," Tuck said.

He was right. There was no way to know at that point what kind of chopper we were dealing with. Maybe it was just an unarmed Blackhawk out on a scouting mission or a fully-armed Kiowa Warrior or Apache. It was hard to say. ARM had been liberating military hardware all over the state from what I heard and maybe the country, too. They could have had just about anything. About the only thing we had to answer back with was the .50-cal machineguns on the Guardians...that was, if we could draw the chopper in close enough.

The atmosphere grew decidedly tense.

"Are we in danger?" Sandy asked.

"Now what gave you that idea?" Robin said.

"Jimmy wants to know what to do," Diane called out.

"Tell him to keep rolling for now," Tuck told her. He called up to Sabelia in the basket. "I'm gonna spell you up there for a bit."

She climbed down and he went up to the remote weapons station. Up there, he could manipulate the .50-cal and grenade launchers. That was the beauty of the Guardian. Like the Strykers I knew so well, you could do all your fighting by remote control while under the hood of the armored turret. Of course, if that chopper had air-to-surface antitank missiles, the basket, like the rest of the vehicle, was about to become an iron coffin.

The chopper made another pass, this time flying less than a hundred feet above both Guardians. They didn't engage any weapons, but I had the nastiest feeling that was about to happen.

"Gotta be those ARM pukes," Tuck called out.

The American Resistance Movement were the primary scavengers atop the bone pile of the country. I refuse to call them predators exactly. I preferred to liken them to rats. We'd had nothing but trouble from them as we fought to stay alive and every chance we had, we gave as good as we got. Something that wasn't always so easy because there were so few of us and so many of them. There were lots of survivalist enclaves out robbing and murdering each other, but ARM was the worst. There were thousands of them, remains of real military units and lots of trigger-happy GI Joe wannabees that saw the fall of civilization as their golden moment to get weapons in their hands and act out their fantasies.

Sandy was shaking.

She'd been through a lot and was not exactly anyone's idea of a hardcore survivor type. She was pretty and blonde and leggy, strictly cheerleader fodder, the baton-twirler sort. Not exactly the person you'd want to share a foxhole with or have watching your back.

"Any last words?" Robin asked her with her usual sarcasm. "I'll see that they put them on your headstone."

"Shut up," Sandy said quietly, a little uneasy about incurring Robin's wrath being that Robin had already belted her once earlier in the day for being a drama queen.

Robin giggled. "Go ahead, just pretend you're writing your senior will again. *I leave my perfectly adorable pretty purple pumps to Buffy and my ponytail rings to Summer and all the wild times at Key Club to Bambi! Kaay! Kaay! Raa! Raa!*"

I felt Sabelia growing tense next to me. It seemed like every muscle in her body had tightened. She was going to tell Robin to shut the hell up—which rarely did any good—but Sandy beat her to it. "How about you just kiss my ass?" she said.

Sabelia loosened next to me and tried not to smile.

"Score one for the princess!" Robin said.

Where it all was leading, I didn't know, and I never found out because there was a loud explosion very close by and the Guardian trembled.

"It's not the chopper!" Tuck called down to us. "But we got incoming!"

11

There were two more explosions, neither of them near enough to do more than rattle us, but they were getting closer.

The radio crackled again and Jimmy, sounding a little shaken, said, *"We're getting shelled...might be mortars...I can't tell."*

He was right. I could hear the thumping of them in the distance, then the whistling/screeching sound as they passed overhead. Two more hit and the Guardian shook with the impact which sounded like trees cracking in half.

Tuck said he hadn't seen the chopper again and Jimmy confirmed that if it was around, then it was flying high. *Whump! Whump! Whump!* The shells were getting closer. Whoever was firing them was trying to march them in on us. I'd been through barrages in Iraq when insurgents harassed us with 82mm mortars. I knew very well the sort of destruction those things could bring down.

In the back of the Guardian, nobody was saying a thing. Even Robin wasn't smarting off for a change. We were all on edge, wired tight with stress. We were juiced with adrenaline, our hearts thudding in our chests. Sweat kept running down my face and gathering under my eyes. The Guardian was essentially a metal box on wheels and it was getting hot in there.

"We got high hills to either side of us," Tuck said. "They must be up there, sighting us in."

There was nothing we could do but pour on the speed and hope we made it out of the breach in one piece.

Sandy was breathing very hard. "I want to get out," she said, the claustrophobia enfolding her like arms. "Please...I really need to get out of here."

"You can't get out," Sabelia told her. "You'd get torn apart out there."

"We got shooters in the woods! We're in a fucking funnel!" Jimmy cried over the radio.

Diane told him to keep pushing on, that we couldn't stop now. There was no going back.

Bullets began to graze the armor of the Guardians. *Ping! Ping! Ping! Thunk! Thunk! Thunk!* They were pouring small arms fire at us from the treeline, but I had yet to hear the bark of any big guns, mostly 9mms and the like I was guessing, some light machineguns. The Guardians could withstand that. Our only real hope was that we'd drive right out of it.

I got up and went up front with Diane.

The jarring of more incoming mortars nearly threw me off my feet. The flashing of their explosions was blinding up in the cab. Bullets were still grazing the outer plating of the vehicle and I could see green tracer rounds coming at us from both sides of the road. This couldn't be a coincidence. This many men all lined up and ready to shoot...no, we had been expected. This was a trap and we had rolled right into it. But it was too late to retreat now.

I could see Jimmy's Guardian directly ahead of us. There were so many tracer rounds flying, it looked like a luminous green spider's web was dropping over it. The slugs threw off sparks as they hit.

Up in the basket, Tuck was swearing.

He did his best work when he was pissed.

He opened up on the treeline with the 40mm grenade launcher, saturating enemy positions with high explosive and white phosphorus rounds. The HE shook them out of their hides and the WP lit their world on fire. He fired the launcher off and on, switching between it and the M2 .50-cal machinegun, ripping apart the real estate and knocking trees down. I distinctly heard men screaming and the firing slacked off some. Jimmy's Guardian was pouring fire into the opposite side of the road, lighting up the treeline.

Both vehicles were moving at top speed by then, shaking and rattling and it wasn't exactly a comfortable ride. Mortars screamed overhead and each time they hit, the vehicle shook and gear flew off the racks. Sandy was screaming, fighting with a belt of machinegun ammo that had dropped on her.

Maybe the small arms fire was tapering off, but the mortars were really raining down. Their blasts made the Guardian jump and lurch and I was thrown down and when I got up, I was thrown down again. I fought my way to my knees and a mortar round exploded right in front of the vehicle with a rocking concussion and a blinding white flash. Shrapnel slammed into the windshield.

Boom! Boom! Boom!

RPGs now. They were landing all around us, mixing it up with the mortar rounds. Sometimes a series of convulsive explosions made the Guardian jump up in the air and come crashing down. But again and again we were in one piece, still pushing forward, unstoppable, it seemed.

Then an RPG slammed into the side of the Guardian and there was a rocketing explosion. Shrapnel came right through one of the windows, even though the outer ceramic plating absorbed most of the blow.

Diane cried out and I saw her cover her face.

Sandy was shrieking.

I crawled up to Diane, jumping behind the wheel. A sliver of shrapnel had creased the crown of her head. No real damage, just a lot of blood. In the chaos, Sabelia got the first aid kit and wound Diane's head up in gauze. It was the best that could be done under the circumstances.

Now we were really in the shit.

Not just mortars and RPGs, but IEDs now. The road had been mined and we were driving right through squalls of shrapnel. Flying dirt and smoke filled the air and I couldn't even see Jimmy's Guardian. It was like being at ground zero in Hell. Tuck was still blasting away, but more selectively and I knew he was running low on ammo. If we didn't get out of this fucking mess soon, we wouldn't get out at all.

"Keep pushing it!" Tuck called to me, as he racked the bolt on the M2. "Don't fucking slow down for a second!"

I had no intention of that.

He hammered away with the .50-cal and I knew he wasn't doing anything but laying down a curtain of suppressive fire to shut down the shooters and particularly the RPG guys.

The smoke cleared for a moment or two and I saw an RPG slam into Jimmy's Guardian followed by a second or third that made it jump all over the road. It couldn't take much more beating.

"I got wounded over here!" He called out.

"Keep rolling!" I told him. "You've got to keep rolling!"

Those words had barely left my mouth when an IED was triggered just beneath his Guardian and the entire thing burst into flame. Then another and another exploded and it was thrown up into the air, crashing down and rolling over…right on top of another IED that went with a thundering roar and the Guardian went up into the air again, crashing down broken and burning, but somehow righting itself.

"JIMMY!" I shouted.

I slowed as dust and smoke enveloped our vehicle and there was an immense explosion, throwing me to the floor and I was knocked cold.

SURVIVORS

There was smoke. Thick acrid smoke that burned my eyes and seared my throat. I tried to blink my eyes and it felt like there was salt in them. I tried to swallow but my throat was dry as dust. I kept going in and out of consciousness, trying to stay awake but finding it very difficult. I couldn't remember the last time I had a decent night's sleep. It was bound to catch up with me, of course, but I could have thought of a better time and a better place.

Voices were calling my name.

I felt hands on me and for a moment or two I thought they might be ARM puss-heads or maybe the dead. But these were not rough hands. They were gentle yet insistent. I think part of my brain came out of it before I was completely conscious because what snapped me awake was my own voice saying, "What the hell do you want?"

Somebody said something and I was dragged outside and placed on the ground.

"Fuck happened?" I said.

"IED," Sabelia said. "Thank God you're okay."

"Is anyone...?"

She shook her head. "No, they're fine. Banged up but fine."

A cigarette was placed between my lips and I took a pull of it. Robin was holding it. "Shit, Big Steve, I thought you were dead."

"Well, I'm not."

"Figures. I already had the music picked out for the service and I was going to recruit a couple deadheads to be pallbearers."

She giggled at that. Nobody else did. Nobody really seemed to understand her sense of humor.

I saw a shape come walking over. It was limping a bit, but I could see it was Jimmy LaRue and he was still in one piece. He was carrying a carbine like the others. "Glad to see you're still kicking, Steve," he said.

He told me his Guardian got hit by RPGs and two command-and-control IEDs. I knew that much. I saw it get blown up into the air, breaking apart and on fire when it came back down. Jimmy survived it okay, as did his crew, miraculously. I thought they were goners. Ginny had taken some shrapnel in her left arm, but she would survive. Carrie was unscathed for the most part. They were all banged-up pretty good, but they were lucky to be alive and whole. Jimmy said he was sore as hell, but nothing was broken. Maybe he was in his sixties and beginning to lean toward seventy, but he had survived a tour with the River Rats in the Mekong Delta back in 1967. He was definitely a survivor type.

Diane came over, her head bandaged like Henry from *The Red Badge of Courage,* one of my favorite books. She laid everything out for me very carefully. Both Guardians were done in. Jimmy's was pretty much totaled. I knew that because I could see it down the road, still burning. The one I had been driving would never run again without a mechanic. But they had scavenged ammo and grenades from it, as well as the first aid kit, water and MREs, the SAW—Squad Automatic Weapon—and several belts for it. Carrie and Tuck were out reconnoitering.

"No sign of ARM?" I asked.

"No sign of *anybody,*" Sabelia put in. "If it was ARM, they must have pulled out after they blew up the Guardians."

That didn't make much sense to me unless that had been their objective all along—to knock us out of commission. Maybe…still, though, I was suspicious. We were about half a city block from the wrecked and burning vehicles. There was plenty of light to see by, but thus far no one had shown.

The others moved off to guard the perimeter, even Robin who had found something of a friend in Ginny. Probably because they both had little patience with Sandy who sat alone, back up to a tree. When they were gone, Sabelia pressed her lips against mine. Maybe she didn't expect me to kiss her back, but I did. I kissed her like I had never felt a woman's lips before. For the longest time I had pretty much ignored her interest in me out of respect for Ricki, but with what I had been through in the past six weeks or so I wasn't wasting anymore time.

"Well, you *did* miss me," she said.

I held her face in my hands. It was a pretty face—high cheekbones, full lips, big dark eyes and perfect olive skin marred only by an old knife scar across the bridge of her nose that gave her face real character and a brooding, exotic sensuality. "Want to go in the woods and fool around?" I said.

She laughed and so did I. It felt good to laugh.

Tuck came back with Carrie in tow. He called us together. "We got a town down below," he told us, stroking his gray ZZ Top beard. "We got to hump it over a few hills and up a ridgeline, but there's definitely a town down there. Good-sized. We can't hang around here."

There was no argument on that.

We formed up with Tuck out front carrying the SAW, Sabelia and I taking up the back door, everyone else in-between walking single file, weapons at the ready save for Ginny and Diane given their injuries. Everyone was carrying M4 carbines, save for Seppy and I who had Mossberg 500 tactical shotguns. The SAW is an M249 light machinegun, an infantry support weapon that gives you the fire power of a machinegun but is portable and easy to handle and very accurate. I'd carried one more than once in Iraq during a few weeks of house to house fighting in Fallujah. We had four soft packs of 200 rounds each for it. Combined with everything else we were carrying, we were loaded for bear.

Robin still wasn't walking real good from the bullet that grazed her leg in Perryville, but she was doing okay leaning up against Ginny. We pushed through the woods, up one hill and down another. As we got up on top of the ridgeline, we could see the town spread out beneath us. It was dark, very dark, but we didn't have much choice.

"I have a real bad feeling about this, man," Diane said.

I was used to her and her prophecies; they seemed to run in the family. Mostly I dismissed them, but as we moved down towards the town I was almost certain that she was right.

DEADTOWN

When we got into the town proper—we still didn't know the name of the place—I was struck by the eerie silence that laid over the streets. Other than overgrown lots and abandoned vehicles, everything looked relatively untouched. The sound of our marching footfalls was unbearably loud and it went right up my spine. I was reminded a little too much of the horror in Perryville. There was no goddamn way I was going through something like that again, just no way.

But I was being paranoid.

I saw no bones in the streets, nothing but debris and some scattered wreckage.

Nobody spoke. Nobody dared to. We were expecting the zombies to show and if not them, maybe the local militia or whatever stripe of crazies that called this place home.

I marched along with the others, unable to shake the unsettling feeling that we were being watched. I don't know if anyone else felt it, but for me it was bad. The moonlit streets seemed to be filled with moving shadows. Every time I blinked, they were gone. It was just nerves. That's what I kept telling myself, but I didn't believe it much as I wanted to.

The paranoia began to increase in me.

It was more than just what Diane said. It was real, almost palpable around me and I couldn't put a name to it. I didn't think this town was like Perryville; I thought it was even worse. But I had no reason to think that.

I saw abandoned cars everywhere. These were not dramatic abandonments, but simply cars left at curbs and in driveways to rust and flake away through the seasons. No one would ever climb into them again. Street by street, the town was deserted. We passed silent churches and moved through neighborhoods whose houses stood like monuments in a cemetery. I was amazed at what seemed to be the lack of looting and vandalism. The windows of stores were not broken, the homes seemed tidy even if their lawns were overgrown. This was not what I was used to seeing. I saw no bones. No wreckage. No evidence that battles had been fought or even simple firefights. The town was like a movie set or a restored ghost town. It was empty, as far as we could tell, but it did not feel exactly untenanted.

"Is it just me, man, or is this place creepy?" Diane said.

Tuck shushed her because he did not want any talking. His military mind was expecting the worst. And that was something which had kept us alive and breathing many times. He was tense, maybe expecting an ambush. I was expecting something, too, but it was nothing of that variety. Just what, I could not honestly say. We were moving in perfect, single-file formation the way soldiers do on patrol in enemy territory. Tuck was on point, about twenty feet ahead of us now, moving carefully and quietly.

Oh yes, he was tense all right.

Very tense.

But was that because he expected trouble or because, like me, he felt menace but could not identify it?

ARM had hit us pretty damn hard out on the highway and we had no reason to think it was over. Yet, none of it made any real sense. Okay, they used a combination of RPGs and carefully-concealed IEDs to take us out, to disable our vehicles. But once that was done, why didn't they come out and mop us up? Why did they let us live? What could be the point?

Unless this *was* the point.

They had to know that we would seek shelter and this conveniently placed town was the first place we would go. It was only logical. Had all the earlier shooting just been to drive us farther down the road to the RPG/IED trap? Or was I just being hopelessly paranoid? As I walked those dark, echoing streets it did not seem paranoid at all, regardless of the planning that would have gone into something like that. Maybe the trap was already set. Maybe they saw Tuck and the others pass in the Guardians and figured they'd be coming back. Christ, I could have filled a bag with what-ifs and maybes.

I decided the best thing to do, was to concentrate on what we were doing and quit speculating.

Tuck kept leading and we kept following. I think by that point, I was all for high-tailing it out and sleeping in the woods. The town was getting under my skin and the further we went, the deeper it burrowed in until it began to gnaw at my nerve endings.

"There's something funny about this damn place," Robin said and from the tone of her voice I could tell she wasn't fooling around.

"You got that right," Diane said quietly.

Tuck paused and looked back at us. "Zip it!"

"Well, I'm not *zipping* it," Robin told him. "You people aren't paying attention."

Tuck looked angry. "You trying to get us killed?"

"No, I'm trying to keep us *from* getting killed," Robin told him and before he could open his mouth, she pointed up at a telephone pole. "Every damn one of those poles has a little box on it. *Look!*"

She was right.

Up near the top of every telephone pole there was a little metal box. I had seen them, but I figured they were some kind of telecommunications gadget. Tuck led us out again to another pole and another metal box. Two more poles a block apart, same thing. He clicked on the tactical flashlight on his M4 and beamed it on the suspicious box. There was nothing about it that would really catch the eye…except in the center of it there was a shiny round black glass orb.

"Looks like an eye," Ginny said.

"Yeah, a *fish*eye," I said. "That's a security camera."

"Well, it can't be working anymore," Carrie pointed out.

True, but I didn't like it. Security cameras were common in urban areas, but not in small towns. I didn't know how big this city was—what I could see of it, I guessed maybe 20,000 people before Zombpox—but I doubted there would be enough crime to warrant the installation of a video security system. It just didn't make sense. It was but another thing about that place that raised my hackles.

"Why cameras? Why here?" Sabelia asked.

"Big Brother's watching," Diane said. "Maybe it had something to do with the NSA or something."

Tuck and I looked at each other and although neither of us said anything, we both damn well knew this was nothing so obvious. Carrie was probably right—it wasn't working anymore. Why would it be? There was nothing to watch over now.

Yeah, but there had been. Once upon a time there was something special about this place. Something very special.

What that was, I couldn't guess.

"It's all history," Tuck said in his most reassuring voice. "Let's not worry about it. You people can argue your conspiracy theories when we get a roof over our heads."

He was right on that.

He got no argument because I think we were all feeling a little paranoid by then and we all needed to get somewhere safe.

CHARNEL HOUSE

Shelter was our priority and exactly what Tuck was looking for. But I knew he didn't want just any place, but something defensible with an exit in case we had to run. I was starting to question the logic of coming into the town at all. Maybe we would have been better off hiding in the woods and coming by daylight. Then again, if the remainders of the force that had attacked us on the road attacked us out in the open, we wouldn't last ten minutes. No, Tuck was doing the right thing.

He led us through an alley and then called us together.

He saw something he liked.

"That house over there," he said, indicating a tall two-story brick structure across the street. "That looks pretty good."

"What's so special about it?" Robin asked.

"It's defensible."

And it was. There were vacant lots to either side of it. If somebody wanted to make an assault on it, they would have to cover a lot of open ground to do it. And it was brick. It could take a lot of punishment. Maybe Tuck was overdoing it, but when it came to our safety his heart was always in the right place.

"Looks like it'll do in a pinch," Jimmy said.

"So let's get moving," Sabelia said.

Born and bred in the urban jungle, she knew very well just how dangerous city streets could be, particularly these days. She was nervous. Hell, she was wired. When I tried to touch her to reassure her, she pulled away. Her back was up about coming into this town in the first place. A sentiment, I think, that was echoed by Diane and Ginny, possibly even Carrie. The others just wanted a safe place to hole up until daylight.

"A few of us better check it out first," I said. "No sense in endangering everyone."

"Good thinking," Jimmy said.

"Brilliant," Robin said with all due sarcasm. "You can always count on Steve to come up with the smart ideas."

"Zip it," Tuck said.

She shook her head. "Can't. I didn't come with a zip attachment. I blame it on my mother."

As Tuck and Robin tried to out-smartass and out-intimidate each other, I was keeping an eye on Scott and Seppy. Like I said, I didn't know much about them. I'd only known them a few hours, but they weren't exactly friendly. They stayed together and barely said anything. There was something funny about that. They were from the Silo crew and I had gotten a vague indication once or twice that Sabelia did not trust them and that was good enough for me.

"How about I take Scott and Seppy with me?" I suggested. "We'll signal you guys with a flashlight when it's safe to come."

"No," Sabelia said instantly.

Tuck considered it, but I knew he hated to be left out of the action.

"Thing is," Scott said. "After what happened on the road, I'm not sure I'm up to it. My nerves are rattled."

Seppy nodded. "Me, too. Sorry, guys."

"Don't matter," Tuck said. "You two are staying here." He looked over at me. "You and me are going to check it out. The rest of you wait here."

My little test failed. I really had no reason to doubt them, yet I did. I was reminded of Phil Boncek, a guy who had hooked up with us in the past. He had been with ARM, but he fought valiantly with us. Tuck told me he had died outside Perryville, overwhelmed by zombies. I knew that much because later I had shot him down. Point being, we hadn't completely trusted him either and he turned out all right. Maybe Scotty and Seppy were okay, too.

"I think we should all go," Carrie said.

But Tuck shook his head. "No, that's too dangerous. Just me and Steve."

I could see that some of them bristled at the idea, but nobody—Robin included—argued with him. When it came down to the possibility of close-in fighting, Tuck got into the zone, into a primitive drive of aggression, and the last thing you wanted to do was argue with him when he got like that.

Make no mistake, Robin would have argued with him like she did about everything else if her leg wasn't still sore from being creased by a bullet. Diane might have, too. Same for Ginny. But they were both hurting from shrapnel wounds. Jimmy was in no shape for the close-quarter stuff either and his age was definitely a factor. I knew Sabelia had serious street smarts and gang-fighting experience from her checkered past in the Bronx. She was tough and would have proved lethal close-in, but only Tuck and I had any real assault training.

So off we went.

Tuck took an M4 and extra mags. I took my Mossberg 500 and extra shells. We both took two frag grenades each.

We left the others in the mouth of the alley and jogged across the street in the moonlight. There was nothing that concerned me in the neighborhood, save more of those fisheye lenses.

At the bottom of the steps leading up to the house, we paused.

"No hero shit," Tuck said. "Let's do this quietly room by room."

We slid our NV goggles on, adjusted the fields, and went up the steps. The door wasn't locked, so we went right in. In the green fields of our NVGs, nothing moved. Down low, weapons held high, we surveyed the room. It was sort of a large foyer or lobby with an antique-looking table, some high-backed chairs, and paintings on the wall. Pretty normal. There were two sets of stairs leading above, one off to the far left and another to the far right.

There was a corridor opening near the left staircase and Tuck moved towards it. "I'll check down here, you take those rooms over there."

"Okay."

He disappeared down the corridor and I turned towards the archway on the right. I moved slowly and carefully, keeping a tight eye on the archway and both staircases. At the archway, I sucked in a few deep breaths to calm myself and chase away the jitters, then went in low, ready to start capping if need be. I was in a lounge or living room of sorts that might have been called a sitting room in the old days. One quick side to side scan showed me that it was empty. A rocking chair. A sectional sofa. A couple comfy-looking chairs by the fireplace. A big HDTV on the wall. Nothing else. Nothing that even made me slightly suspicious. There was a closet, but nothing in it but coat hangers.

I went through another archway into a dining room and a connecting kitchen. There was no food in the cupboards, but other than that it was untouched like the other rooms. I got back to the foyer in time to hear Tuck call out to me.

"Pigfuck," he said.

It was the password he came up with so we didn't shoot each other.

"Nothing back there," he said. "A bathroom, an office, a kind of game room with a pool table, a doorway leading outside that's locked."

I told him what I found. "Food has been scavenged from the cupboards. Not so much as a can of beans left. That's about it."

"Funny," he said.

Yeah, it was funny, all right. Usually empty places get trashed by scavengers. They're always looking for food or weapons, drugs and booze. Anything that'll give them an edge or take their pain away. Sometimes they just wreck places simply because they can. There's no law left to stop those animals.

"Let's go upstairs," Tuck said.

"I thought you'd never ask."

"Shut the fuck up."

Any other time, we might have laughed and traded a few insults. But not there. There was a clear sense of threat, a sense of impending danger that I think we both felt but could not quite put our fingers on. But it was definitely there, thick as fog in the air.

"Let's do this," I said. "I don't want the others waiting out there too long."

Our plan was simple.

Tuck would take the left staircase and I would take the right. We'd meet above somewhere after we cleaned out our sections…if there was anything to clean out.

But I had a real good feeling there would be.

FEAR OF THE DARK

Again, I moved very slowly, taking it step by step. I knew how this had to work. Though I was with a mechanized infantry unit in the war, I'd done some house to house fighting of course, in places like Mosul and Fallujah, but my real experience had been since the Necrophage outbreak. As I climbed, I kept my eye on the landing above. All of my senses were highly attuned. I listened. I watched. I felt my way through the darkness with that vague but electric survival instinct we all carry inside us.

I got to the landing and waited there.

I saw nothing in the green field of my NVGs, but still that feeling of danger persisted. In fact, it was heightened. My heart was pounding. My mouth was dry. I could feel the adrenaline coursing in my veins.

I know you're here, I thought. *Show yourself, goddammit. Show yourself already.*

The field of my Night Vision Goggles made everything look freakish and surreal like something out of a found-footage horror movie.

My breathing sounded like rasping bellows.

My footfalls were the rattle of snare drums.

It was all subjective, of course, but everything in me was amped up.

It all reminded me too much of an operation in Al Doura during the war. Amongst the wreckage and rubble of buildings decimated by an airstrike from F-16 Fighting Falcons, we were mopping up insurgents, chasing them from one blasted structure to the next as their snipers fired down on us from rooftops.

I had winged a Johnny Jihad—as we called them—insurgent and he hobbled through the doorway of a gutted building. I went after him and found him upstairs. He was dead, bled out. I must have clipped an artery when I shot him. Judging from the blood trail he left behind, I wasn't surprised. I lowered my rifle and at that exact moment, a filthy boy of eleven or twelve stepped out of a doorway. He was carrying an AK-47.

He was as surprised as I was.

He looked at me.

I looked at him.

I remember thinking, *Don't...please, dear God, don't do it...*

But he did, of course. He made to bring up his AK, a look of absolute hate on his young face. I reacted instinctively and put three rounds into him, ripping out most of his throat. He hit the floor, squirming and trying to cry out but all that came from his mouth was a liquid gurgling as blood bubbled between his lips and spurted from his neck.

Twenty seconds later he was dead.

I was practically in shock. Two of my squad had to lead me out of there. I was physically ill over killing a kid for two days. There really was no choice because his mind was so twisted up from the poison the extremists had pumped into it, but that didn't make me feel much better. And now, standing in the house, I could feel it again—a mixture of fear and grief, guilt and self-loathing.

Knock it off, I told myself. *Focus, focus.*

I snapped out of it quickly enough because that boy reminded me too much of my own son and dammit, I was going to see Pauly again. I was determined.

I sensed movement as I stepped down the corridor. I didn't hear anything and I didn't see anything, but the alarm bells of a deeper sense rang off.

I brought my Mossberg around and a zombie pushed out of the darkness at me. What I saw looked like a homeless person. It was a man in dirty work pants and a Carhartt jacket stained with gore that was just as black as engine oil. He had long scraggly hair and a bushy beard stiff and crusty with dried blood. His face was pale and graying, set with open sores the size of nickels. He had no eyes, just two ragged holes that looked like they'd been cored with a knife.

Though he couldn't see me, he knew right where I was. His face split open in a grin of discolored teeth that jutted from gums speckled black. He tried to say something and it sounded like a man retching with dry heaves.

I experienced all this in a few seconds.

He reached out for me with fingers blackened by grave earth. By then, I had the Mossberg up and I squeezed the trigger. From the nose on up, his head vaporized in a spray of tissue and bone. His brains splattered against the wall like a handful of thrown mud.

He collapsed immediately, his hands flailing. As his ass hit the floor, his jaws clamped shut with great chomping force, several teeth snapping free and clattering over the floor like thrown dice. He trembled for a second or two, an inky fluid spilling from him and then he was dead again.

It was at that moment that I heard gunfire.

The staccato burst of an M4 on full auto.

Tuck was shooting over there and by the sound of it, he was fighting for his life.

MORTUARY

I ran down the corridor, ever mindful of several open doors, and came to a dead end. I had thought the hallway would connect the left and right wings of the upstairs, but I was wrong. The house was a duplex, a two family dwelling. I should have figured that from the two sets of stairs, but sometimes big old houses like that one had dual staircases. But that wasn't the case. The left stairs led to the rooms of one family, the right to another, and they both shared a common downstairs, I guess, kitchen and dining room etc.

Growing up in Yonkers, I remembered that lots of Italian families lived in duplexes like that so they could be apart but still connected for meals and social activities.

Dammit.

Tuck needed my help and I couldn't get to him; at least not quickly.

In vain, I tried the other two doors that shared a common wall with the left side of the house. No dice. The first was a bathroom and the second...the second was a bedroom that smelled like a morgue.

And there was a very good reason for that.

As I entered the room, a zombie which had been laying on the bed like the corpse it was sat up and looked at me. It was a naked woman with sloughing white flesh that was stained with whorls of fungus that looked like knots in pine. One breast was a shriveled, drooping cone, the other was immense and swollen like an overfilled water bladder. Strands of ivory-white hair were glued to her face with blood and a snotty sort of nasal discharge. She opened her mouth and black jelly gurgled out.

She was one of the most singularly horrifying creatures I had ever seen.

She sat there, grinning at me, crinkling up her face, the skullish triangular cavity of her nose making a rubbery sound like popping cartilage. Then she swung her legs off the bed, standing up to face me and I took a stumbling step backwards.

She moved towards me with an uneven gait.

One of her hips was disjointed and she limped awkwardly, her foot facing inwards. That's when she did the most revolting thing—she grasped her bloated breast, squeezing it, and a stream of dark juice squirted at me, just missing my face as I jumped aside.

I shot her point blank.

Why I hesitated that long, I don't know.

Her head flew off her shoulders in an explosion of blood and meat. She flopped back on the bed, her arms shuddering at her sides. Then she sat up again. She should have been done, but she wasn't. Headless and leaking black blood from the stump of her neck, she stood up, shambling towards me like a white, fleshy puppet. Her hands reached out for me with sticklike fingers and ragged nails. She made it maybe three feet, shook violently, and hit the floor, breaking apart on impact into a disgusting watery slough of blood, tissue, and protruding bones that washed up against my boots. I saw that the only thing that seemed to hold her together from the inside was sinew, ligament, and threads of some sort of pale phosphorescent fungus.

I turned away, fighting to keep my stomach down.

I leaned there in the doorway, breathing hard, nearly giddy from the warm stench of decay that reminded me of rotting, fly-specked fruit. I stumbled down the hallway, nearly delirious with horror. If another zombie had come at me at that moment, I would have been done for. I wouldn't have had the strength to fight.

Sucking in some cleaner air, my head cleared.

I heard Tuck shooting again, firing nearly non-stop as if he was surrounded or hemmed into a corner. Then I heard a grenade go off with an echoing roar.

There was no time to lose.

I jogged down the hall towards the landing…and skidded to a halt. I saw forms coming up the stairs. For one mad moment I thought it was my friends, but it was the dead. Four of them were coming up to meet me. The one nearest the top was another naked woman, grinning at me with stark white teeth. Her blackened gums had receded and her jaws looked like the fangs of a wild beast.

My NVGs chose that moment to malfunction.

The green field flickered, dimmed, then died. The last thing I saw through them was the burning, luminous eyes of the things that had come to devour me.

I swore and pulled the goggles away from my eyes.

What saved me at that moment was the tactical flashlight bracketed to the rail of the Mossberg. I clicked it on and the brightness of the beam momentarily blinded me...then I saw the monster coming for me.

It had been a woman, yes, but Zombpox had turned her into something else again.

She was skeletally thin to the point of emaciation, her skin like white clinging rubber. Her pelvic girdles jutted like wings, her ribs standing out like the rungs of a ladder. Her face was shriveled dead-white, mottled by purple sores, eyes bulging from black-rimmed sockets. When she grinned, her teeth seemed to slide out of the gums like those of a shark.

Here was death coming for me again.

I think I froze for a second too long. The sheer terror of the situation made me hesitate. It hadn't been the first time. Sometimes the fear that the walking dead generate is just too much and it overwhelms you, strips your gears. Anyone who says that it doesn't is lying.

The undead woman, I think, was counting on my fear paralysis. Though in general there's not much going on in the heads of the risen, now and again you'll see something more, a stark glimmer of evil beyond imagining. And that's what I saw in the drowning pools of her eyes—a cold, mocking intelligence, the way I'd imagine a spider might look at a fly trapped in its web. That's what I saw. A sense of triumph that she had me and there wasn't a damn thing I could do about it.

Or so she thought.

She reached for me and I squeezed the trigger.

One second she was smiling at me with a terrible death rictus, white scabrous fingers reaching for my throat...and the next her head was blown off, raining down on the others in a gory rain of blood, brains, and pellets.

The others were still coming.

No hesitation now.

I fired, racked the pump, and fired again. By the time I was done, the stairs were red with dark corpse drainage, limbs and bones.

I jogged down through the human detritus, pausing at the bottom to reload the Mossberg.

And that's when the front door crashed open.

HIDE AND SEEK

I brought the Mossberg up and then lowered it because the intruders were Jimmy, Sabelia, and Carrie. They speared me with the beams of tactical flashlights, M4s trained on me.

"We heard the shooting," Sabelia said.

Of course they did. I would have come running, too, only I really didn't want them here in harm's way.

"Tuck's upstairs," I told them, mounting the left staircase. "He needs my help."

"We're coming," Jimmy said.

"No," I called down to him. "It's too narrow up there. We'll bottleneck."

That stopped him, but not Sabelia.

"Steve…" she said.

"Stay down here. I'll holler for you if I need you."

I felt like some fool hero from a cheap action movie. *You just wait thar, honey. This ain't no place for a woman. This here's man's business, so don't worry yer pretty head none.* She didn't appreciate it and I knew it, but the less crowding up there, the better.

It was unbelievably black up there, but I hated announcing my presence with the tac light. The corridor was empty as far as I could see. I took off my NVG set and rapped it against the wall. I remember doing it in Iraq once and it worked. I got lucky: it worked again.

I clicked off the flashlight.

I studied my surroundings in the green NV field. Nothing that I could see. I checked the first room, then the second. Both were empty. The layout was slightly different on this side of the duplex. The corridor abruptly ended, then turned off to the left. I came around the bend quickly.

What I saw was disturbing.

The blast from the grenade was obvious. The wall was burnt, the plaster pitted with shrapnel holes. Several of the ceiling tiles were blown free above, others dangling and ripped apart. On the floor, I saw the remains of what must have been two deadheads. They had been blown to pieces, anatomy splattered in every direction, blood and bits of tissue splashed right up the walls.

I stepped over a trunk.

Several fingers squished under my boot.

I saw a leg, part of an arm, and a head that looked like it had been split by a cleaver. In a pool of blood amongst all this, I found an M4 rifle. It was glistening with hemoglobin that looked black in the NVGs. A bit further on, I found Tuck's ammo bag. The extra magazines were in there, but the other grenade was gone.

I had a very sick feeling in my gut.

There were bullet holes in the walls, but no sign of Tuck.

By that point, I guess I wasn't expecting to find him alive, but I was determined to destroy his corpse so he would not walk again. He was like a brother to me and I owed him that much.

I moved down the corridor.

Ahead, it ended in an archway that led into a room. There was blood and other fluids on the floor. A smeared trail led down the hallway and into the room at the end.

I heard movement behind me.

I turned quick and two zombies were coming at me.

One of them was a pouchy middle-aged woman in a filthy bathrobe. She had one fluffy slipper on, the other foot bare. Her face looked like raw, moist suet, one eye fixed on me, the other staring blankly up at the ceiling. With her was a man in a dress shirt and tie. He looked like a guy who'd just come home from the office…save for the fact that beneath his nose his face was a mass of ruptured pustules. It hung in frayed jowls, teeth and gums chomping.

I blew both of them away with head shots.

Then I approached the archway.

Sucking in a deep, nervous breath, I stepped into the room. The first thing I saw was a girl, maybe seven or eight at the time Necrophage got her. She was squatting on the floor next to a mutilated corpse, digging her hands into its stomach cavity and stuffing loops of entrails into her mouth.

I thought she was feeding on Tuck.

I really did for a moment…but the corpse was that of an overweight man whose head was blown apart. It had opened like a flower, gray matter spilling to the carpet.

The girl had her feast; she had no interest in me.

She looked at me with eyes that seemed to glow in the NV field, her face black with blood from her meal that she continued to gobble ravenously. I blew her head off and then others started coming out of the darkness of what looked to be a large living room. There were seven or eight of them. They came after me and I dropped two, turned, and three more were coming through the archway. I shot them down, racking the pump on the shotgun as fast as I could. I only killed one of them, but I took the arm off one and blew a hole the size of a dinner plate through the other.

They dropped, but I knew they would not stay down.

I ran through the archway, kicking out at the one without the arm and driving him into the other. They both stumbled into the living room and I popped the pins on both of my grenades, and threw them in there as I dove to the floor down the hallway. There was a deafening concussion as they went off nearly at the same time. Smoke and dust blew out of the doorway. Then I went back in and killed anything that still moved.

I stood there, the room painted with zombie remains.

They oozed down the walls and dripped from the ceiling. I stepped through the wreckage, sighting a closet door that was slowly swinging open. I moved towards it, my Mossberg held high for killing and I found myself looking at the bald head of Tuck.

"Nice work," he said, palming his last grenade.

Sighing, I relaxed. "You have no idea how ugly you are when seen through NVGs."

"Piss off."

By then, Sabelia, Jimmy, and Carrie came through the archway, flooding us with light.

"It's okay," I said. "I killed the others, but I saved the ugly one."

Tuck ignored me and gave us a truncated version of events. When he went up the left staircase, it was quiet. Then the maggot-eaters came from every direction. He shot down a few, blew apart some others with his first grenade, and then it was strictly hand-to-hand fighting. They got his rifle and ammo pouch, but they didn't get him.

"So you hid in the closet?" Sabelia said.

He scowled. "Just me and my grenade. If they got through, I was pulling the pin."

Nobody commented on the grim tragedy of that.

"I figured I'd come out when the time was right," he said, trying to lighten the mood.

"That's right," I said. "It was only a matter of time before he came out of the closet."

The four of us shared a brief laugh, but not Tuck. He stomped past me, giving me a playful thump on the head with his knuckles.

"Just you wait, smartass," he said.

PSYCHO CITY

By this point, it was after three in the morning according to Robin's watch. We were all exhausted and strung out from the lack of rest. We decided since we had fought so hard for the house, we might as well go and enjoy it. The downstairs anyway. The only thing that concerned us was that we had never checked out the cellar. We canvassed the lower floor and found no door that might lead to one.

Satisfied, we linked up with Robin and the others and made an organized retreat back to the house. The streets were quiet and it seemed like a good sign. We were all looking forward to some rest.

We set up downstairs since the upstairs was a little too full of remains for comfort. We found some candles and chased away the gloom. We chose the game room that Tuck had told me about. Once we hauled the pool table out of there, it was plenty roomy enough for the lot of us. Besides, it had a stout door with a lock on it and that was the most important thing of all.

Robin, being her nosey self, started looking around in a closet. After some looting around with Ginny, she came back with an expanding multi-pocket file folder tied with string. She emptied out its contents on the floor.

"Charles and Vivian Emery," she said. "Tax returns. Let's see what old Charlie boy was up to."

Diane had joined them now, too, as they looted through the private papers of Charles Emery. It kept them busy and pretty soon Carrie was involved in it. Tuck kept his eye on the door. I smoked a cigarette, sitting on the floor with Jimmy and Sabelia. It was going to be a long night and I doubted any of us were going to get too much rest.

"What do you got there?" Diane asked.

Robin held a paper up, bringing it closer to the candle. "A W-2 form for 2008. Charlie, damn, you made three-hundred grand after taxes. Not bad, buddy boy, not too fucking shabby at all."

"What the hell did he do in this shithole to make that kind of scratch?" Diane said as she looked through some bank statements.

Robin didn't answer right away. She brought the paper even closer. "Hey, this lists Charlie's occupation as a research biologist/virologist. Funny place for a guy like that to live." She looked over at me. "It says he was employed by the CDC. Isn't that the—"

"Center for Disease Control," Sabelia said.

Nobody had picked up on the significance of that or maybe they had and preferred to keep quiet about it. I went over and sat by Robin. She handed me the paper. I read it through two or three times.

"Funny, eh?" she said.

It was funny, but I wasn't laughing. "CDC SPB," I said.

"What's that?" Tuck asked.

"Special Pathogens Branch," I said. "They deal with unknown infectious viruses, the sort of things that could start plagues like Ebola and the like."

All eyes were on me by that point.

"And how do you know something like that?" Sabelia asked.

Some of those there had already heard my story of encountering a village in Iraq during the war that had been infected with Necrophage, but I went over it quickly again. The village had been called Et Ukhbar—now destroyed—and it was full of the walking dead. The infective organism was called *Necrovirus,* but it was just an earlier version of Necrophage.

"The point being," I said, "is that after the mission we were debriefed by a couple labcoat johnnies from the CDC's Special Pathogens Branch."

"Maybe Charlie just retired here," Robin said.

"Yeah, I'm sure that's all it is," I said.

Diane lit a cigarette and walked over by Tuck. "What else could it be? A research virologist just happens to retire to a weird town with cameras everywhere. What could be more normal?"

Nobody bit and I was glad. We had too much on our minds and we hadn't had enough rest to really properly process it all. Seppy and Scott never said a word through the whole thing. Maybe they were smarter than I thought.

We ate some MREs and then stretched out. Sleep came right away. Dead, dreamless sleep that was black and heavy like the night itself.

Unfortunately, a few hours later, somebody was shaking me awake. It was Sabelia. "Sandy's gone," she said. "And so are Scott and Seppy."

I should have been more surprised than I was, but I figured there was something going on with those two guys. The more I thought about it, the more I was certain they had never really been up to anything as I originally feared. They just wanted out. And when we were asleep, they went. Sandy, apparently, had gone, too. Unless she saw them leave and followed. It was hard to say. Sandy's brains were so scrambled by that point I don't think she even made sense to herself.

"Maybe they slipped out to take a leak," Tuck said.

"Girls generally don't go off to piss with guys," Ginny pointed out.

"They may have left ten minutes ago for all we know."

Jimmy shrugged. "Could be. But my guess is that it was once we were all sleeping soundly. Who knows why? But if they went outside, just about anything could happen to them."

"Then they brought it on themselves," Tuck said, clearly not interested.

We hashed it out for a few more minutes. Tuck was against going to look for them, saying it was crazy for the rest of us to risk our necks because they were being reckless. He had a point. Robin agreed with him. So did Diane. Jimmy, Sabelia, and I thought we should go find them. At the very least, just make a quick tour of the neighborhood and see if they were in any kind of trouble. Ginny and Carrie thought we should just wait because they might come back on their own.

"Well, I'm going to look," I said. "Just to be sure."

Sabelia volunteered to go, too, and Jimmy said, "Count me in. Sleeping on the goddamn floor is killing my back anyway."

"You're wasting your time," Tuck said.

"We're going anyway," Sabelia told him.

"Don't do it, Big Steve," Robin said and I knew there was serious concern for my safety behind her words. "They'll come back when they're ready and if they don't, fuck 'em."

She talked tough but I knew that had her leg been better she would have been coming, too. Same went for Diane and her head.

We took M4s, extra magazines, and grenades. I told them we'd be back in fifteen or twenty minutes. I really wasn't trying to play hero. I just had to know if they were okay or not. It was a motherly impulse I had.

Before we left, Tuck stopped me. His hands gripped my arms and I could see real concern in his eyes. "Steve...*Booky*...don't do this, man. It's not a good idea."

"I have to."

He stared into my eyes like the caring, loving older brother I'd never had. "Just watch yourself...just do that, will you."

"I will. You know I will."

"Shit," he said.

At the door, I turned one last time and looked at him. We smiled at each other.

"See you when I see you," he said.

He wanted to come with. I know he did. But to do so would have been admitting he agreed with my fool's errand and he couldn't do that. And it wasn't pride, it wasn't that at all. No, he was thinking of the unity of our little group and trying to reinforce the fact none of us belonged going out there. That unless there was a common consensus, no one had any business threatening the well-being of the all.

He was right.

I knew he was right.

But I was worried about Sandy, so I went anyway.

They locked the door behind us and out into the streets we went.

As earlier, it was quiet out there. Quiet, but tense, as if the city was just waiting, every muscle and sinew drawn taut and bunched, waiting to spring. We moved down the block until we reached the end. There was nothing. No sign of violence, no sign of anything.

Jimmy said, "You want my opinion, Steve?"

"Always."

"Well, they hightailed it back to the Silo."

"It would take them a week to walk back up there," Sabelia said.

Jimmy nodded. "Sure, but when people get scared and desperate, they don't think straight. They run. And I think Scott and Seppy ran and Sandy went with them. I don't think it would have taken much convincing for her. She was looking for a way out and any offer would have sounded better than what she had."

He was right about Sandy; I had no doubt of that. But as far as the other two went, I didn't know them. I couldn't adequately judge them other than the fact that I didn't trust them. They gave me a bad feeling and I said so.

"Your feeling was right on," Sabelia said. "You didn't get to know them like we did at the Silo. We all worked together to make our lives better, but those two were always trying to get out of work, always in collusion about something."

Jimmy agreed. "That's true enough. Now, I don't think they were disloyal to our cause or cowardly or anything like that. I knew guys like them in the Navy and when I worked in the shipyards. Just the sort that like to get out of things and make it as easy for themselves as they possibly can. Opportunists, I guess. Even when we decided to raid Perryville—and we ended up finding you and the girls—they didn't want to come. That much was obvious. You're talking about two shiftless sort of guys here. The sort that like to pass the buck. Why should they risk their necks if they could get someone else to do it?"

I had a pretty good idea of the kind of characters they were. I'd known guys like them myself. We all have. Sometimes, though, if you could separate people like that from one another they would turn out okay. Honestly, though, they weren't my main reason for going out in the streets again. Sandy was. Sure, she was a pain in the ass and a weak link under the best of circumstances, but I still worried about her and I still felt protective of her because she was so messed-up. I mean, hell, I'd been there when she watched her sister die in the streets of Perryville and it had been an absolute horror.

We moved on.

I led the way around the corner, suspicious of every shadow and darkened doorway. None of them held any true threat; it was all in my mind. I was becoming professionally paranoid and the only thing that would cure that was downtime and a lot of sleep. And I knew damn well I wasn't going to be getting much of either in the foreseeable future.

By the time we got to the end of the block, we began to see a lot of wreckage—buildings hit hard by artillery rounds or rockets, facades scarred by gunfire, houses burned down to frameworks. This was the sort of thing I expected to see when we entered the town. Somehow, it relaxed me to see these things. As we moved past gutted ruins, stepping over bricks and around overturned cars, I saw telephone poles had been knocked down and trees split in half. In the distance, I could see that a tall building had been obliterated and its remains filled the street, blocking it entirely.

"Looks like somebody had themselves a real shooting war here," Jimmy pointed out.

"And then some."

I started to get nervous. I don't think I was the only one because Sabelia had grown very quiet and Jimmy, on the other hand, was chattering nervously.

As we prowled the streets, moving silently and low to the ground now, our eyes were in constant motion, looking, searching, hoping to avert a catastrophe before it happened. At any given moment, some nutbag could open fire on us from the roofs or windows or from behind wrecked cars, as well as an infinite number of other places.

That was the ugly reality of urban guerrilla warfare.

No jungle in the world had so damn many hiding places.

Sabelia paused, breathing hard. "I have a feeling we're not alone."

I had that feeling, too, and I'd been having it for sometime.

"Let's scout to the end of the block and then make a hasty retreat," Jimmy suggested.

We all agreed silently with that.

We moved forward. Sabelia was leading now. I'm not sure how it happened, but she was out front. Not walking point or anything, just ten feet or so ahead of Jimmy and me. She was stalking like a cat, rifle up and eyes fixed, every line of her body wiry and feline and somehow dangerous. She had been in more than one girl street gang in her teenage years, so this came almost naturally to her. Stealth and combat in the streets was part of who she was...or had been, I reminded myself.

"Keep your eyes peeled," Jimmy muttered.

Sabelia flinched as if he had broken her concentration.

I was starting to sweat. I hadn't seen anything unusual or even remotely dangerous...yet, I was certain we were being watched. It was coming from no particular direction, but it was heavy and ominous in the air. I didn't think it was the dead. This had nothing to do with walking carcasses and their insatiable hunger, this was directed, this was secretive, this was intelligent.

"I got a real bad feeling that I'm way too old for this shit," Jimmy said.

"*Quiet,*" Sabelia snapped. She had paused, cocking her head, scanning her weapon back and forth. She had picked up on something and I was plugged into the same source. The nape of my neck was tingling. My lips were so dry they were stuck together.

"Listen," she whispered.

I could hear the soft padding of bare feet. Many feet. On the roofs, in the alleys. Whoever was here was about to show themselves and there was no doubt that they were hostile. Ordinary, peace-loving people did not run around barefoot in October. That was the sign of unhinged minds. At least, that's what occurred to me.

Sabelia backed up and nearly bumped into me. She put her lips against my ear. "We're practically on top of them."

Up ahead was an overturned school bus, weathered orange with rust. All of its tires were gone. It was a good place to hide behind, to spring an ambush from and I had a nasty feeling that's what was about to happen. I slipped my NVGs over my eyes, hoping they'd work and they did. There was plenty of moonlight to see by, but I wanted an edge.

I motioned Sabelia to get behind me and I edged in closer.

I scanned around the bus. I knew they were hiding behind it. I could feel them out there getting ready to pounce.

Then I saw something.

A hint of movement…a lock of hair blowing in the breeze from around the side of the bus. Someone was waiting for us. My body felt like coiled springs, my heart was racing. It was the way I always felt before the shit started flying.

I motioned Jimmy and Sabelia to pull back even farther.

Quietly, I dug a WP grenade from the canvas sack looped around my shoulder.

Closer.

I pulled the pin. Pungent white smoke twisted in the breeze.

Closer still.

I let the spoon fly and tossed the grenade over the top of the bus. It clattered to the ground and went with a great *Whoosh!* of fire and smoke. Flames spread out behind the bus. There were screams and bestial howls. About ten people charged out at us wearing little more than rags, their hair long, their eyes hateful, their mouths hooked into grimaces of hate. They carried clubs and knives, nothing more.

We pulled back and started shooting.

It was no contest.

We dropped the attackers within seconds. Their bullet-ridden, blood-soaked corpses twitched in the street. Others stumbled out from behind the bus and fell, burnt and smoking near their comrades. I moved in cautiously and turned one of the dying over with my boot.

It was a man, age indeterminate.

His hair was long and unkempt, snarled and streaked with soot. His eyes were open, his cracked lips attempting to form words. He and the others had gone feral and I really didn't know why. Was there another germ floating around out there that I didn't know about? Judging from the look of them they might have been homeless people before Necrophage swept the world into the graveyard. Maybe they had taken the next step into barbarity.

The smell of burning flesh and pooling blood was nauseating, so we began our retreat before any more crazies showed up. I wasn't naïve enough to believe that there weren't more out there.

Sabelia cried out and started shooting.

Jimmy and I whirled around, bringing up our weapons.

Five of the savages were charging from across the street and three more followed in their wake. Sabelia dropped two of them, then she was beaten to the ground by the other three as they jumped at her, knocking her rifle aside. They were fast and violent.

One of them turned in mid-stride and charged me. I drilled three rounds into him, blowing his face off in spray of flesh and blood. He screamed and stumbled in a circle, ripped muscle and shattered bone attempting a grimace. Then he fell.

Jimmy was firing on full-auto at the other three and a dozen more that had crept from the shadows brandishing axe handles and baseball bats.

I hesitated in firing with Sabelia lying there and one of them vaulted out at me. I cracked him in the face with the M4 and kicked him in the head when he went down. I took out another with a spray of bullets, opening up his belly. The guy went to his knees, trying to push his internals back in as they bulged between his red, dripping fingers. I dropped him with a kick to the temple and killed the other one with a barrage to the chest. He went down, too. Several others that had shown up turned and ran. I shot their legs out from under them. Behind me, I saw, the one I'd cracked in the face with my rifle was rising with a sneer, his face a bleeding mess, his fingers hooked into claws. I blew his head apart.

As Jimmy fired off into the shadows to drive the others away, I went to Sabelia. She was all right, just stunned. She'd taken a fist to the forehead and was bleeding, but other than that she would be fine. I helped her to her feet and handed her her rifle. I put my arm around her to support her, but she shoved me aside and started putting rounds into the shadows, too.

"YOU MOTHERFUCKERS!" she screamed. "DIRTY FUCKING SONSOFBITCHES!"

They were gone by then.

Jimmy and I just looked at each other, knowing we were witnessing her violent Latin temper that had made her a real terror in the streets of the Bronx when she was a teenager.

She stopped firing and balanced her M4 on her shoulder. In the moonlight with her dark good looks she looked like a pinup girl for a revolutionary army. "Sorry," she said. "But I had to get that out."

46

Well, if I hadn't known it before, I knew it then: Do not piss off Sabelia Cortez.

BARRAGE

Then the shit really started.

It began in the distance with scattered small arms fire. We all heard it and it stopped us there in the street. It was answered by the distinctive burning hiss of RPGs and their attendant explosions. And these were very close because the noise echoed through the streets and the flashes were very bright. A chopper flew overhead and I heard the sound of running feet, many of them.

"What the hell's going on?" Jimmy said.

The thing was, I didn't know, but I had the oddest feeling that we were standing dead center of a siege. Now there was gunfire from the roofs and the clattering of machinegun fire. More explosions. Fire belched into the air down the block as an abandoned car burst into flame. The crazies were shaken out of their hides and ran down the sidewalk as bullets torn into the facades of buildings they passed.

"COME ON!" I said.

We dashed towards the protection of the buildings on the other side of the street and good thing, too, because a light machinegun opened up, rounds ripping holes in the pavement. The LMG kept sweeping back forth and we huddled behind a pickup truck that had been abandoned on the sidewalk. But with the RPGs, that was definitely not a good place to be.

"Are they after us?"

"No," I said. "Not specifically. I think we're caught in the middle of something here."

Two APCs rolled across the intersection in the distance. I couldn't tell what they were, but they were both firing .50-cal machineguns and nothing means business like a .50-cal. One of them was hit by an RPG and the concussion was deafening. A ball of red flame rose into the night and a man began to scream his head off. I think they had targeted the .50-cal gunner and taken him out. He continued to scream and the volume of fire intensified.

It was getting closer.

The heaviest fighting was probably two blocks away, I was guessing, but it was moving towards us from two different directions and we were going to be caught between two opposing armies. I wasn't about to let us become collateral damage.

I could hear vehicles rolling in our direction, search lights sweeping around. Assault rifles were firing nearly nonstop. Bullets were pinging all around us. A chopper passed overhead again, casting lights into the street. I saw figures moving out there, caught in some weird strobing effect by the clouds of smoke in the air.

"Let's go," I said.

We left the protection of the truck and right away it was strafed by bullets. We jogged up the block. There were shooters now on rooftops and in doorways across the street who ignored us for some reason. As an APC turned the corner behind us, it took a heavy volume of fire from windows above. An RPG was fired from the rooftop and it passed just over the APC, striking a dumpster with a booming metallic sound that threw the dumpster ten feet into the air. It came down with a clanging reverberation, rolling end over end.

Jesus, we were really in the shit.

I was worrying that Tuck and the others might try and come after us, but I knew that wouldn't happen now. As I snuck up to the corner and peered around, I saw the fighting in the streets was heavy down by the house. There were explosions and gushing clouds of fire, lots of small arms fire. The vehicle down there was almost certainly a LAV-25 and it was firing its chain gun, tearing up the real estate around it, attempting to suppress enemy fighters.

By that point, I thought I had a fair idea of what was going on.

The choppers and APCs were no doubt part of an ARM contingent. The other fighters moving by foot were guerrillas of some sort, probably people from the town who would not submit to ARM control. Maybe, maybe not, but it definitely sounded like a good guess.

Some of the rounds were getting too close, so we ran across the street, taking advantage of the blowing shrouds of smoke. The APCs behind us were coming and so was the LAV-25 from the opposite direction. We were about to become the meat in a sandwich. There was absolutely no way we could make it back the way we had come. The closer the vehicles rolled, the more intense the fighting grew. It was only a matter of time before we were caught in the crossfire.

Sabelia spotted an alley down the way and we ran for it, making it, luckily, in one piece as heavy guns hammered and I could hear the booming of artillery pieces in the distance, the ground shaking each time a shell landed.

As we got to the end of the alley that opened up onto a street with burning buildings, I saw fighters scurrying around in the rubble. One of them must have seen me and he fired in my direction as he ran off. The rounds didn't come anywhere close. I saw more fighters in full retreat now, making for the shell of a building just up the block. Then, out of the rubble came soldiers. They were definitely ARM. In the light of the fires I could see they wore Russian shadow camouflage.

Jimmy and Sabelia brought up their M4s to shoot, but I told them to lower them. This wasn't our fight. We wouldn't get mixed up in it unless we had no choice.

Now the ARM pukes and the guerrilla fighters were firing back and forth, tracers flying like hot embers. Grenades were thrown. ARM troopers positioned a machinegun to fire on the building the fighters were hiding in. They burned off thirty or so rounds, just strafing the building and shooting through the missing windows. Brave, suicidal fighters kept darting out, firing, then leaping for cover.

ARM pushed in.

The machinegun was giving them the necessary cover. They crept in. One of them was hit and dropped shrieking in the street. When two others tried to retrieve him, they were hit, too. The fighting got heavier as more ARM troopers pushed in. The firing was going nearly nonstop now. The snout of an LMG pushed out of one of the windows and started firing on ARM positions, driving them back. The ARM machinegun answered. Then an RPG hissed from the rooftop and hit the ARM machinegun crew with a devastating blast. When the smoke cleared, the gun was destroyed and there were body parts everywhere, the pavement shining with blood.

"We have to get out of here, Steve," Sabelia said and I knew she was right.

ARM was worked up into a kill-happy froth, a boiling frenzy where their own lives were immaterial and the only thing that mattered was payback for their dead comrades in the street. I could almost feel it in the air. The ARM force lost all cohesion and discipline and there was a lot of shouting and screaming. They were taunting the guerrilla fighters, calling out about what they were going to do with their wives and daughters. When that happened, it was only a matter of time before the men started losing it.

And they did.

One by one or in pairs, they charged the building, all of them getting cut down almost instantly and that just drove the others wilder. Their commanders were yelling at them to pull back, but unit discipline was gone and more charged out. I heard a rumbling and I knew what the commanders were up to. A LAV-25 rolled down the street, opening up with its chain gun on the building, blowing great holes in the walls. Some rounds went right through windows and exploded with crashing sounds. I heard men screaming in the building. A pair of crazy fighters raced from the ruins, opening up with what looked like old Vietnam-era M-16s, their bullets pinging harmlessly off the LAVs armor. A gunner on top fired with his 7.62mm machinegun and cut them nearly in half.

We ran and I'm not even sure what direction we went.

It was sheer chaos.

Everywhere, it seemed, there was gunfire and explosions, burning vehicles and smoldering structures. There were bodies in the streets. The lucky ones were in pieces or had drowned in pools of their own blood. The unlucky ones were still breathing, maimed and mutilated things that were missing limbs, punctured with shrapnel, cored by bullets, burnt and suffering wrecks that crawled under porches and into gutters to die slowly and painfully.

Their screams and ragged, desperate moaning seemed to come from every direction.

And still the guns never ceased and the incoming never stopped falling as the faces of buildings were erased or cracked open, and the roofs of houses collapsed and piles of rubble were further reduced to pulverized fragments whose dust twisted in the wind.

After we watched ARM blow the shit out of the building where the guerrilla fighters hid, we took advantage of the chaos and ran through clouds of acrid smoke, leapfrogging corpses and debris, hiding behind bullet-pocked vehicles, and seeking one safe zone after the other. Most of which were gradually compromised as the war pushed in closer, dragging itself to us on worn, bloody feet.

We hid in a courtyard between two blasted buildings, secreted in the shadows of an immense rubble pile.

"Do you even know where the house is now?" Sabelia asked.

I was honest: "No."

Jimmy chuckled, his breath wheezing from his lungs. This was hard enough on me—a guy in his thirties—and Sabelia—a woman in her twenties—let alone poor old Jimmy who was getting so close to seventy that the seven and zero were casting a shadow over him. But he never complained and his age never became a factor. He fought with us and worked as hard as anyone.

Once, just after The Awakening when we were still at Tuck's tower and had been going through some rough action fighting deadheads, I said to him that it was a hell of a way for a man to spend his retirement.

He said, "Hell, Steve. As bad as all this is, it beats the shit out of wasting away in a rocking chair, watching the world go by and the nursing home getting closer. I haven't felt this fucking alive since I was nineteen giving Uncle Ho's pissbags hell in the Delta."

It wasn't that he liked any of it. No sane person *liked* what Necrophage had done to the world. Yet, fighting for survival had invigorated him and renewed him in many ways and I understood how it made him feel better about himself and gave him a reason for being. My greatest fear was that his luck was going to run out one of these times. He was an old friend and practically like a grandfather to my son. His death would be bad, very bad.

He wasn't a suicidal type of guy, but there was an undercurrent to his words whenever he talked about getting old and sick. "Ain't no more nursing homes," I remember him saying once. "A man can't afford the luxury of dying in bed, pissing himself like a pig in the straw. These days, when a man goes, chances are he's going to die like a man. He's gonna go down fighting."

And my guess was that's exactly what he wanted and the idea kind of scared me.

Anyway, the three of us rested there, silent and alert. I don't think any of us were worried about our predicament; we were thinking about the others. I was just hoping that They were lying low.

The fighting went on, the heaviest stuff a few streets over to what I thought was the west. It was a constant jarring cacophony of urban warfare over there—machineguns clattering like typewriters, small arms fire, RPG strikes, and artillery barrages. Now and again, I'd hear a chopper coming in low on a fire mission. It was such confusion on the ground that I bet the gunners never knew whether they were hitting the enemy or their own men.

After ten or fifteen minutes of downtime, we got up and Sabelia stopped us before we moved.

"Listen," she said.

I heard the clomping of boots in the street.

By firelight, I saw two ARM troopers coming up the sidewalk out there. I knew they were ARM because they wore Kevlar helmets. One was helping the other along who was clearly injured. They chose to rest not twenty feet from us, sitting down and putting their backs up against a shelf of fractured concrete. They waited there, muttering and smoking cigarettes.

We were pretty much stuck.

If we wanted to leave, it meant we'd probably have to kill them and I don't think any of us wanted to do any killing that wasn't absolutely necessary. Besides, the shooting might draw others in.

We waited.

Down the street there was a horrific explosion that was either a missile or an artillery shell. The ARM duo pressed together, covering their faces. Flames rose up from down there, casting flickering light. It was then that we saw four and then five shapes creeping stealthily up on the soldiers.

"Crazies," Jimmy whispered and our hands tightened on our weapons.

There was no doubt that he was right. They were spidery, inhuman shapes, ratlike and stalking, moving in ever closer to their prey. They were very patient, eerily so. When they were but a few feet away, they dove on the soldiers. It took everything I had to remain hidden and not intervene on ARM's behalf. The soldiers were quickly beaten down with clubs. One of them was not killed outright and I heard him whimpering, saying, *"Oh please...don't kill me...please don't kill me..."*

One of the crazies picked up a slab of concrete the size of a cinder block and crushed his head with it. Something in all of us snapped. We just couldn't take it anymore. We jumped up, bringing our M4s to bear.

The crazies heard us and froze.

One of them hissed.

Another gnashed his—or her—teeth.

We opened up and dropped them alongside their victims. And as we did so, someone across the street began to fire at us. Slugs punched into the rubble around us. There were snipers over there and I spied a muzzle flash from a second-story window.

We pulled back and got away. Not two minutes later when we were out of harm's way, a chopper came swooping down. It opened up with miniguns, saturating the courtyard with rounds, chewing up everything. There would have been nowhere to hide if we were still there.

Breathlessly, we ran down another street.

We saw more night fighters firing at fleeing bands of ARM soldiers. They fled in our direction. We cut down another alley and out into yet another street. The fighting had been very hard there. I saw dozens of corpses, mostly ARM troopers. Pools of blood glistened in the moonlight. The night fighters were dressed in black. Amongst them were a variety of weapons—M-16s, M4s, AKs, riotguns, you name it. From what I could see, they all carried gas masks. That disturbed me.

But there was no time for closer inspection because we weren't alone.

The dead were coming.

ZOMBPOX

The question that kept coming back to me again and again like a ghost haunting the ruins of a deserted house was this: how long could we go on? We'd been through so much shit by that point that it was like a stink that clung to us. We were dipped in it, had it rubbed in our faces, and shoved up our noses…and this particular shit smelled like death, gassy and hot and putrefying. The world all of us had known, the world we had grown up in and lived in and trusted, was gone. It was dead. We were trudging through its remains day by day, all clinging to some hope that once the dead were put back down and the crazy survivalists were buried with them that we would be able to put it back together again like the pieces of Humpty Dumpty.

Some days I believed it.

Other days I didn't believe it at all.

But that's what we were fighting for. That's the thing that kept us going and we all dreamed about it, we all fantasized about the day it would come and we were safe and happy and relaxed, the corn was growing high and the children were singing happy songs and the sun was bright and warm. As the days ground into weeks and the weeks became months, it got harder to believe it. The life we led, the life all sane survivors led, was ugly. This wasn't a crappy horror movie or a silly comic book or some ridiculous video game, it was reality. A world hunted by the walking dead and the survivors were frightened rabbits scurrying from one hole to the next.

That's what it was like day after day.

My little band had camaraderie. We all put on a strong face for one another, but I knew inside that we were scared to death. Scared of the crazies out there and the zombies and maybe scared of ourselves for the dark, inhumane things we had to do just to stay alive. Necrophage, or Zombpox as we called it, was out there, smoldering like old bones in a crematory pit and we knew it. It was the shadow that haunted us continually. The fear of contracting it was the greatest fear of all. Everything else paled beside it. What would you do when you got it? And, worse, what would you do when someone you loved got it?

INTO THE SHIT

There was nowhere to escape to.

A mob of the dead saw us and moved in our direction, faces and bodies torn, mouths chomping and fingers reaching. Behind us, down the alley, the fighting picked up and we heard the thudding of heavy machineguns and the rumbling of vehicles out in the streets.

We had no choice.

As the dead came on in a revolting, maggoty arm, we took up firing positions with our backs to a building. Despite the fear we felt, we opened up on semi-auto, choosing targets and dropping zombies, blowing their heads apart and splashing their brains across the pavement.

Still more came.

We hopped behind a rusting car and I tossed a few WP grenades at them. The grenades exploded with blinding flashes of light, engulfing the dead in mushrooming flames. The air was hot with the smell of seared corpses. Several zombies struggled still forward, white phosphorus clinging to them and continuing to burn. They blazed and sputtered, pieces of them dropping off and eventually the last few stragglers collapsed as the WP melted the flesh from their bones.

But it was hardly over.

Attracted by the stench of roasting carrion, more zombies came out of the darkness. Most of them fell on the remains in the street. Men, women, and children cursed by Zombpox and turned into ravening cannibal corpses, began tearing apart the corpses of soldiers and night fighters, gnawing on limbs and yanking organs from bellies and smashing heads to get at the buttery folds of brains.

The more adventurous ones went after the burning dead, ripping them apart and chewing on crunchy, blackened meat. The crispy gnawing sounds were almost more than any of us could take.

We moved away down the street, past the burning hulk of a disabled LAV-25 that was split into three pieces. It must have been hit by an armor-piercing shell or an antitank missile. The body of an ARM trooper was hanging from the wreckage, impaled on a four-foot shard of metal. A naked teenage zombie boy was chewing on his throat with slobbering, gluttonous sounds.

He turned as we approached, grinning at us with a blood-smeared face. Great sections of his flesh were missing as if he had been peeled. He went back to his meal and we got out of there as fast as we could.

After that, we were constantly dodging zombies, ARM patrols, and stalking night fighters. Every time we found a place to lay low, we were forced from it. We were bone tired. We needed rest badly.

We cut down an avenue into a residential section, thinking we were getting away from the action only to stumble into the killing fields once again. It was dark in the neighborhood with no fires burning, but we could smell death all around us. Worse, we could see shapes moving.

We clicked on the tactical flashlights fixed to the rails of our rifles and saw everything in detail.

More corpses, but not ARM troopers or night fighters but what looked like ordinary men, women, and children than had been lined up and gunned down. It was an atrocity.

All those cold cuts brought out the zombies in numbers, of course. Bodies were spread all around us and we were right in the middle of a human buffet. Most of the walking dead had plenty to eat and were completely disinterested in us. But some ghoulish gluttons tossed aside what they'd been eating and came right at us.

This time, there was no wall to put our backs up against.

The best we could do was to form a sort of triangle and fight.

As the other maggot-eaters continued dining, I started blowing away the dead that came for us. Jimmy and Sabelia were doing the same. A woman brandishing the well-stripped arm of a child moved at me and I put a round in her forehead. The entrance wound was clean, bloodless, almost surgical, but the exit wound took out the back of her skull. Hell, it *kicked* it out like rotten wood.

She fell and two more replaced her.

It became a killing frenzy then.

They wanted us and we did everything we could do to keep them from getting us. We were firing and firing, hot shell casings piling up at our feet and still they came, more and more all the time, it seemed. For every one you dropped, three more came at you. We emptied magazine after magazine and still the tide was not turned. And the worst part, the very worst part, was that there was no real exit for us. We were hemmed in tight.

Something had to give.

Or, better, I had to *make* something give.

We were still managing to hold the dead off at about twenty feet, but that wouldn't last forever. I had to punch a hole through the wall of them. I had two frag grenades left in my pouch. I took out one, pulled the pin, and tossed it. The three of us went down. There was a booming explosion and zombie fragments rained down over us.

"FOLLOW ME!" I cried.

The grenade had pulverized four or five zombies and driven a dozen more back that were hit with blazing bits of shrapnel. The wall had weakened. Before the dead could recover, I charged into them, shooting and batting them aside. I didn't know for sure if I was immune to Zombpox, but I had been bitten once and survived it, probably due to being infected by a weakened strain. They reached out for me and it was such close quarters that it was near impossible to get a decent shot off, so I smashed them with the stock of my M4, battering and beating them aside. I kicked and punched and swung the rifle. One of them got an arm around my neck and I flipped him into a trio of others.

We were free, or nearly.

I gunned down four more and then we were running, stumbling, tripping over partially-devoured corpses in the street. Sabelia and Jimmy were still with me, thank God, both of them shooting and dropping the dead as we charged ever forward until their numbers became insignificant and there was light at the end of the tunnel.

We slipped between a couple of houses and turned our lights off, hunkering down in the darkness.

"Anyone get bit?" I said.

"No," Sabelia said. "I can't believe it, but I didn't."

"Jimmy?"

"Oh no," he panted. "I'm fine. Tired as hell, but I'll live."

I had a feeling he was in worse shape than he was admitting, but at least we made it out in one piece. Given the odds, that was a miracle in and of itself. We sat there for maybe ten more minutes, enjoying the downtime. The fighting was tapering off now and I only heard random gunfire in the distance.

Were we safe?

I doubted it, but we were in better shape than we had been earlier. That was something. It was about that time that we heard the marching of what seemed dozens of feet. I reconnoitered back the way we came and saw what appeared to be an army of the dead heading in our direction. In the fading moonlight, I could see that they were literally everywhere. We would never be able to sneak around their lines.

I went back and told the others.

"Best thing, maybe," Jimmy said. "Is to get into one of these houses."

"If they come after us, we'll never hold them back," Sabelia said. "I'm on my last magazine."

"Me, too," I said.

Jimmy nodded. "I can't have much more than a dozen shots left."

Which put our armament at a serious disadvantage. I had one frag grenade left and a knife. Yeah, we were definitely in the shit. And as we hashed it out or attempted to, the dead were pushing in closer and closer and we began to smell the stench of their corruption.

We got to our feet, checking out the houses around us.

Most of them had been hit hard. Their walls were scathed by gunfire, windows shattered, doors torn off hinges. I guessed that ARM had hit them, that the corpses we saw in the street had been the people from these houses. We continued on, checking them out and finding nothing promising. A zombie woman stepped out of one and I shot her between the eyes.

I could hear the army getting closer.

Though the dead were most assuredly slow nearly all the time, it was their numbers that were frightening. And from what I saw out there heading in our direction, I knew we didn't have a chance in hell of holding them off.

Then Sabelia said, "Look."

In the backyard of one of the houses there was a fort of sorts suspended up in the air on four pillarlike posts. It was basically just a square box with a roof, no windows, open on all four sides. It was about thirty feet up in the air and must have been built as a kind of playhouse for kids. I clicked on my light and saw a rope ladder hanging down.

"The dead aren't much for climbing," Jimmy said.

My greatest fear was that once we were up there we'd never get down. I was envisioning the three of us up in the fort while down below hundreds of zombies waited with that unnatural patience of theirs, hour by hour and day by day. Not that it would realistically go on that long—if Tuck and the others didn't get to us, ARM probably would—but what if?

"What do you think?"

"I like it better than waiting here," Sabelia said.

Jimmy nodded. "Me, too."

The zombies were getting closer so there was no time to really hash it out. In fact, three of them had already shown and were moving in our direction. They had to go and I knew it. If they started mulling around, others would come and do the same thing.

Jimmy and I held the rope ladder while Sabelia climbed up it. She went up fast with her usual athletic agility.Then I held it while Jimmy climbed. He was not quite so fast. He moved up it almost painfully and I had to wonder just what sort of aches and pains he was suffering from that he wasn't telling us about. I noticed also that he seemed to be favoring his left arm. That gave me concern.

Finally, he was up.

As I grabbed the rope, I noticed the sky was brightening in the east. Sunrise wasn't far off.

"Steve," Sabelia called down, "you want me to pop those three maggot-eaters?"

Honestly, I didn't want her to. I was afraid the noise of gun shots would draw unwanted attention and I didn't like the idea of being trapped up in the fort and having to fight against some particularly randy ARM troopers, but those deadheads had to be put down before they attracted more.

"Yeah, go ahead," I said.

She was quick and efficient. *Crack, crack, crack!* went her rifle and down went the zombies. She was a damn good shot, getting better all the time. I hurriedly climbed the rope ladder and pulled it up behind me, shutting the trapdoor.

The fort, as I said, was essentially a box on stilts, looking kind of like a guard tower of the sort you see on *Hogan's Heroes* or one of those old TV shows. It was about eight feet long and five wide, benches set along the walls which rose up to about belly level and then it was open on all four sides with a roof overhead.

Realistically, there were advantages to the fort.

We were safe from zombie incursions because, as Jimmy pointed out, they weren't much for climbing. Being thirty feet off the ground made the climb real difficult even for a normal person, let alone one of them. Up there, we had control of the surrounding terrain and could drop anyone who dared to get too close.

The advantages were many, yes, but so were the disadvantages. Sooner or later, we had to come down from our roost. And if somebody wanted to take us out bad enough an RPG would easily do the trick.

The three of us waited there, leaning on the sides of the fort and watching the dead come. At first, it was dozens and then many dozens that became hundreds as they filled every open space down there—yards and alleys, streets and vacant lots. There were so many that some simply pushed right into houses or garages, seeking any opening they could find. There's a dread feeling you get when the dead mass like that. It's the same sort of feeling in your gut you get when you see swarms of flying ants take to the air in August. There's just too many and it makes your skin crawl because it's just damn unnatural. It's not, of course, at least as far as ants go.

After a time, the sun started rising so we sat on the floor so our guests down there wouldn't see us seeing them. We were exhausted, but we didn't sleep. The sun was warm and baked the chill from the air. We were dirty, spattered with gore, cut and bruised and sore. We didn't say a damn thing. We all just stared at the floor. Now and again, one of us would peek up over the walls and see how the zombies were making out. They were still there, but they were moving, slowly, slowly moving, guided somewhere by a force we would never understand.

The stench in the air was gaseous and sickening, a sickly-sweet stink of putrefaction that we didn't even notice after awhile. The sun had heated things up and made the dead smell even worse. It had also activated clouds of late-season flies that found us up in the fort and crawled over our arms and faces. After a time, we didn't even bother swatting them. I sat there next to Sabelia and smoked the cigarettes that Robin had given me. I had two of them and I smoked them one after the other, trying to chase the flies away but it really did no good.

The city was quiet out there and I couldn't hear anymore fighting. There was nothing, just the slow shuffling of the zombies below.

After a time, an hour maybe, Jimmy nodded off and it was then that I started studying his left arm which he kept pressed to his belly. There was blood all over the sleeve of his shirt. It was drying now, dark and crusty. It was certainly possible he had cut his arm in any number of ways.

But I didn't believe it.

And I didn't think Sabelia did either, judging from the look she gave me.

Jimmy had been bitten.

DEATH MARCH

I must have drifted off.

I didn't think it was even possible, but when you reach the point of absolute exhaustion the transition between being wide-eyed alert and dead to the world can take place in the blink of an eye. I woke up because Sabelia was shaking me. Not roughly, but just enough to rouse me. And I must have really been out because the sun was high in the sky and my back was stiff, my legs numb from being folded underneath me.

I heard rumbling and shouting voices, a gunshot now and again.

"What's going on?"

"Ssshhh," she said. "They're everywhere."

I poked my head up over the ledge and I saw that the zombies were gone, but they had been replaced by soldiers. From my vantage point up in the fort, I could see over the rooftops of the ranch houses that made up the neighborhood and what I was seeing was like something out of a slavery movie. Out in the street were people. Not just five or ten, but what looked like hundreds. Men and women all roped together like steer and being driven by ARM troopers with rifles. They were marching four abreast, throats encircled by ropes that tied them to each other and the people behind them. I watched the procession and it kept going and going and going.

"They must have the whole town out there," I said to Sabelia. "They must have kicked the doors in on every house in town and taken them one by one."

She nodded. "That's what we came into last night. They must have been holding out against ARM, so ARM hit them hard last night, broke the backs of the defenders, and taken them all prisoner at first light."

Their fate could have been any number of things.

Maybe they were being marched out to a place of execution or to a blood farm like the one Robin and I had been held prisoner in or to a slave labor camp. It was really hard to say. I didn't really think they were going to be executed. If they were, why go to all the trouble of tying them up and marching them out when they could have been blown away in their houses?

I looked over at Jimmy.

He was still sleeping. He looked very old, very used-up. He was dirty like us, face streaked with grime. For a moment there, I thought he was dead but then I saw that he was still breathing. If he had been bitten—and I couldn't say absolutely that he had been—then I wondered how advanced the germ was by that point. When Necrophage took hold of someone, it wasted very little time. Your immune system was overwhelmed within a matter of hours and then it was all downhill from there.

I looked over at Sabelia.

Her dark eyes were intense and shining. "I don't know," she whispered to me. "He might have it and he might not. We should see something pretty soon if he does."

We were in a real mess, that was for sure.

All I really wanted was to get to the Silo in the Catskills that I'd heard so much about. I wanted to see my boy. Hell, I *needed* to see him, but it seemed the more I wanted that the farther away it became. It had been going on that way for well over a month by that point. The thing was, as much as I wanted to run up to the 'kills, I knew I couldn't. Whatever was going on with Jimmy had to be sorted out first and I had to find Tuck and the others. I just hoped to God they hadn't been captured. If that was the case, I might never see any of them again.

Sabelia sighed. "If he does have it," she said, meaning Jimmy, "then…well, we can't let it happen, can we?"

There was compassion and sensitivity in her voice, but there was also something brutally practical behind her words. I knew very well what she meant. I had done it before when someone was infected. "If he has it, *if* he has it, I'll do the right thing."

She hung her head and I put an arm around her. What a sad state of affairs life was when you even had to be considering putting a bullet into the head of a guy who'd practically been a father to you.

Suddenly, Jimmy opened his eyes and looked at us. "I can hear you both yammering, you know. When I decide to eat your brains I'll let you know."

Sabelia and I just looked at each other. We were like two kids caught in the act. I didn't know what to say, but she did.

"We're worried about that wound in your arm," she said.

"I got that much."

"If you were bitten..." I started.

"If I was bitten, you were trying to hash out who gets to put me down like a rabid dog," he said. "Well, for your damn information, I snagged my arm on some sheet metal. Pretty sure I ain't gonna rise and chew on livers because of that."

The relief was liberating.

"You're sure?" I said.

"No, I'm making it up, bonehead."

That got a chuckle from me. I wasn't completely relaxed about the situation, but I was feeling better. Sabelia filled Jimmy in on what was going on out there. The three of us peeked over the ledge and we saw that the procession had thinned out considerably. Within about ten minutes, the last of them were marched away and I saw fifteen or twenty soldiers followed by a LAV-25, its .50-cal machine gun aimed at the marchers.

In the distance, I heard a few more gunshots.

"That's what happens if you try to escape, I'm guessing," Jimmy said.

I was sure he was right. Wherever they were being marched to and for whatever reason, attendance was mandatory. ARM did not care much for those who turned down their RSVP.

Jimmy poked his head up again. "Give it another ten minutes, then we better get our asses out of here."

"Then we'll go find the others and split," Sabelia said.

Neither Jimmy or I commented on that. She was being optimistic and we both knew it. The chances of them not getting rounded up or killed when they refused were very remote. Tuck was a survivor. So were the others. But there were still only five of them. Five fingers can make a fist that can give you a good slug but it's still only one hand and ARM has dozens and dozens of them. The outlook was not good and I knew it.

Sabelia seemed to read our pessimism. "They may have slipped away last night, you know. Tuck might have gotten them out of there when he heard the APCs and soldiers. The house might have been hit by artillery or something. They may be outside town, waiting things out, waiting for ARM to leave so they can come back in and find us."

"I can't see Tuck leaving until he knew we were safe," Jimmy said.

"Or dead," I put in.

Sabelia gave us both hard looks. Here was a woman who'd been through the shit in her lifetime, but she never knuckled under or gave up because it wasn't in her to do so. It was an admirable trait. She always set her mind on some distant point when things would be better and focused all her energy on getting there. She would accept nothing less.

"Well, I don't have time to listen to you two pouting and giving up. I'm going to find them and I'm going right now. You can either come with me or stay here with your doom and gloom."

She grabbed her rifle, her ammo bag, and opened the trapdoor, lowering the rope ladder. She didn't even look at us as she climbed down. We followed, of course. Nothing could have stopped us from doing so. We followed her like moths drawn to the same burning flame.

DUSTED

We hadn't made it twenty feet before something happened that was quite literally beyond our experience. There was a sort of popping noise that reminded me of a smoke grenade and, true to form, a cloud of yellow gas suddenly came blowing in our direction. We heard two more similar popping sounds and before we knew it, immense clouds of yellowish smoke had immersed us from all sides.

I heard Sabelia cry out and I saw Jimmy hit the ground, gasping.

My throat felt raw, my chest felt tight, and my head spun like I was on a merry-go-round. I tried to stay on my feet. I tried to grab Sabelia, but the vertigo got the best of me and the next thing I knew I was on my knees, then I face-planted right into the ground.

I could seem to think or concentrate and I doubted, at that moment, if someone had asked me my name I would have been able to tell them. Everything became very confused and unreal. My face felt flushed, my eyes watered, and when I tried to call out to Jimmy and Sabelia, my tongue felt like rubber. I couldn't think and I definitely couldn't speak.

The gas dissipated quickly enough, but the symptoms were ongoing.

Somebody had thrown non-lethal grenades at us and it had to be to weaken or subdue us, but it wasn't like anything I'd ever experienced before. I'd been through gas training when I was in the Army, but this was not smoke, OC or CS. I had no idea what it was, only that it was extremely unpleasant. While I was engulfed in the cloud, it felt like millions of tiny insects were crawling over me. It was so extreme that I involuntarily began scratching myself. It was a weird, phobic sort of reaction.

Then it was gone and I tried to pick up my rifle, dropped it, tried to pick it up again and fumbled it. My muscles didn't seem to want to obey my brain. My hands were useless. It was like trying to do fine, detailed work with oven mitts on. I tried to stand and I went back down again.

Jimmy was out cold, but muttering like somebody going through a bad nightmare.

Sabelia had a dopey grin on her face. She was staring at me with wide eyes that ran with tears. Her lips trembled. She kept trying to talk, but nothing made any sense. Either my brain couldn't process what she was saying or she was unable to say what needed saying. We just sat there on our knees, staring at each other. She held a hand out to me and it trembled. She started giggling and I wanted to, too. This was all incredibly funny, but I wasn't sure why.

I looked up and it seemed as if the sun had traveled across the sky a good distance since we climbed down out of the fort. Was that possible or was I just delirious? I finally got to my feet, knowing there was not only something wrong with me but all of us. Sabelia's giggling was disturbing, but I wasn't sure why.

I forced my feet to move and it felt like my boots were filled with cement. One, two, three steps. My muscles began to respond but my stride was drunken and uneven. I couldn't have pissed a straight line let alone walked one. I guided myself along the side of a house until I could see the street where all the people had been marching. I saw several dead soldiers and more than a few civilians. There was a dog sprawled over the curb whose guts were hanging out. I had to look away because it seemed like its intestines were crawling.

Get it together, get it together, get it together, a voice kept repeating in my mind. *You've been drugged. There was something in that smoke. It's got you all fucked up. Get it together.*

Something wet touched my arm.

I brushed it away with my finger. *Plink, plink.* More drops. I was scared for a moment because I thought for sure it would be blood. That the sky was about to open up like an artery…but it was merely boiling gray with clouds and the only thing falling was rain. More drops fell that became a gentle shower. It was cool and refreshing. It picked up in intensity until it was a real down pour. I was soaked to the skin in what seemed seconds. But it felt good, washing the dirt and grime from me. Rivers ran along the curbs. I could see lots of gleaming white bones out in the street.

I turned and went back.

Jimmy was still out, completely oblivious to it all. Sabelia was up, spinning around and around like a kid trying to make herself dizzy. She would whirl and whirl, then fall laughing to the ground and do it all over again. Everything was a mess. Nothing was making sense. We were acting erratically. There was danger, I knew. Danger in this town and everywhere else but I could not put a name to it much as I tried.

We had to do something.

But I honestly could not think of what that was.

Jimmy. Yes, Jimmy.

The rain was coming down in gray sheets and he was still laying there, his face spattered by mud as the earth seemed to go liquid around him. I went over there and grabbed him by the shoulders. I had to get him somewhere dry. That much was making sense. I dragged him over to the back porch of the nearest house. Sabelia came over and helped me, giggling like a little girl, happy and filled with life. It took some doing, but we got Jimmy up on the porch where it was dry.

I went inside the house and found myself in a kitchen.

Sabelia was standing behind me and I could hear the water dropping from her to the tile floor. Rain pattered against the windows. It sounded like a torrent coming from outside. Knowing I had to do something, but unsure what that might be, I started looking in drawers. I found silverware, cooking utensils, a drawer of odds and ends—everything from batteries to old cell phone chargers to castoff screwdrivers and rubber bands. There was a rolling pin in there. A novelty rolling pin about five inches long and made of finely polished wood.

I tried it on the countertop and it really rolled. I was fascinated by it. Sabelia couldn't stop laughing and I began to wonder if the rolling pin was really that small or, somehow, I had grown really large. It makes no sense, but it did then. That's when I saw something I hadn't noticed: there was writing on the rolling pin. Fine black script. BLUE ROOF CABINS, it read. TWIN MOUNTAIN CATSKILLS. And if you revolved the pin, it read in smaller script, WHEN MAMA'S IN THE KITCHEN YOU DON'T HEAR NO BITCHIN'. I started laughing myself. The rolling pin was just a kitschy tourist item as was what was written on it. Sort of thing that made you giggle at the time, then you threw it in a drawer or it ended up in a cupboard in the garage and one day twenty or thirty years later you pulled it out and said, *Hey, Martha! Lookee what I found! You remember dis? Remember dat shop where dey sold da moose knuckles and porcupine jerky? Ho! Now dat was a hoot, weren't it?*

I had to stop laughing so I handed it off to Sabelia.

She gratefully took it and rolled it along the counter. I had things to do even if I couldn't remember what they were. I had been scavenging things for so long by that point that it was ingrained in me. I looked in the dusty, abandoned fridge whose door was propped open with a clothespin. I searched around in the cupboards, but there was no food. Just dishes and spices and an old bag of red licorice that was hard as a brick. In another cupboard I found half a fifth of Jim Beam and I pulled off it and so did Sabelia.

I sat there staring at her as if there was something very important I needed to tell her, but it just wouldn't come. Then she unbuttoned her wet fatigue shirt, tossing it to the floor and her eyes were huge and dark, simmering almost black, it seemed. I took her in my arms and kissed her and her tongue was burning hot in my mouth. I pulled my shirt off, desperate to feel my skin against hers and the touching was almost electric. Then I was squeezing the full cones of her breasts, the nipples brown and hard under my fingers. I put my mouth on them, sucking them into my mouth and licking them and she was moaning, saying things which I couldn't seem to understand.

As I loved her breasts, I unbuttoned her pants and they were so wet I nearly had to peel her out of them. But I found the line of dark hair between her legs and followed it with my fingers until I found the hot wetness and worked two fingers into her. She unzipped me and fondled my cock which felt immensely swollen like it might burst. I worked her with my fingers until she came with a little cry and the entire time I could not take my eyes off the tattoos on her thighs—a four-leaf clover and a coiling serpent.

The next thing I knew I had lifted her up onto the counter and entered her. I rode her hard until she came again, her nails cutting into my back painfully. I kept pushing into her harder and faster as if I had to release something inside both of us. It took me a long time to climax—at least, it seemed so—and when I did, she did again, rocking and bucking and laying my back raw as she pressed herself tightly against me and bit down on my ear, making a high-pitched sort of squeal in her throat.

I dropped to my knees on the floor and she slid down from the counter, leggy and loose, like something poured from hot liquid.

Then, later, minutes or an hour, we were laying naked in the dining room on the carpet, sipping from the bottle of Jim Beam. I kept exploring her olive skin with my fingers, feeling her taut muscles and the bones beneath. She put her head down between my legs and took me in her mouth, sliding her wet lips up and down until I was hard again and then she climbed up on top of me. She pressed me down with her hands and rode me with violent gyrations of her hips, our flesh slapping wetly together. I drew her breasts into my mouth, marveling over the rose tattooed on one and the numbers 182 on the other. It took me longer to get off the second time and she shook with orgasm after orgasm, a hungry and hot thing that moaned and cried out and finally fixed me with eyes that looked black with hate.

Then we were laying there, side by side.

Sabelia was breathing hard like she'd just ran a marathon and her flesh was cool with sweat.

I can't say how long we laid there.

Finally, still not talking about anything the other understood, we climbed back into our wet things and went back into the kitchen. By then, and I think the sun was beginning to sink low in the sky, we had started to come to our senses.

"What the hell's going on?" I finally asked.

"I don't know," she said. "I really don't know."

We pulled off the bottle a few more times and the alcohol seemed to help, as if it was canceling out the other drug inside us. We stood there for a time and then I heard boots out on the porch. Jimmy was standing in the doorway.

"You find a bottle," he said, "the right thing is to share it."

We both laughed and then stopped because it seemed to strike us suddenly that none of this was funny at all. In fact, it was scary.

There was real terror going on only we'd been too stoned to notice it.

Jimmy pulled off the bottle. "We were dosed," he said.

That much was true. I wasn't sure about any of the rest of it, but that much was true. The question was *why?* That's what I couldn't figure and what scared me. If somebody was close enough to toss some sort of chemical grenades in our direction, why didn't they just kill us? It would have been easy.

Because they don't want you dead, dummy, that voice in my head said. *They want you confused and trippy and disorganized. They want you to doubt what you see and hear. They want you incapacitated.*

I was starting to make connections, but I had the worst feeling that what was inside us was not done with us quite yet. It was still in there, smoldering away like fissionable materials that were buried but still very active and deadly.

Sabelia started to cry.

I saw it happen. She was perfectly calm one moment, then the next she was backing away from us as if we were horrible slime-dripping monsters. She would have kept going but her ass bumped into the stove. Then she started to cry. Tears rolled from her eyes and there was a dry, wracking whimpering coming from her throat. Through the sobbing, I think she was trying to convey to us exactly what was going on, but we couldn't understand her. When I went to her, she struck out at me like an injured animal. She sank to the floor, hugging herself, tears still rolling down her face, her entire body shaking with the fear that gripped her.

"Just leave her," Jimmy said, leaning up against the counter. "Let her work through this. It's all you can do."

He looked like hell. He was pale and blotchy, eyes red-rimmed and fixed, unblinking. Clear mucus ran from his left nostril. He was shaking as if he had the chills. But was I *really* seeing that or was I imagining it?

Sabelia coughed, then made a gagging sound. Then she was on all fours, vomiting out a watery discharge that led to more coughing and dry heaves. Gasping for breath, she said, "I saw...I saw...I saw the hole under the ground...the dark spaces...and *everyone* was dead...everyone..."

Though it was nonsensical at the time, the meaning of it became all-too apparent later on. Jimmy was mumbling, barely staying on his feet. I couldn't seem to breathe so I stumbled out on the porch and I was overcome by the feeling of being watched and studied closely. It wound me up in a shroud of darkness until I stepped off the porch.

Problem was, I forgot to use the steps and I came down in a mud puddle.

Then everything went black.

DEAD IN THE HEAD

I was losing it and I knew I was losing it and that was the really scary part. They say if you think you're going insane you probably aren't. But what if that wasn't true? Because it didn't feel true, none of it felt true. Hell, the truth was a butterfly with radiant, auroral wings flitting about in the back of my head which felt like a glass jar and as subjective and fucked up as that sounds, it made sense to me. My mind had cracked open like a walnut and I knew it.

I couldn't think straight and it seemed almost worse than before. I wasn't even sure if any of that had happened. Memories kept colliding in my head. I saw my house in Yonkers. I saw my son playing in the backyard. I saw Ricki taking the Thanksgiving turkey out of the oven. And then zombies in the streets, armies of them, ravenous hordes. Tuck's tower and Claymore mines and Strykers rolling through the streets of the Bronx. I saw Sabelia watching me with dark eyes and Diane holding my son and Hillbilly Henry offering me meat and Sonny Boy peeling a man with a knife and Spider's swollen, grease-shining face as he sucked the blood out of Robin's throat. These things had happened in one way or another, but most of them were mixed up and reinvented in my head.

Finally, I got up on my knees and cried, "ENOUGH!"

That's when some of it cleared and I saw the world again, at least enough of it to realize I was kneeling in a mud puddle, still in the yard of the house and there was the fort before me rising up on stilts.

Then, the world began to fade around me and I saw something like shining shards of glass coming at me. I blinked and they were gone. I was still in the yard, still, apparently, tripping my fucking brains out. I couldn't trust my thoughts and I couldn't trust my instincts. In fact, I simply couldn't trust myself. Images of Sabelia and Jimmy passed through my head and I knew I had to get to them…but how? Wherever they were and where I was seemed miles apart.

I reached down to touch the grass to root myself to the real world, only the grass did not feel like grass but like...a floor. A smooth and polished floor that felt oddly like tiles. I could see grass, but I could *feel* tiles. It made no sense. There was a disconnect between my brain and my fingertips. I wanted to scream, but I couldn't. It just wouldn't come out.

Then...then I saw a room. I was in a dream or a nightmare and I saw a man standing there with white hair and the coldest gray eyes I have ever seen. There was a grin on his face that looked like stretched latex.

There were tables lined up, stainless steel tables like the sort they do autopsies on. And on each one, a zombie. They were strapped down and straining to be free, their eyes glassy and white and they all wore the shadow camouflage of ARM.

The man was studying them intently. Then, slowly, like the head of a puppet turning, he looked over in my direction and I saw that he had a carefully-trimmed steel-gray mustache. There was something inherently evil about him that made me shiver, made my bones feel cold under my skin.

Well, awake are we? Taking a little breather from it all? Good, good. He stepped in my direction and I trembled with absolute terror. He had a needle in his hand, a hypodermic syringe. I could see that it was empty. *Now, my friend, all I need is a little bit of what you have and then we can begin. That's not asking so much is it?*

He moved closer to me and I had never known so much terror before. I tried to move, but I couldn't. My body was loose and rubbery. He came in closer with the needle and I tried to scream again, but it stuck in my throat like a chicken bone and try as I might, I could not hack it out.

No need of that, my boy, no need for theatrics. I won't hurt you. And you can't stop me from doing what I'm about to do, so just...relax.

"I'm crazy," I heard my voice say. "I've cracked up."

No, no, no, he said, *his voice weird and wavering. You're not mad. You're not mad at all. At least, not yet.*

Then, like a switch was flicked, the room was gone and I was laying on a bed. A cot, really. It was narrow and not terribly comfortable, but the mattress pad was soft, so soft. I had been feeling its softness for some time, not at all sure of its reality. The wild dreams or weird impressions I had been having seemed to disappear and there was a nasty, metallic taste in my mouth. And a voice in my head said, *that's what doom tastes like. Now you know.* I looked around the room, but I didn't see the man.

Then I blacked out again and the dreams came back. Actually, only one dream came back—if it was a dream. I was kneeling in the mud puddle outside the house and when I tried to move, I fell into the puddle and I crawled, crawled on my hands and knees through the wet grass, knowing I needed to get away. That nothing had ever been so important.

Then I saw boots.

White rubber boots.

I looked up and three men were standing there. They looked like spacemen, but they weren't from outer space. Just guys in white self-contained biohazard suits, staring down at me through the plastic bubbles in their hoods. I could hear the hiss of their respirators. They were dressed like the special ops people in Et Ukhbar and probably for the same reason.

The last thing I was aware of was them dragging me off by the ankles and the sound of Sabelia crying in the distance.

Then I woke up screaming.

Maybe it was hours later or days…God, there was no real way to know. I was screaming my head off in the darkness and then a light came on and Sabelia was there, she was holding onto me and I was on the cot again in a long narrow room with a door at the end. It was a steel security door with a small pane of unbreakable glass up at eye level.

"It's all right, Steve," she said. "I'm here with you…*ssshhh*…it's okay now."

The first thing I said was, "Is this real or am I still tripping?"

"It's real."

She looked like Sabelia and felt like her as I touched her, but I was still on the edge of panic and I was suspicious of everything. There was a sheet covering me and it was damp and sour-smelling as if I'd been sweating out poisons in my sleep.

I looked Sabelia in the eye. "Where are we?"

She shook her head. "They won't tell me. They all wear suits...like radiation suits or something. They took us from the town. Do you remember?"

I sighed. "I remember a lot of things. I'm just not sure which are real."

"They gassed us, Steve. Dosed us with some sort of hallucinogen. Everything is kind of gray after that...but I remember the men in suits taking us away."

"Jimmy?"

"He's here. He's pretty sick, Steve. He's across the hall. We can go see him if you want. They let us do that."

I took it all in. There was a logic at work here that my tripping mind had been unable to grasp with its hallucinations, temporal disruptions, and subjective nightmares. Things began to occur to me. I got up off the cot and I was naked.

Sabelia smiled. I smiled back.

She showed me where the shower stall was and I took a hot shower. Everything was provided for. I soaped up and washed my hair. In fact, I did it twice. I had a pretty good growth of beard but there were no razors. I stepped out and toweled off and slipped into a bright orange jumpsuit like the one Sabelia was wearing. We looked like convicts.

Then, I did some thinking.

The town, whatever it was called, had cameras everywhere. The house we found had tax document from a CDC scientist. And now guys in biosuits had taken us away to some sort of biomedical complex by the looks of it. It all fitted together.

"And they've told you nothing?" I said.

Sabelia shook her head. "When I came out of it, they were bringing you in. You had a bandage on your arm. They took it off and dumped you in bed."

The man. The man with the needle. She showed me where the bandage had been. Yes, there was a tiny red needle prick on my forearm. Had the man taken blood? The syringe was empty. But could I trust my memory?

I sat down on Sabelia's cot with her. "In the house...we..." I broke off. How did I put it? "You have a four-leaf clover on your left thigh and a snake on the right. Is that true?"

"Yes, Steve."

Her eyes grew very sultry as she answered and I was sure that I had not dreamed we made love. Still, I wasn't completely satisfied.

"I'm going to do something and I don't want you to get angry, okay? It's going to seem weird."

"Okay."

Her arms were folded across her chest and I moved them. Then I grasped the zipper of her jumpsuit and started pulling it down. She did not try to stop me. In fact, I think she was excited by the idea. I unzipped it to her waist and then I opened it so I could see her breasts. Yes, there was the rose on her left breast and the numbers 182 on the right. I touched them with my fingers and I could feel her begin to breathe faster.

"There's also a dragonfly on my back," she said, "beneath my left shoulder blade if tattoos are your thing."

I zipped her back up. I felt embarrassed and guilty and I didn't know all what. "Why 182?"

She chuckled. "East Tremont in the Bronx. East 182nd Street and Crotona Ave was the stomping ground of my posse when I was sixteen. We all had the rose on one tit and 182 on the other. Satisfied?"

I was. Well, I guess I hadn't hallucinated our relations. I told her what I remembered, tactfully skipping over certain details. Then I told her that I thought this place was some kind of secret CDC research lab and that the town with its cameras and what not was probably part of it, too.

"But it can't still be in operation," she said. "The CDC doesn't exist anymore."

"No, but maybe places like this are still running, still working on Necrophage or things like it. I rather doubt they're run by ARM, but maybe something like them or a piece of our government that's still active. Who knows?"

"So what do they want with us?"

"That's the question, isn't it?"

LOCKUP

The next morning we got our answer. It came in the form of a little angry-looking man with white hair, a thick neck, and a big cigar. He came through the door about an hour after we had our breakfast which consisted of bacon and eggs, the former freeze-dried and the latter powdered. But it all tasted good. Maybe it wasn't exactly fresh, but I ate every bit of it and so did Sabelia.

The little guy introduced himself as Colonel Pratt and apologized for keeping us locked down in what he called "sterile confinement" but they had to be sure we weren't infected. They had seen us enter the city and would have made contact if it wasn't for the fighting with ARM.

"They've been fucking us pretty hard," he told me, then looked at Sabelia. "My apologies, ma'am. I've got a dirty mouth and a dirty mind, but a clean heart and a good soul. You ask anyone around here and they'll tell you Billy Pratt is a good sort and then some. And if they don't, I'll personally kick their asses."

Sabelia was not won over by his wit. "Who are you and what is this place?"

"This place was an underground CDC research laboratory. I was head of the security contingent that safeguarded it. Basically, it's a bunker."

"Beneath the town?" I asked.

He shook his head. "We're about half a mile outside town right now. The bunker is—or was—connected to the town by an underground passage. It's flooded now."

The town was called Baneberry, he said. All the houses and land were bought up by the government back in the late 1940s under the guise that the nearby Delaware River was going to be dammed to create a reservoir here in the valley. But it never happened, of course. Instead, back in the 1960s the NCDC—National Communicable Disease Center, forerunner of the CDC—covertly built an underground containment facility beyond the city limits and the houses were given to the employees, scientists, technicians, support staff, and the security team that kept an eye on anyone that passed through town. No outsiders were allowed to move in.

The way he described it, it was like a company town and everyone who lived there were involved with the bunker somehow.

"Down here, there's about thirty of us left. We're surviving the best we can. A lot of that's due to the facility we're in now which is nearly impregnable and a lot has to do with the doctor."

"The doctor?"

"Dr. Cripps. He was the chief research scientist here and, as such, the head of the whole ball of wax. He oversaw everything and still does. Thank God for him."

Sabelia and I looked at each other. The awe in Pratt's voice was more than a little alarming like this Cripps was the fucking messiah or something. I had a feeling I'd already met him. He had to be the guy with the white hair and the cold gray eyes. The one with the needle. That part of my trip must have been real.

"In Baneberry, as you saw last night, it's chaos. Utter chaos. There's a group of survivalists hiding out there that ARM has been trying to throw out. Why? Because they're guerrillas and they harass ARM units constantly. They're led by an old school ex-paratrooper named McTeague. He's tough and so are his people. We have a sort of uneasy alliance with him because he trusts no one." Pratt shrugged. "Anyway, now and again when ARM rolls into town, we hit them as hard as we can. You saw that last night. We hit ARM pretty hard and they hit right back. They suffered heavy losses, but so did we. We don't have the numbers to strike like that again."

"I saw them marching people off like slaves," I told him.

"Sure. Squatters, mostly. People who came here, found empty houses and decided to stay. Mostly transients from the larger cities. ARM believes them to be allied with McTeague, but I doubt that they are."

"Where are they taking them?" Sabelia asked.

Pratt shrugged. "Labor camps? Blood farms? Take your pick. Those that are willing will probably join ARM. Those that aren't...well..."

He explained to us that we had been hit by a psychochemical weapon that was generally known as *fear gas*. It was a new toy ARM had been playing around with and no doubt had its origins in the dark catalog of PHOBIC, who I knew were the puppet masters of ARM. He said that this fear gas was very similar to anticholinergic 3-quinuclidinyl benzilate, an incapacitating agent tested by the U.S. Army back in the 1960s and called BZ for short.

"The Iraqis had limited stockpiles of it, we discovered, during the Gulf War. They had used it against their own people more than once," he said.

I had heard of BZ when I was in the Army.

"So it makes you terrified? Drives you insane?" Sabelia said.

Pratt shrugged. "The experience can be very subjective, Miss, and vary from person to person. Some people scream with terror and others can't stop laughing, sometimes it alternates between the two. From what I've been told, it causes detailed illusions and panoramic hallucinations, confusion, blurred vision, speech difficulties, sporadic mood swings, violent behavior, incapacitating fear, even what's known as *primal regression,* in that people act like animals. They tear their clothes off and crawl around on all fours or sit around picking imaginary nits off one another. Lots of weird, strange, very fucked up things."

He told us that the point of BZ was to hit the enemy with it in aerosol form, creating absolute chaos, disorienting them and the civilian population in general. A good dose and it would be impossible for them to organize a defense. They'd be too terrified and weirded out, most of them tripping their brains out.

"We tested it on our own troops back in the '60s," he said. "Volunteers...or so I was told. They were so out of it they couldn't even recognize men in their own units. Their best friends were strangers. Hostile strangers they had to run from or fight. Terrible stuff, all right."

"But a gas mask would protect you?" I asked, remembering that some of the night fighter corpses had them.

"Yes. But a heavy enough concentration on the skin might be absorbed, but not with as much of a dynamic effect."

"So can we leave?" Sabelia wanted to know.

"No," Pratt said, puffing off his cigar. "Not until we're sure."

"Sure of what?"

"Sure of two things, Miss. The first being that you're not carrying Zombpox and the second being that you're still not dosed on fear gas."

"We're fine," I told him. "Neither of us have been bitten and we're over the gas."

"We're running blood tests on both of you just to be sure. It's strictly procedure with us, you understand. The problem with fear gas is that it can have a lingering effect up to forty-eight hours. We have to be sure. There's enough berserkers out in the streets as it is."

The *berserkers* were the crazies we saw in the streets. They were people who had been dosed again and again by fear gas until they were no longer normal, hysterical and raving and savage.

"They're dangerous. Many of them have even changed physically…but for the most part, you have to pity them."

He said there was a rumor going around that the berserkers were really just homeless people plucked from the streets and experimented upon by PHOBIC, dosed continually with high concentrations of fear gas and then released here in Baneberry to cause trouble with the local insurgents.

He pulled off his cigar. "Maybe, maybe not. Thing is, they just started appearing in the past month or so. Who can say?"

"So tomorrow we can leave?"

"Yes. Or you can stay here with us. It's up to you."

"We're looking for some friends," I said. "We just want to find them."

"Ah, yes, I'll bet you do. Do they have names?"

"Tuck," I said. "That's short for Tucker. Diane, my sister-in-law. Robin, Ginny, Carrie."

He smiled. "I'll see what I can find out. If they're around, chances are they've been seen. But for now, you have to finish your time in isolation."

Sabelia didn't look too happy about it, but what choice did we have?

"We'll get you out of here just as soon as possible. We tend to be cautious…maybe too cautious."

"I'd like to see Jimmy, the guy we came in with," I said.

Pratt was no longer smiling.

GOING TO YOUR GOD LIKE A SOLDIER

Jimmy was strapped to a metal-framed bed. He looked very old, much older than I had ever seen him as if he had aged a decade in a matter of hours. I sat with him for two hours and he never woke up. The nurse who watched over him wore full biohazard gear. It was a man but I never saw his face. He made me wear disposable latex gloves and a mask so I would not breathe in any airborne particles or blood if Jimmy sneezed. I didn't bother telling him I didn't think it was necessary in my case.

It's never easy to watch an old friend die and in Jimmy's case it was even worse. He'd always been so good to us. When I was off in the war he took care of Ricki and Paul like they were his own. He was a kindly old guy with a good heart and enough great old stories to fill a book. I sat there by his side, staring down at him, tears running down my cheeks. It wasn't going to be easy to tell Paul about this when I saw him. Jimmy had been like a grandpa to him.

I went back to my room and slept for about four hours. Sabelia was sleeping and I didn't bother her. She was fond of Jimmy, too, but her roots with him didn't run as deep as mine.

Around seven a.m. I went back over there.

Things were getting worse.

The nurse said it wouldn't be too much longer. He carried a 9mm sidearm and I knew exactly what he was planning on doing with it. I think if it wasn't for Pratt, they would have just marched Jimmy outside and put a bullet in his head. The fact that they were allowing any of this was simply out of respect for us.

Jimmy thrashed from time to time, chattering his teeth and smacking his lips very loudly. Sweat poured from him in rivers as his fever spiked. Now and again, his eyes would open and they would roll back into his head as he strained at the binds that held him.

I knew in the next few hours the real ugly stuff was going to start and the idea of it broke my heart. Hell, it broke everything inside me.

After I'd been there about an hour, his eyes opened again. They were bleary, but they looked over at me and he managed a lopsided smile that was about as close to a grimace of pain as you can imagine.

"Hell, you doing here, Steve?" he asked in a scratchy voice.

"Just visiting. They got me and Sabelia bunked in across the hall."

He coughed and gritted his teeth. "You got that...that pretty long-legged woman over there and you're nursemaiding an old duffer? You get the hell out of here...I'll manage..."

But, of course, he wasn't going to manage and we both knew it. I think he *did* want me out of there, though. I don't think he wanted me to see him this way, to witness his suffering and degradation. He wanted very badly for me to remember who he was and not what he was becoming.

"What is this place, Steve?"

I told him the best I could.

"You...and Sabelia be careful. I got a bad feeling. A real bad feeling."

"We will."

He coughed a few more times. "When...when I was in 'Nam, I had a Viet girlfriend. She was a wash girl. She'd come around..." his voice trailed off, his eyes closing, then they snapped back open. "...she'd come around the base and wash clothes for us. Pretty, petite thing. We hooked up and I spent every minute I could with her. Her skin was like Sabelia's, her hair real dark."

"What happened to her?"

Jimmy laughed, then coughed. Pinkish sputum ran down his chin. "She was...she was VC, Steve. All those washer girls were VC. She just disappeared one day. I heard she got executed...who knows. Stories over there, crazy stories...guess I'll...guess I'll take 'em down into the deep with me..."

"C'mon, Jimmy," I said, wiping tears from my face. "You can beat this. You'll get better."

He smiled at me again, but didn't bother commenting on the absurdity of what I had just said. "Laying here...thinking stuff, lots of stuff."

"What sort of stuff?"

His breathing was very fast and it seemed to take great strength on his part to get it back under control. His teeth chattered and more of that pink drool ran from his mouth. "Remembering things. Lots of things. When I was kid...back before the war, me and my old man...we'd go up to Morgan Lake. Rent a cabin every summer, spend a week fishing for bass and pickerel. Those nights by the fire...stars out...more than you'd ever see in Yonkers...pan-frying fish and listening to the old man's stories about being a teenager in the depression. Ha...funny shit, chasing ice wagons and stealing potatoes, the CCC camps. He had some wild yarns."

"Those must have been some times for you and your dad," I said.

"Sure. Good to go to sleep remembering...remembering how good things were when you were a kid. The sky was the limit then." He broke into a coughing fit, his entire body trembling. "You tell Skip...you tell him I died fighting, Steve. I don't...I don't want him to know I died in the straw like this. I want him to think good of me."

"Skip" was the name he always called Paul. I never knew why and at that moment I knew I never, ever would.

"Steve...I need to turn over...loosen these straps...I won't try nothing."

I did, helping him roll over onto his side. Then I tightened them again. I knew the nurse was outside the door and he was watching us through the observation port.

Jimmy's breathing got a little easier. "That's better...getting the bedsores, I swear." He made a hoarse chuckling sound. "Remember how Skip...how he'd get a real kick out of those foot long hot dogs I'd get at the deli...sure, we'd grill 'em up in the backyard, me and you and Ricki...oh dear sweet old Ricki...and the boy. A cold beer, a hot dog, Yankees on the radio, crickets chirping, and stars out above...those were times I felt good about the world and I think...I think it felt good about me, too..."

"Jimmy," I said. "Do you need anything? A drink of water or something?"

"No, I'd just throw it up anyway. What I need you to do is listen *real* good, real good. See, now I ain't looking into your eyes and you ain't looking into mine and it'll be easier…what you have to do. Real easy. I'll just yarn on and you can put me to sleep so nothing gets worse…okay, Steve?"

I knew what he was asking. I knew what he wanted and if I was a real friend, if I really loved him, then there was no way I could refuse. No way in hell I could let him become one of those things. It would have been an insult to our friendship and all that it stood for. But the idea was almost more than I could take.

"Anytime, Steve, anytime," he said. "You're like a son to me and I wouldn't ask it of you if I didn't love you so much."

I motioned the nurse in and asked him for his sidearm. He hesitated, then he seemed to understand. He gave it to me. It felt cold and deadly in my hand. I could barely hold it still because I shook so much. It felt like everything inside me was draining out. Tears ran down my face and I had to clench my teeth to keep from crying out.

Jimmy shuddered and made a strange barking sound. "Hurry…Steve…hurry…I can…I can feel things happening…*please…*"

I walked over to the bed and my feet felt like they weighed a hundred pounds each. I pressed the muzzle of the gun up to the back of Jimmy's head. My entire body was shaking now, my breath coming very fast, rushing in and out of my clenched teeth as sobs broke loose in my throat.

"…you were off to war and I said to Skip, I said, Skip let's go do us some camping and we'll catch our fill up to Morgan like me and my old man did," Jimmy said, his voice scraping like a knife, old and dry and wheezing. "So up we goes, me and Ricki and little Skip, pitching our tent and what a weekend that was. All the time…we…we thought about you, Steve. Sure…sure we did. It was just like it was with my old man…the sun was warm and the water was blue and flat, frogs hopping and fish jumping and Pauly's eyes were bright and the air, the air smelled so fresh and sweet and, dear God, if I could just go back there…just for a minute…just for…"

I pulled the trigger.

Then I stumbled away from what I had done, half out of my mind, seeing that lake and Paul there and Ricki so pretty in the sunlight and Jimmy, good old Jimmy on the grassy shore smiling at me and waving goodbye.

GIMME SHELTER

I wasn't much good for anything after that.

When I got back to my room, Sabelia was awake. She had heard the gunshot, of course, and she saw the wreck I was. I sat down by her and all I could say is, "He's gone now. He won't be coming back."

We laid there together for an hour or so and she soothed me as best as she could, but there was no peace and there was no comfort. I was bleeding inside and I knew I always would be. Days would pass and the memory would dim, put parts of it would always be crystal clear and the pain would always be real and cutting.

I did what I had to do and I did what Jimmy wanted me to do, but that made me feel no better. I had just killed a man I loved and respected more than anyone else. And if it makes any sense, I did it out of love and for no other reason.

NICKEL TOUR

The next morning, Pratt came and got us, telling us we were all done with our period of isolation and we could re-join the real world. He muttered a few condolences about Jimmy and told me that his remains had been cremated. He went through it all quickly as if it made him uncomfortable and I'm sure that it did. He moved us to a different room that was much smaller, but at least we got to stay together.

"You're welcome to stay as long as you like," he said. "You're welcome. I imagine you're not leaving the area until you find your friends."

"No," I told him. "We have to know one way or another."

So he gave us the tour which didn't take too long. There were two underground levels to the bunker. Most of it had been laboratory space but had been converted into sleeping quarters and the like. We visited the supply rooms and armory, dining hall and kitchen, walked down a lot of long grim concrete corridors. We met people and they smiled at us and chatted informally, but none of them really had anything interesting to say. Pretty much, *Hi, how you doing? Glad you're with us. It's bad out there but we're getting by in here.* Nothing much more than that. If they had anything more to say, they weren't saying it. But, then again, we were strangers and with the way things were you didn't automatically trust people until they had proven themselves.

I understood that.

I practiced it.

You had to.

It probably didn't help that Pratt was with us. If he was the commander of the bunker, the man in charge, then they weren't about to speak their mind. I wouldn't have either, I guess. For the most part, the people there were as gray as the walls that hemmed them in. Theirs was a sunless, subterranean existence. Living like moles, I knew, was not conducive to the human mind or the human spirit. Under such conditions, people tended to lose their focus and to degrade morally and ethically. Sooner or later, they just didn't give a shit. It was the sort of psychology you found in any situation where people were confined. And these people, I thought, seemed lackluster and disinterested in general. They were on the edge.

Later, we sat in the dining hall which was gray and utilitarian, tables lined up in rows, bored-looking people sipping soup and barely talking. There was not a spot of color on the walls, not so much as a cheap print or still life. Nothing. I wasn't much into interior decorating, but even I with my purely male lack of style and ambience could have improved on the place. The people were equally as colorless. As I spooned some soup into my mouth—chicken noodle—I kept looking around as Pratt blathered on about this and that. The dining hall reminded me less of a school cafeteria and more of a mess hall in a prison movie.

"I haven't seen any children," Sabelia said.

"There aren't any right now," Pratt explained. "In general, they've been real susceptible to Necrophage. We've lost quite a few." He lowered his voice. "Some of the parents are still here so you need to watch what you say."

After lunch which, I have to say, wasn't much even by post-apocalyptic standards, Pratt took us upstairs. The top or cap of the bunker was built right into a hillside with firing ports to all four sides. The men up there were armed with M107 .50-caliber sniper rifles. Outside the firing ports, I could see they had a clear killing field of about a hundred yards in all directions. At the outer perimeter there were a series of concrete berms and crash barriers, as well as row upon row of razorwire emplacements. Trying to attack the bunker would have been suicide.

"Even if they make it through the wire, the inner perimeter is mined," a guy named Jeggs told me. "And I guarantee if they get through that, they won't get through us."

"Which brings up an important matter," Pratt said. "The reason why both of you will need to stay with us a bit longer."

I saw a darkness pass over Sabelia's face. She was suspicious of this entire set-up and it was plain from the look on her face. If you didn't know her, then it simply might look like she was emotionless, not reacting to anything anyone said. But I knew better. Her back was up, but given her background, she wasn't about to let anyone know that. She was noncommittal.

"What's that?" I asked.

"Jeggs," Pratt said. "Let Steve here borrow your weapon for a moment. It'll be easier to see what I'm talking about with the scope."

I got into position and he handed the M107 to me. I put my eye to the sight and adjusted it. What I saw out there beyond the berms and wire was zombies. Hundreds and hundreds of them massing out there as if they knew there was food to be had but they did not know how to go about getting it.

"We're locked in," Jeggs said.

I handed his weapon back to him. There was a circular corridor in the bunker that connected it to each firing port. Pratt had me check out the outer perimeter on each side. It was the same everywhere: zombies. I can't say there were more than I'd ever seen before because I had seen thousands of them in New York City, but there was enough to make my knees feel weak.

Pratt said, "All the fighting in Baneberry has attracted them like flies to shit. All those corpses out there. It's like a buffet and now, as you see, quite a few of them are zeroing in on us here."

"So we're trapped," I said.

"Yes. But we're safe. Very rarely one or two will make it into the inner perimeter but they never get through the mine fields and none have ever made it past our snipers."

"So we just sit here and rot?" Sabelia asked.

That took Pratt back some. He looked confused for a moment or two as if no one had ever asked him such a question. "No, no. If it goes on for any length of time—and trust me, it won't—we'll go out there and clean them out."

He said it had been done before and it would be done again, if necessary. The military man in me wanted to know how they went about it. Pratt told me they first saturated the area with grenades and RPGs, then it was a shooting war from atop the berms. When the dead were culled to acceptable levels, teams with flamethrowers marched out and lit up the rest.

"Sounds like you got it all planned out," I told him.

"I like to think so."

I was trying to give him the impression that I had complete faith in him and his bunker. I didn't, but I didn't want him to know that. Keep your enemies closer, as they say. I didn't know *who* my enemy really was inside the bunker, but I was getting more than one bad vibe about the place.

We went back to where Jeggs and another man watched the perimeter. The wind out there changed direction and then we could smell the mulling dead out there. Pratt said he had some business to attend to and that left us alone with the snipers.

I had a cigarette with Jeggs and started asking him a few questions.

"What's the worst you've seen here?"

"Shit. That would have been before we got the barriers and wire up. The dead used to come at us in waves. We had machineguns up here then. We'd drop wave after wave of them and then we'd go out and mop up." He shook his head. "That was something. Crawling over hills of corpses and body parts, putting out hundreds of rounds and still they kept coming. It was plenty bad."

I imagined that it was. I sympathized with him because I had been through things like that myself.

"But now it's not so bad," he said. "We rarely have to even shoot. We've got a pretty good thing going here. The Doctor watches over us and keeps us healthy. Thank God for him."

Thank God for him.

Which was exactly what Pratt had said.

Maybe it meant nothing, but I saw it had registered with Sabelia, too. Pratt returned and took us down to the lower level and showed us some of the old biocontainment areas and an immense iron blast door that was locked at the end of the corridor.

"That used to lead to Baneberry. There was a passage that's flooded now."

"No way through at all?" I asked.

"Not unless you have a boat."

Later, we went back to our room and we didn't leave it. We passed on dinner that night because if it was made by the same people who ladled out the soup, then I had a feeling it would be barely digestible.

"Everything's bland here," Sabelia said. "The food, the people, everything."

After we had taken a shower, we went to bed. Lying there, entangled in each other, she propped herself up on one elbow in the dark and said, "He's lying, you know."

"Pratt?"

"Yes."

"I know. I'm just not sure about what or why."

"I'll bet that passage isn't flooded at all."

"Maybe not."

She laid back down. "I tell you one thing, Steve, we better start thinking of how to get out of here."

Which is exactly what I was thinking.

CONFINED

It had been a long day and I fell asleep in Sabelia's arms—at least, I think I did—and when I woke, I was alone. I couldn't feel her next to me. But even so, it didn't matter because I knew she wasn't there.

I tried to move and I felt sluggish.

I tried to cry out and my mouth felt numb like I'd been shot up with Novocain. For the life of me, it felt as if there were thirty pounds of bricks on top of me. It was a dream. I knew it had to be a dream. That's what I told myself. One of those crazy dreams where you can't run even though someone is chasing you like your shoes weigh a hundred pounds or you're mired in mud.

Then a voice, the crystal clear voice of reason, in my head said, *You're not sleeping, dumbass. You're not sleeping at all.*

But if I wasn't sleeping...

The first thing I realized was that I wasn't even lying down. I was sitting with my back up against a wall. The room didn't have that medicinal smell I'd gotten so used to, the after-odor of medical disinfectants. It smelled...metallic. Like steel and rusted rivet heads. And dankness.

I wasn't in the room with Sabelia.

I had been taken somewhere else.

As I sat there, working my limbs so I could get some feeling in them, weird thoughts flashed through my brain. The weirdest of all—and probably the most prosaic—was that I had an absolute, overpowering craving for McDonald's. I wanted, hell, I *needed* a Quarter Pounder with Cheese and a large fry. A chocolate shake, too. And maybe a Filet-O-Fish and some Chicken McNuggets. It was insane, but I could almost taste the Quarter Pounder. I hadn't had fast food in many months, of course, burger joints being in short supply since The Awakening, but I could have killed for some at that moment. I kept seeing the image of the golden arches in my head and my mouth was watering. Christ, I could smell the fries.

Then, as quickly as it had popped into my head, it was gone.

Like a faucet being turned off. Not only was it gone but the very idea of a burger and fries made me physically ill. The food paraded through my head and bile came up the back of my throat. I gagged and spit it out. The inside of my mouthy tasted like cold grease.

Then that, too, was gone.

Maybe this is what Pratt meant by an after-effect of the fear gas. And maybe I was just losing it. Regardless, that didn't explain where I was or how in the hell I'd gotten there. And it didn't explain how I'd gotten dressed. I knew that when I fell asleep I didn't have a stitch on. Neither had Sabelia.

My sense of reality was fractured.

It had been to a certain extent even since I was gassed. And as I sat there, I doubted everything in the blackness of that unknown room.

That's when I heard something.

It was a wet slobbering sound like a dog lapping from a bowl of water. Then a moist tearing sound. It sent fingers of fear through me. There was silence for a moment or two and then I heard a gnawing sound like a hound working on a meaty bone.

And I smelled something awful. Something I had not been aware of before—the dark, corrupt odor of decay. I knew that odor too well by then. There was a zombie in the room with me and it was feeding. It could have been something else, another animal, but I knew better.

The fear became terror that settled deep into me as I listened to teeth scraping on bone.

By then, the numbness was almost gone. I moved my legs and then my arms. I shifted a bit and bumped my elbow against the wall behind me which gave out a sort of hollow noise. The gnawing stopped immediately. I froze, holding my breath.

Wait.

Just wait.

The gnawing started again and I relaxed a little.

I was in a real shitty situation anyway you cut it. I was in the dark with one of the living dead and maybe more than one for all I knew. In general, I knew they usually wouldn't attack as long as they had something to eat...but not always. I didn't have any weapons or any way to get my bearings. My only hope was that my possible immunity to Zombpox was still working. Regardless, the idea of dancing in the dark with a ravenous corpse was not exactly appealing.

The gnawing went on unabated.

What the hell now?

I couldn't just play dead and hope that the creature went away. And I wasn't about to sit there in the dark without knowing where I was. I stood up as silently as possible. There was nothing in the pockets of my pants. But in my shirt pocket, cigarettes and a disposable lighter. They hadn't been in there earlier. Somebody had put them in there. The last thing in the world I wanted was a smoke, but the lighter gave me ideas.

The gnawing stopped and I heard a tearing sound again.

The zombie was probably tearing off a new piece of flesh to eat. I heard a crunching sound that reminded me of someone chewing on a chicken wing.

I had to do something and I knew it.

DEAD FRIENDS

I brought the lighter up and flicked it.

The first thing I saw was a body.

It was spread-eagled on the floor, laid open from crotch to throat. It looked like rats or wild dogs had been eating on it, biting out chunks and gorging themselves. But I knew it wasn't rats or dogs. The body was that of a man and it looked like he'd been shot through the head at close range. The pattern of blood on the wall told me he'd been standing up when it happened. It was a disgusting sight, but it wasn't the most shocking thing.

That was its identity.

Because I knew who it was.

It was Seppy. And if he was here, then I was pretty certain Scott and Sandy wouldn't be too far away. The lighter started burning my fingers so I let it go out. I could still hear the gnawing. It went on uninterrupted.

Where the hell was I?

In the glow of the lighter, I saw steel bulkheads which meant I could have been just about anywhere in the bunker…unless I was still in bed, still tripping out on fear gas. But I didn't think I was. The walls were maybe fifteen feet apart. Feeling my way along the one nearest me, I moved away from the gnawing. I kept going until I came to a flat wall with a steel door set in it. I felt around, but there was no knob or latch.

I flicked my lighter to be sure.

There was nothing.

I was sealed in with that gnawing thing.

I moved back along the wall until I came to the corpse of Seppy. Before I got there, I bumped into something. A table. That's what it felt like. An ordinary little table on wheels that rolled when I pushed on it.

I flicked the lighter again.

There were two things on the table. Two things I suppose I was meant to find: a flashlight and a K-Bar knife, a fighting knife. This entire thing had to be a game or a test. It was all arranged too conveniently.

But I *did* have a weapon.

And a light.

I moved along the wall until I reached Seppy's body. I nearly stepped on it. The knife in my right hand, gripped tightly, I decided not to use the light until I had to. No sense alerting my position. I moved around the body, feeling my way forward by instinct and instinct alone.

I could hear the chewing of the zombie very clearly.

Its smell was rancid.

I could hear it ripping into cold flesh, the chomping and biting sounds, teeth against bone. When I was sure it was only about ten feet from me, I turned on the light.

I saw it.

It saw me.

The zombie was a girl, a teenager, and the body she was feeding upon had been mutilated to the extent that it looked like a mass of raw hamburger. Blood had flooded out from it in a sticky puddle, loops of entrails cast about like dead snakes. I saw a severed hand, a leg that had been twisted off at the knee, bits of flesh and organ meat that looked like they had gone through a meat grinder. There was no way to tell the corpse's sex. Its genitals were gone, eaten down into a bloody trench, the skin peeled from its flesh. Even its face was gnawed down to the red-stained skull beneath.

The zombie cast aside a femur pitted with bite marks.

It stood up to face me.

I put the light full on it. In life, it had been a slender, tall girl with long blonde hair. In death, it was a livid nightmare. She was naked and spattered with gore, her fingers looking like they'd been dyed in red ink. One eye was huge and white, threaded with scarlet vein tracery. The other was a lidless, scarified pit.

But it was her mouth that drew my attention.

It was like a bloodstained bear trap, the teeth pink and filed to sharp conical points. Blood oozed down her pale chin and strings of meat dangled from her chomping jaws. There was no way in hell any of the risen had even the rudimentary smarts to file their teeth like pulp horror cannibals. Someone had done it for her and most likely to heighten the instinctive terror she inspired.

She came at me, her feet slopping through the blood, her hunger insatiable.

I was going to have to fight her.

I would have to kill her with the knife.

I stepped back. "Please just go away," I said, knowing it was hopeless. It was like trying to talk an axe out of splitting your skull. "Just go away…I don't want to do this, Sandy."

Because it *was* Sandy.

Necrophage had made her into this monster, but it hadn't done it alone. Judging by the filed teeth, it had had help.

She lunged at me and I sidestepped her.

She came around fast for one of the living dead and I nearly didn't get out of her way. I dropped the flashlight, but thankfully it didn't go out and I had light to fight by. When she attacked again, I slashed her remaining eye, blinding her. It split like a sliced grape, yellowish ichor bubbling from it. She seemed to barely notice, vaulting at me again and this time I got behind her and away from those teeth. I hooked an arm around her throat, pulling her head to the side and sliding the blade of the K-Bar beneath her right ear and up into her brain pan. It was no slick, fluid sort of kill like a commando on TV. No, it was sloppy as all hell and the first two times I botched it, stabbing her in the ear and the neck.

But then I had her and she knew it.

I held onto her, twisting the knife, blood spurting over the back of my hand. She bucked and fought, her nails laying my forearm open as she frantically scratched at me. But I kept twisting the knife and finally I felt her go rigid. She made choking, gurgling sounds and vomited out a black bile that smelled so foul I let her go and hit the floor. She moved around in drunken, uneasy circles, trying to paw at the knife buried in her head.

But it was too late.

She went to the floor on her knees, making a shrill sort of pained sound in her throat and then face-planted with a wet, splatting sound.

Breathing heavily, feeling like I was almost hyperventilating, I picked up the flashlight and panned the beam around. The room was almost like a tunnel, as I suspected. I got to my feet and followed along the wall until I found another door. Like the other one, it had no knob. I tapped on it with the butt of the flashlight and it rang out. I could hear the noise echoing out on the other side.

"Hey!" I called. "I killed her, so let me out!"

I waited for a few more minutes, but there were no sounds. Nothing at all. No voices. No approaching footsteps. I sighed and dug out a cigarette. As I pulled off it, relishing in the odor of tobacco smoke that cancelled out the pungent and sickening death smell, I was more certain than ever that this was no trip, no chemically-induced nightmare.

"All right!" I shouted. "The game's up, okay? I performed for my fucking supper, so let me out!"

Still nothing.

There was nothing to do but wait, so I waited. Twenty, thirty minutes later I heard a key in the door and I stood up, ready for freedom. The door swung open and a blinding light exploded in my face.

I thought I heard a hissing sound like an open gas valve.

"Hey!" I said.

Then I felt blackness rushing up at me and I went out cold.

COLD CUTS

When I came out of that madness, I was down on my knees, but in a different room entirely. It was maybe fifteen feet long by fifteen wide, lit by a naked bulb hanging from the ceiling. Like the other room, the walls were gray steel, institutional-looking. I came out of it slowly as before, hearing a voice singing in a droning, squeaky sort of voice. It was a song I recognized from childhood. Was it "Puff, the Magic Dragon"? I think it might have been. The voice terrified me for some reason until I realized it was my voice.

I blinked my eyes.

I had to come out of it.

My first real sensation was that I was starving. I felt hungrier than I had ever been in my life. Images kept drifting through my mind—juicy roasts of beef, well-marbled steaks smothered in mushrooms, thick-cut pork chops striped with grilling marks, barbecued chicken and glazed fat hams. As these things went through my mind, filling my belly with sharp waves of hunger that bit so deeply they seemed to have teeth, I realized I had a hand braced against the wall. I looked down and I was wearing only fatigue pants. My body was horribly emaciated. My stomach was sucked in and my ribs jutting out. Even my arms were spindle-thin. I touched my face and there was a bristly growth of beard. But I knew I had shaved yesterday.

I knew I had.

Then...weirdly enough...my body looked normal again, even though I was still starving, my stomach growling loudly. The beard was still on my face, though, and if I had to judge, I would have thought it was at least five or six days worth of growth.

My second real sensation was that I was not alone.

When I craned my head over to the side, I saw a body. It was not some revolting slaughtered corpse, but the body of a woman that was hung by the feet. Her ankles were roped together and tied off to a beam overhead.

I sat there, staring at her, fearing for a moment that it was Sabelia. But it wasn't. This woman was a redhead and her long shiny locks were brushing the floor as were her fingertips. From what I could see, there didn't seem to be a mark on her so it was really hard to say how she died.

I crawled over to her.

Unsteadily, I climbed to my feet. It took some doing. When I finally stood, I was dizzy and nauseous. The room spun and then spun again. I held onto the wall until it passed. Sweat ran down my face and my teeth chattered uncontrollably. I felt like I needed to throw up, then I thought I was going to pass clean out.

Don't fold up now, I cautioned myself. *This is all part of it somehow. This is part of the game, the test, whatever this is about.*

The world slowed down and I began to feel better. Again, as surreal as it all was, I couldn't convince myself that it wasn't real. I knew it was real.

So I would play along.

I had no choice.

I walked over to the corpse of the redhead. The nausea was gone. The hunger, however, was back. Again, I'd never known such hunger before. I felt woozy, lightheaded. Christ, I would have sold my soul for a cracker or a slice of cheese.

I stood there, staring at the corpse.

The redhead had been an attractive woman, athletic but not sinewy. Her thighs were meaty, powerful-looking, her breasts heavy. She was the sort of woman a man would have wanted badly in life. Her lips were full, cheekbones high, a sort of exaggerated sexuality around the mouth that made me want to kiss her, to suck her tongue into my mouth. I wanted to nibble on her lips…no, that wasn't true. I wanted to *bite* them. I wanted to sink my teeth into their juicy plumpness until her blood ran free and filled my mouth.

Jesus.

The desire was so strong I stepped back. What I was thinking was insane. It was…cannibalism, ghoulism. But the hunger was so intense it had nearly driven me to it. Even as I backed away, it chewed at my insides. I turned away from the body. For the first time in my life I was actually afraid of myself, afraid of what I was and what I was capable of if I didn't maintain control. There was something in me. Something that did not belong. The animal at the core of my being was trying to claw to the surface. If it got free, if

I turned my back for a moment or let my resolve weaken, it would take over. It would rise up, fangs bared, and begin devouring the woman.

This was what must have been at the root of the zombies themselves: voracious animal hunger laid raw. Intellect, culture, ethics and morals—all of it was pushed aside, cumbersome baggage rejected, and the savage, gluttonous, primeval reptile brain lorded over all.

Somehow, it had been set loose in me.

It took every ounce of willpower I possessed to keep it at bay, to suppress its horrible appetites. My entire body was shaking. I was caught in an internal struggle to save my dignity, my humanity. My muscles strained and stood out like cords under my skin. It was all I could do not to turn and look at the woman.

And in my head there was a voice, a mocking guttural voice that constantly tormented me. *Don't be stupid, Steve. You have to eat. All things have to eat. Nobody will ever know. I won't tell. You won't tell. We won't tell. C'mon, look at her hanging there, soft and luscious. Think how sweet her juices would be, how delectable the meat of her thighs. Think of how wonderful it would feel to seize her in your mouth, to rend and tear until her blood flowed like red wine and ran down your chin. Her breasts would be the softest loaves, her lips tender and sweet, and that delicate budding flower between her legs would explode with honey when you bit into it—*

No!

Glut yourself, Steve! Fill yourself! Use your fingers, your teeth, let the beast free!

NO! NO! NOOOOO!

Oh, don't be a dumbass, Steve. I'm talking survival, I'm talking continuation here. You're empty inside and I'm empty inside, but together we can be full and satisfied. You don't want to starve…do you? Do you know what that's like, Steve? Do you have any idea? The hunger pangs do not go away, they only bite deeper and deeper until it feels like your belly is filled with razors, forever slicing and cutting until you lose your mind! When that happens, Steve-o, when you reach that point where every pang is excruciating, you'll eat anything! Anything! Insects, toads, snakes, dead rats, even your own fingers! You'll kill Sabelia so you can taste her meat and pull the blood-juiced mass of her heart fresh and pumping from her chest! By God, you'll even feast upon your son's cold corpse—

At that point, I screamed and kept screaming until the voice was gone, until it was expelled from my head. I wouldn't listen to it. I wouldn't allow myself to taste human flesh. I had once before but that was trickery, it was not choice. I'd never taste it again. I'd kill myself first.

Still...I could feel the draw of the corpse hanging there like a succulent side of beef. Its pull was practically magnetic. But I wouldn't look at it. I would not sink my teeth into cold human flesh. I had been tricked into it once, I had eaten human bacon, but never again.

Then you'll starve, boy! You'll starve like a rat in a cage!

I ignored that.

There was a door on the other side of the room. It had no knob like the others. It was locked and I couldn't move it much as I bashed my shoulder into it again and again, kicking it, and beating on it with my fists until my knuckles were skinned and bleeding.

It did no good.

There was only one other thing in the room besides me and that corpse: a little cabinet pushed against the wall. It had three drawers. I went over to it, getting precariously close to the corpse of the redhead. Two of the drawers were empty, but the third held gleaming stainless steel cutlery. It looked very much like the set of Rada that I had gotten my wife for Christmas before I went off to Iraq. A meat cleaver. A butcher's knife. A carving knife. A long roasting fork. Two paring knives. And all of them, I knew, surgically sharp.

The tools of a butcher.

And like the K-Bar and flashlight in the other room, placed there for the job I was expected to do: the gutting and filleting of the woman. They would have made it all very easy. And like the voice said, nobody would ever know.

Except that wasn't really true, now was it?

Somebody would know.

The very same twisted asshole that had arranged all this and put me in this predicament in the first place. Whatever sort of fucked-up games or tests or feasibility studies these were, I was being watched and I knew it. I was a rat in a maze and the cheese was hanging only a few feet away.

But I wasn't going to bite.

I slid the drawer closed.

I went over to the door and sat there with my back up against it. The hunger pangs hadn't gone away. They were worse if anything. Absolutely debilitating. They came and went in peaks and valleys. The valleys were about what you got when you hadn't eaten all day, but the peaks…a living hell that actually made me cry out. Maybe not even peaks. That wasn't descriptive enough. More like spikes and stabbing blades that were so agonizing, I kept doubling over.

"This can go on for a month," I said out loud, "but you won't break me. I swear to God, you won't break me."

You're wrong, Mr. Niles. You're already broken.

"The fuck I am."

The mind games grew even more intense then because as I looked over at the body, I saw that great sections of flesh had been cut from the thighs. The breasts had been carved free, spongy red cavities in their place. Somebody had been at her. As I saw this, the hunger in me was gone. I was full. I was stuffed.

I had been eating her.

And how you enjoyed every morsel and every bloody mouthful.

"Bullshit!" I cried out and the rage in me overcame the hallucinations I was being fed. I looked over at the corpse. It was untouched. Completely.

I got it then, or at least part of it.

This was all as real as I had thought, but suggestions could be placed in your drugged mind. Suggestions so powerful that you would not doubt their truth and your overheated imagination would do the rest. I had to guard against these fictions, even if my mind wasn't entirely my own.

"You can't break me," I said and I heard a voice laughing at me with an evil cackling. It took me a moment or two to realize that as I said this, I had been staring hungrily at the corpse…and salivating.

DR. CRIPPS

You can wake up now, everything is all right.

I heard the voice and it was like a hypnotist's fingers snapping me out of trance. I seemed to jump from sleeping to full wakefulness very quickly, then I fell back into the former only to once again emerge into the latter, back and forth, back and forth like a bouncing rubber ball.

I said you can wake up now. Open your eyes.

There was something commanding about that voice and I didn't dare refuse it. If it wanted me to be awake, then I wanted to be awake, too. My eyes opened and stayed open. I could hear a voice speaking, but I couldn't be sure of what it was saying. Was it speaking English? It sounded like gibberish to me.

"Why don't you get the shit out of your mouth?" I said.

The voice droned on and on and I still couldn't be sure what it was saying. It was like half my brain was awake and the other half was still sleeping. Was that even possible? It seemed so at that moment.

Then I could not only hear the voice but understand it and I knew I had heard it speaking many, many times. "...is something we use, Mr. Niles. Do you see? Fear exists in the human mind. It is a mechanism like any other. That's what I need you to understand."

I was strapped to a bed. I knew that much. And sitting at my bedside was the old guy with the white hair and steel-gray mustache. The one I remembered from my dreams. The man with the hypodermic needle. *Now, my friend, all I need is a little bit of what you have and then we can begin. That's not asking so much is it?* Yes, his voice had a flat, droning quality to it and his eyes were dead like chips of tombstone marble. This was Dr. Cripps, the engineer of nightmares, the mind-stealer and brainwasher. *Thank God for him.* Oh yes.

"What the fuck have you done to me now?" I asked him.

He scribbled on a clipboard. "I've put you through another series of tests to determine if you're of the right caliber to continue on with the drug trial."

"I don't want any part of it."

"You don't have a choice. I selected you," he said, as if he was talking about a kitten he'd plucked from a litter. "You meet the necessary qualifications in just about every way. You're an excellent subject."

"Where's Sabelia? What have you done to her?"

He smiled. His lips were thin, his grin arrogant, the whites of his eyes nearly pink. "I've done nothing to her. I really have no plans for her…of course, if you don't cooperate that could change. How much fear do you think she could take?"

I wanted to rage at him and tell him she could take more than a candyass like him could ever hand out, but I knew it wasn't true. Cripps was an expert at breaking minds. He knew how to do it. You didn't want to taunt or toy with a guy like him.

So I kept my mouth shut. A first for me.

Cripps hovered over me, shining a light in my eyes and testing my pupil reactivity. "Right now, Sabelia is fine. She's living in the bunker above with the others, going about her life and attending to her tasks and asking no more." He grinned again and it was big grin of gums and yellow teeth. "She doesn't remember a life before the bunker and you are a stranger to her."

"Like all the others up there," I said. "Mindless slaves."

"Peaceful people who are working towards the common good. Not a single revolutionary or troublemaker among them. They are the future, Mr. Niles. They are my people."

"Your puppets."

"Have it your way." He grinned again. "Not to sound like a heavy from a bad movie, but resistance is really futile. You can't stand against us. The future is coming and they are part of it. People like you will either fall in line or they'll be crushed."

"You're part of ARM, aren't you?"

"Yes."

"And so are they?"

"Yes…only they don't realize it which is fine. They are a test group. One of many."

Cripps explained that he had been part of the original PHOBIC research program whose aim was to amplify latent psychic abilities in the human mind via implants in the brain. Those with implants were considered too special to die out with the rest of us, I knew, so they had their blood replaced with a synthetic hemoglobin called X-Plasma. Unfortunately, while it kept them free of Necrophage infection, it created a mutant strain of Porphyria which made them anemic, mentally unbalanced, and in need of fresh human blood to rejuvenate themselves. They were called *Bloodlords.* And I knew all about them and the way they could manipulate your mind just as I knew about the blood farms they ran where people were kept like cattle, their blood siphoned off drop by drop.

"But you're not one of them are you? You're not a member of the PHOBIC Consciousness?" I asked him, referring to the powerful uplink shared by the Bloodlords.

He shook his head. "There was more to PHOBIC than the creation of psychic supermen. Its original aim was behavioral science. Developing certain psychochemicals that could be used by the military. We searched for the perfect compound and found it in a derivative of BZ which is—"

"I know what it is. Pratt reeled off all the info you programmed him with."

He smiled again. "Of course. What we came up with was something called Agent 17. Depending on its dosage, it was something of a miracle. Undiluted and sprayed down on an enemy population, it would create confusion and panic, incapacitating fear and paranoia by unleashing all the phobias and secret fears of the subconscious mind. But that was at full strength. Diluted, it could render an enemy population into a herd of sheep who were extremely susceptible to behavior modification techniques and hypnotic suggestion. Hence, you have the residents of the bunker."

He went on to say that had been the original plan. Dose an enemy population before you invaded and they destroyed each other, running wild and confused. Then, before you hit the beach, you dosed them with a highly diluted dose and there were no more enemies, only friends that would help you reach your goals even if said goals were their own enslavement.

"But then came the implants and all that and our funding was severely curtailed…but now all that's changed."

Yes, it had changed, all right. The PHOBICs—as the Bloodlords liked to call themselves—were not many in number. They lorded over ARM, but that wouldn't last. They were dying out. ARM was in the process of changing from a destructive force in the world to a *constructive* force.

"They are the antidote to chaos, Mr. Niles. Already we have several towns out there that are safe zones. The inhabitants work and live together. They marry and have children. They are re-creating what Necrophage took from us. And as the walking dead are eradicated, there will be more and more towns until once again we have states and nations," he told me, a despotic gleam in his eye. "Like it was before, but much better. Mild doses of Agent 17 will assure that. No more fighting, no more racism, no more religious persecution, no more political division, no more hate and violence. What we will have is a positive force that will create a positive world free from strife and poverty and disease and starvation."

Yes, a doped-up world.

But Dr. Cripps didn't see what was so alarming about that. The United States for example, he said, was already doped-up on booze and drugs, sex and violence, greed and self-indulgence. Such narcissism would be a thing of the past. Our egocentric, self-destructive behavior would no longer exist. And as a unified people on a unified planet no longer divided by religion and politics and social boundaries, there was no limit to what we could achieve.

I had to admit, it sounded pretty damn good in some ways, but doping people was still doping people. They were still the same under the skin and in the depths of their minds. Sooner or later, all the dark and negative urges were going to reassert themselves one way or another and when that happened it would be like a human atomic bomb. Besides, even all that aside, Cripps' plan left out certain things like human dignity, freewill, and choice.

"And what do you want with me?"

"I want you to be part of the process."

"Another brain-dead puppet up in the bunker?" I said, even though I knew it couldn't be that or I'd already be up there with them. "Another sheep?"

"On the contrary, a *wolf.*" He let that lay with me a few moments. "You see, Agent 17 can do more than incapacitate, confuse, or sedate. Combined with other psychotropics it can create killers. It can set the animal within free. And with proper hypnotic control, those violent tendencies can be turned off and on like a switch."

That was my job.

I was to be an *exterminator*, as he put it. My job and those like me would be to clean out Baneberry block by block, putting down zombies, berserkers, ragtag survivalists, and insurgents like McTeague and his raiders. That's what this was all about and what my testing had led to.

"Consider it a clinical drug trial," Cripps said. "We want Baneberry. It will be our next settlement. We already have the people waiting to move in there, but first it has to be cleaned out and mopped up. And that's where you and others like you come in. We want that town and you're going to get it for us."

"The fuck I am."

He grinned again and his eyes almost seemed to glow like those of a cougar seen by night, shining and huge. But it wasn't their physical appearance, I knew, but what was behind them. The power Agent 17 gave him. The power to make and break people as he saw fit, to play with them like toys. To cherish them if they performed correctly and crush them if they did not.

"Oh, you will, Mr. Niles," he said. "Be most assured that you will do everything I say and you'll do it happily."

I started to tell him what I thought of him and his ideas for this pristine, sterile, and bloodless new republic of his, but all that got me was a syringe in the arm. Then I was sinking away into the darkness and I could hear his voice speaking to me. I liked the sound of it and I wanted to do whatever it told me.

THE DEVIL'S DISCIPLES

Make no mistake: Cripps was a monster. Maybe he had lofty plans for creating a peaceful brotherhood of man where hand-in-hand we all walk into the sunlight, but his methods were unthinkable and sinister.

Everything he said was either true, absolute bullshit, or a clever concoction of both, a seamless scarf that he could wrap around your throat so easily you wouldn't know it was there until you were bug-eyed and green-faced, your lungs sucking dust.

But one thing was true: with Agent 17 he could do just about anything. He could make minds better, fill them with purity or drag them through the blackest anti-human reaches of subconscious nightmare. Given at full dose, injected intravenously, Agent 17 could strip your mind in minutes, completely debilitating you with fear, reducing you to a screaming, rubbery mass of terror as every nightmare you'd ever had and every phobia you'd ever known clothed itself in flesh and claimed you for its own. Given at half-strength in diluted aerosol form and delivered with, say, a gas grenade, it created panic, confusion, hysteria, and utter disorientation. You either became a mindless zombie wallowing in its own shit, head filled with dead snakes, or you lost all inhibitions and danced naked in the falling rain or laughed hysterically at kitschy sayings on rolling pins right before you fucked like an animal in heat. And at its lowest dosage, delivered orally through food and water, you became like the residents of the bunker—blank-eyed, complacent, Wal-Mart smiley-faced, your head filled with warm gray putty waiting to be kneaded. You became an extra wandering the streets of Mayberry R.F.D. and glorifying in the banality of Norman Rockwell and Thelma Lou's cooking down at the diner. *Yes sir, no sir, two bags full sir.* You looked out through your eyes, but like glass balls they did not really see. And like an empty box, your brain did not really think other than reminding you when to piss, when to shit, when to eat and when to sleep. And very often it told your mouth to say, *Thank*

God for the Doctor, which you did almost constantly…which was like buying the guy who raped you a drink or letting the monster that sucked out your brains marry your daughter.

Enough said.

My memories after that point range from being almost hallucinogenically vivid to blurry and indistinct. But let me lay it all out for you the best I can.

The area of Baneberry where Sabelia and I and the others first came in was a relatively peaceful place, give or take. The zombie situation was not out of control. There were berserkers, but not too many. Very few survivalists were fighting it out.

Downtown in the heart of the city it was a whole 'nother story.

The Main Street area comprised something like eight square blocks and was the hardest hit sector in the city. It belonged to no one and anyone. Sections of it were bombed out and there was rubble and debris everywhere, burned-out cars and trucks, bones in the gutters and rats in the alleys. All the heavy fighting had turned it into a no-man's land of corpses and wreckage, a maze of deserted buildings and garbage-strewn byways patrolled by survivalists and militias, the living dead and the insane, religious cults, cut-throats, psychopaths, and wild dogs. At night, the berserkers came out and snipers capped rounds from rooftops and fanatics sacrificed people on street corners to the rising moon.

If it was insane, inhuman, deranged, unbalanced, or just plain freaky, it hid out in the Main Street sector.

An afternoon out there was enough to make you feel like a Jonah, and fill your belly with creeping dread. A night would strip your gears entirely. Anything that moved was prey and anything or anybody that didn't walk at your side was the enemy. This was my hunting ground and I stalked it with blank eyes, bent nerves, hatred and resignation, terror and a kill-happy death lust that wired me together into one piece.

My unit was known as Kilo India Alfa-9 or, KIA-9. A little joke on us, I guess. "9" because there were nine of us. There were four other KIA units out there, but we never came in contact with them. If we had, we would have killed them or them us. That's how it worked in Death City, as we called our sector.

KIA-9's main objective was finding the enemy and whether that enemy was living or dead it did not matter. We were sort of an advanced scout unit that looked for the enemy and killed them when possible, set-up booby traps and ambushes, and called in the heavies when we were outnumbered or came across a sizeable force. The *heavies* were mech infantry units with Guardians and LAV-25s and close air support from Kiowa choppers. KIA-9 was made up of me, Smitty and Scales, Mongol and Loony, Mad Mike and Doc Feelgood, Big Bird and Little Gun. I was known as "Dog." What anyone's real name was, I never found out anymore than I found out where they came from.

In KIA-9 there was only the here and now.

That was something we practiced with zeal.

We were quite a crew. Saints, sinners, psychopaths, homicidal maniacs, pathological murderers, take your pick. We did what we did when war came to town and our programming was foolproof. Our balls and brains had traded places and our souls were burned black. We were push button killers manipulated by an egomaniacal hand and there wasn't a damn thing we could do about it.

THE KILLER ELITE

One morning after some serious close-in fighting with a survivalist group known as the Omega Clan, Scales said to me, "When you come down to it, you better know it's about the grease—who gets it and who don't. At the end of the day, you don't think about who you put down, who you greased, you just walk away." He had a habit of saying things like that and I never knew if he was talking to me or to himself or maybe both of us.

There were about thirty corpses out in the street, in whole and in part, along with a few wild dogs we'd capped just for kicks. Smitty, who was nuts and just liked to blow things up or make them burn, had wired the bodies with a couple bricks of C-4 and we were hiding in the shell of a building down the way, waiting for the dead to show. Waiting for the *boom!*

As we waited, Doc Feelgood cleaned his fingernails with the tip of his K-Bar and Mongol used a machete—which he kept razor sharp—to peel off some beard stubble under his chin. I sat there smoking with Scales, both of us listening to Smitty going on about the fact that since he could not remember his past it was highly likely that he had been abducted by aliens and reprogrammed…which in its own way was precariously close to the truth.

"Who's to say we're still on Earth, man?" he asked us as he stroked his detonator. "Maybe we were sucked up in a force ray or something and taken away to Arcturus or Altair Four. Maybe that's where we are now and this is just a stage and we're just performing here to keep our masters amused."

Big Bird and Little Gun were tense. They wanted to fight. They wanted to get out there and take lives. Nothing else satisfied them. Zulu waited patiently with her chainsaw and Mad Mike scanned the streets with dead eyes. He was a gigantic bulk of a man, battle-scarred and grim. Holding the SAW in his hands, bandoliers of ammo criss-crossed over his shoulders, he looked like Sgt. Rock.

"We got a nibble," Zulu said and all eyes were on the corpse pile.

She was right: a couple of deadheads had smelled the goodies and wandered in for a snack. I couldn't tell if they had been men or women in life. They were just ragged-looking things, their scalps sloughed away, dead-white eyes puckering in black sockets, teeth chattering as they contemplated the offering. They wasted no time, dropping to their knees and digging into open bellies for soft, chewy goodies. Being the animalistic, stupid things they were, they fought over the same body, playing a grisly game of tug-of-war with the same blood-greased hose of entrails, pulling back and forth on it. If it hadn't been so fucking sick, it might have been funny.

"Don't give you much faith in the future of zombiedom," Zulu said and I giggled. She looked over at me and winked.

Big Bird and Little Gun were just beside themselves. Here was something that moved that should not move and they could take care of that with a few squeezes of their triggers but Doc Feelgood wouldn't have it and they knew it. I watched them. They were both shaking. Have you ever watched a cat stalk a pigeon? They creep forward silently, every muscle quaking with the primal call of the hunt. That's how Big Bird and Little Gun were.

Scales elbowed me, grinning, directing my attention to them but it was already there. They looked like they were going to explode. It was not easy to hold back the *Kill! Kill! Kill!* imperative that juiced through them. It was like willing your heart not to beat. They kept looking back at Doc Feelgood, KIA-9's leader, hoping he'd turn them loose, but he just sat there impassively, cleaning his nails. About the third or fourth time they looked back like anxious hounds wanting to run, Mad Mike spit a stream of tobacco juice into Big Bird's face and Big Bird nearly opened up with his weapon. Only a look from Doc kept him from doing so. I think Mad Mike wanted him to try. He would have cut both of them in half with his SAW.

Mad Mike was hard to figure.

Sure, Sgt. Rock in the flesh…if Sgt. Rock was not only battle-worn, crusty, and pissed-off, but a fucking maniac to boot that loved killing simply for killing's sake. He would have turned the

SAW on us had Doc suggested it. He had no allegiance to anyone or anything. He never spoke. He never smiled or frowned. His eyes were always dark and simmering with hate. Just one big killing machine. Beyond that, he was hard to figure.

Two or three other zombies showed up now.

It was no surprise; there were hundreds and hundreds of them in the Main Street sector. We dropped a lot of them, but they just kept coming and coming, meatflies attracted to the smelly garbage can of Main Street, Baneberry, US of A. I don't know what senses still worked in them. Some of them seemed to be able to see real good, others were nearly blind, still others had no eyes at all. But they could hear pretty good and I'm guessing they could smell carrion like sharks smell blood.

Mongol was grinning as the zombies began to swarm.

He was probably crazier than the rest of us, which was really saying something. He was dressed like we were in camo BDU pants, desert boots, and a tactical vest fitted with spare M4 magazines, frag, incendiary, and smoke genades, the works, but in twin sheaths at his back were two double-edged machetes. All he had to do was reach back with both hands and clutch their handles and slide them free and he had serious killing power ready to be used. And make no mistake, he *liked* to use them. He had a long, thin drooping mustache that hung down to his jawline, a sharp little beard, and his head was bald and shiny save the warrior scalp lock he sported. That look, combined with his Asian ancestry, made him look like a badass from a kung fu movie.

He looked over at me, eyes like black glass. "Confucius say: When zombies go boom, wise men bow heads in thanks." He laughed at that with a low growling sort of sound.

As the zombies pressed in, I started to get anxious myself. I wanted to charge out there and do some serious killing. The need to kill, to destroy our targets was hardwired into us and when it was denied, I would get a sort of hungry feeling in my belly. I was like a starving man being denied food.

Doc Feelgood was doing a mental count of how many heads we had out there. "We got forty-three maggot-eaters," he said. "That should be good."

Smitty was shaking with excitement. Sweat ran down his face. He wanted to fire the detonator. At that moment, it was his entire world and until he did, it was like being denied a building orgasm. He kept gnashing his teeth and licking the salt off his lips. He had enough C-4 wired out there to bring down a house and he wanted to get it done.

"All right," Doc said, "everyone get down. Smitty…do your thing."

Smitty held up the detonator and pressed the firing button.

There were a few milliseconds when nothing at all happened—then *WHUMP! WHUMP! WHUMP!* The C-4 went off. None of us had our heads down, of course. We all wanted to see and see we did. The explosion was blinding, the noise like rolling thunder, and for the zombies out there it was like sitting on the spout of an active volcano. They were vaporized in a resounding eruption of force, flames, and flying debris. We were down the road a piece from them, but it didn't protect us. What goes up must come down, as they say.

And it came down, all right.

Blood and gore and flaming guts dropped from the sky and rained down into the street and we were pulverized with it. It lasted but a few seconds, but when it was over, we were busy wiping blood from our faces and picking bits of tissue from our equipment and clothes. Smitty found an eyeball in his hair. Zulu was nearly cold-cocked by a severed arm. There were legs and feet and hands around us, a flaming skull not two feet from me. Scales was bitching while he disengaged a smoldering set of entrails from himself and Doc Feelgood was using a tweezers from his medical bag to pluck shrapnel from Mad Mike's arms which turned out to be human teeth.

It was quite a scene.

Smitty couldn't stop giggling, red streaks running down his face like tears. Little Gun and Big Bird were busy cleaning each other of debris like monkeys plucking nits from one another. There was something funny *and* disturbing about that.

I reached in my vest pocket for a cigarette and pulled out a yellowed human finger. I tossed it aside.

Zulu was spitting something out. "It even got in my fucking mouth," she said.

Mongol was smiling about it all. "Confucius say: April showers bring May flowers," he said to us. He tossed a hand to me. "What is the sound of one hand clapping?"

I caught it and was amazed that it was a woman's hand, wedding ring still in place. I found that hilarious. I bet when her husband slid the ring on her long finger, he never imagined where it would end up.

TROPHIES

One day Scales told me, "For awhile there, it was getting like fucking Vietnam or something. We had little kids coming at us, Omega kids, with bombs strapped to 'em. We had this dude named Rafe with us before you got here—don't get me going on him, I saw him fucking a corpse once, funniest thing I ever seen—and he got blown away by one of those kids. I wasn't too far from him and after I picked my ass up, I saw that pieces of Rafe were all over the place. My hair was red with his blood. Hard to believe a man has that much blood in him. So, the next time we come on a kid, living one I mean, Mongol grabs her and says he's going to skin her. He says he knows how to tan skin, any skin, into the softest leather, only he don't remember where he learned it. So he ties the girl down and starts peeling her…and *shit,* did she scream. Doc comes over. Fuck you doing? He says. Mongol says, I'm skinning her. And Doc says, Well, use my knife, it's sharper."

We laughed at that story.

It's hard to believe, but we did. It was pure comedy to us. Now and again when I'd hear something like that, something inside me would hesitate for a second as if to say, *man, that's not funny, it's sick,* but then I'd laugh anyway.

In a normal, sane world we would have been charged with war crimes and strung up for the things we did. But our world was hardly sane and we sure as hell were not. Dr. Cripps was Dr. Frankenstein and we were his monsters set loose to ravage the world. And ravage it we did. It wasn't just the zombies we put down, but anything we could find. Sometimes we'd hang people up and sit around watching zombies disembowel them. We'd throw people off roofs, bet on the width of splatter patterns, then run down to the streets below to see who won. We lit people on fire, we tied them up, cut them open and let the dogs and rats have them. We played soccer with a woman's head in the streets until it finally fell apart.

We liked taking what Zulu called "mementoes."

These were usually ears which we strung on wire around our throats and when we were bored we'd trade them back and forth. Mongol slit the breasts off a dead woman one time, wired them together and wore them on his chest until they turned black and drew too many flies. There were always sick, brutal, and very unfunny things like that going on that we got our kicks from. For several days, I remember, Mongol wore the death mask of a woman he had killed. He peeled it off her, scalp and all. He looked like something from *The Texas Chainsaw Massacre*. Finally, Doc told him to get rid of it.

Smitty carried a digital camera around with him. He told everyone that it was his job to document what we saw and what we did and who we did it to. I don't know if it was his idea or not. I suspect it was one of those little jewels that Dr. Cripps had programmed into him. Regardless, he went around taking pictures—*after-action photos,* he called them—like some kind of combat photographer. Doc Feelgood wouldn't allow him to take any while we were fighting, but when it was done and the corpses were sprawled in the warm sunlight, that's when Smitty would get right down to it. He would take shot after shot of dismembered bodies, zombies blown to fragments, even throwaways that we lined up against walls and executed. *Throwaways,* were what we called the transients and squatters who weren't insurgents or part of any militia or survivalist group.

Smitty and his camera, oh yes.

If he had only taken photos of the dead it would have been one thing, but there were worse things than that. Mongol, for instance, liked to pose with what he had killed like some great white hunter. Sometimes it was relatively inoffensive (at least to our mindset) like him holding up a couple dead ones by the hair or him sitting there with his arms around a couple gored deadheads like they were old pals...but it got much worse than that. Mongol sticking his dick into the mouth of a dead woman. Mongol with a naked and very dead girl on his lap. Mongol pissing on burning bodies as if he was trying to put them out.

But it wasn't just Mongol.

There were gruesome, sickening shots of Zulu cutting a guy in half with her chainsaw. Militia members running around on fire.

Mad Mike carving his initials into the forehead of a dead woman. A half-dozen survivalists strung up from an overpass. Corpses arranged like they were having sex. In one shot, there had to have been at least twenty of them in some bizarre post mortem orgy.

It went on and on.

Maybe there were even pictures of me doing things I'd rather not recall. It wouldn't have surprised me. We were disconnected from morality of any sort. We did not think beyond the killing and maiming. There was nothing else and we didn't even know really who we were. And whenever the subject of somebody's past came up, the others would just politely turn away. For them it was like trying to decipher the nature of God. Some things could not be known and you had to be content with that. There were lots of zombies out there, but the members of KIA-9 were the real walking dead, sleepers who could not wake from their nightmares, killers and sociopaths and sleepwalkers. That's what we were. There was nothing else. We were Dr. Cripps' wind-up soldiers, his terrible toys and demonic play things, and we did what we were conditioned to do in the way that he wanted it.

STREET FIGHTERS

We went in heavy with a LAV-25 rolling in behind us, chain guns and .50-cal machine gun awaiting our orders. If we got ourselves into a fix—and we did quite often—the LAV would fix it. There was a certain amount of comfort in that, a confidence that could not be taken away from us.

"Mother's got this feeling we just stuck our cocks up the wrong hole," Zulu said, adjusting her equipment load. "Stuck 'em up there real, real deep."

With her bald head and perfect bone structure, she looked like some Amazon warrior on the prowl, fearless and bloodthirsty, an M4 in one hand and a combat knife in the other, a Stihl chainsaw at her back in a sling. At 6'3, lithe and long-limbed, she cut an imposing shape in the light of the setting sun which painted her smooth black face amber and golden.

She impressed me.

Hell, they *all* impressed me but not always for the right reasons. Natural-born killers, I would always think as I saw our shadows creeping along the bullet-scarred face of a building. But there was nothing natural about any of us. We were synthetic things.

"What do you think, Dog?" she asked me.

"I think mother is right."

Dog was the nickname they gave me because everyone had to have one. I'd seen it in Iraq and I'd heard of it in Tuck's tales of Vietnam, that need for a handle. As if when you went into combat you were like Batman putting on his cape, donning your alter-ego, role-playing. You were an actor that created a character that would do terrible, inhuman things, but when you went home, you'd dispense with it and just be yourself. Thereby, the guilt would be on your alter-ego's soul and not yours.

Doc Feelgood told us to hold our position and we waited there on the deadly street, all of us anxious to kill because we honestly didn't know anything else.

Doc was chatting over the Icom with the LAV crew. I pulled my earpiece out so I didn't have to listen. He held his fist up in the air which meant we had to be quiet. He was KIA-9's leader and we always did what he said. There was never a thought in our little reptilian brains of doing anything else. Doc was a real cool, easy sort of cat. But his mellow nature was disarming—if you fucked-up, he'd simply smile and put a bullet through your head. He did it my first day with KIA-9 (it was *10* then). A dude named Motorhead couldn't keep his dick in his pants. He found a cute little throwaway and raped her on the sidewalk while a trio of shitheads (insurgents, guerrillas) ran our flank and tried to send us to the happy hunting ground. If Motorhead would have kept his eye on his zone it wouldn't have happened.

No biggie, I thought. Mad Mike read the gap and sprayed down the three stooges with his SAW. No harm done. But that's not how Doc saw it. He waited until Motorhead was done—six last jackhammer thrusts to the girl that made her cry out—and had zipped up, shouldering his weapon.

Doc said, "Nice work. Now drop your weapon."

"Why?" Motorhead asked.

"Because dead men don't carry guns," Doc told him, pulling his Beretta 9mm sidearm and shooting him through the left eye.

That's how Doc was.

He never got mad. He never raised his voice. He never even swore. He was calm as could be when he dropped Motorhead. When he saw Big Bird and Little Gun watching the raped girl crawl off, he was still calm. Calm as you please as he took her by the hair and slit her throat so no one else would get any dumb ideas.

"Nothing like free pussy for the taking to cause trouble," he said. "Ain't that right, Zulu?"

"Mother believes it to be so," she said. "Sometimes Mother gets this awful fire down below, but she don't pay it no mind. No mind at all. She always feels better when she pulls the trigger."

Anyway, that's why you did what Doc Feelgood said, because he had a way of striking fast and unseen like a rattlesnake in the dark.

While he chatted away with the crew of the LAV, probably making us stand out there in the open to draw fire, I had a cigarette with Scales and Smitty. Three men on a match. Shit. Mad Mike and Mongol scanned ahead for trouble while Zulu held her ground and Little Gun and Big Bird were crouched down in firing positions just aching to make contact. They looked like hounds on a leash that just wanted to run.

"Funny how those two are," Scales said, blowing smoke out of his nostrils. "Like Siamese twins, cut but still connected. Both fucking wired. You go up behind 'em and snap your fingers, they'll start capping."

Smitty considered that. He got that deep, faraway look in his eyes as he often did because he was so stoned all the time. It looked like he was contemplating the deeper meaning of it all, but it was probably just the drugs. If he was thinking of anything it was probably just blowing something up.

"Sometimes I wonder where they even came from," he finally said.

"Sometimes I wonder where *any* of us came from," Scales put in.

But none of us knew. Who we were or where we came from or what we were about was a big mystery. It seemed like we'd always been doing what we were doing and there had never been anything else. I saw faces in my mind sometimes but when I thought too hard about who they were or what they meant to me I'd get a real bad headache. So I tried not to think because it only brought me pain.

"Okay," Doc Feelgood said. "Cut down that alley. We got movement on the next street. Big Bird? Little Gun? Lead us in."

He gave us a hand motion and we moved out.

The LAV lumbered behind us at a distance. I loved the sound of its purr. It made me feel easy and sure. Mad Mike and Mongol hung back as we edged into the gap, ready to provide us with covering fire if we needed it. We moved quickly before anyone could draw a bead on us, over crevices in the pavement, bomb craters, and the debris of half-demolished buildings.

"Contact!" Big Bird called out over the Icom.

He and Little Gun gave us the signal to hang back and wait it out. Contact was half a dozen deadheads that had been walking around too long and were beginning to fall apart. Their faces were like raw meat, eyes sunken white marbles in flesh morasses. A woman closing from the left—wearing granny underwear and nothing else—looked like she had a confetti poncho on but it was just her own sloughing skin. It had cracked open and split from the bones beneath like dried-out bamboo.

Big Bird and Little Gun opened up with three-round bursts.

Zombie heads started breaking apart like soft gourds, skull fragments and brain matter ejecting in red-black cascades of rot. They dropped the six and a dozen more came dragging themselves in.

Zulu and I went into the breach next, jumping in and opening fire. I dropped three, putting out rounds on full auto, and they tripped on their own entrails and hit the pavement. Zulu took the head off a big bald guy whose face was like a flap of mildew and drilled a seemingly unstoppable pregnant woman with six or seven rounds who came apart like her seams were burst. What she'd been carrying in her belly—whether living, dead, or undead—hit the ground before she did, the birth sac opening like a bag of meat and discharging a fetid pink and green mass that hit the pavement and exploded in a gushing slop of seedy, stringy pulp like the guts of a pumpkin.

I think it actually moved for a few seconds, one baleful yellow eye appraising us with hate.

As the dead pushed in, we took them out, our weapons smoking in our hot little hands. The more we killed, the better we got at it. At first, when they came at you, you just started popping rounds, anything to drive them back. But that was fear and the heat of the moment. After that, you calmed and aimed strictly for the heads.

When the dead were scattered on the ground, Mongol came in with his flamethrower and lit them up. There was pure joy on his face as he did that, as the flames rose higher and plumes of dirty smoke twisted in the air. The stench was gagging.

Doc Feelgood called out that our objective was the row of battle-scarred houses across the way. Already I could see zombies swarming around them, others pouring from doorways like worms from warm, spoiled pork. We grouped and prepared to charge, but a hail of bullets stopped us. They ripped up the street in front of us, the shooters marching their rounds closer and closer to us.

We were taking fire from a crumbling three-story building on a hilltop just above us. We ran from rubble pile to rubble pile, keeping low as bullets flew all around us. We shot back, doing little but punching more holes into the brick façade of the building, hoping to drive the shooters back and give us some time.

"Quit wasting ammo," Doc Feelgood told us over the Icom. "Grab cover and scope it out."

It was easy enough to scope: our shooters were in at least three different windows up there. They had little accuracy, just throwing a lot of rounds in our general direction and keeping us bottled up. Maybe that was their intention. As I pulled off a cigarette, crouched with the others behind the remains of a well-blasted wall, Zulu and Mongol fired an occasional burst up towards the windows. They were trying to draw the shooters out so Mad Mike could paste them with his SAW. But they weren't having any of that. Two of them were on the second story, the other on the third. They would each individually dart to their respective windows and fire quickly down at us, taking turns but never with the same pattern. By the time we returned fire, they were always gone.

"Fuck is Doc waiting for?" Scales wondered out loud. "Bring that fucking LAV in and hit the building."

But I knew Doc.

He was careful. LAVs certainly didn't grow on trees and he was very protective of ours. He wasn't about to let it get drawn into an IED trap or a RPG nest. We had all seen things like that before. And without the LAV, we were just infantry grunts crawling through the rubble like rats, fighting and dying for every inch of ground we took.

But something had to happen.

Across the road, the zombies were getting a little randy over by the houses. They knew where we were and several were already headed in our direction. That's how it would start. First a few sniffing us out like recon scouts and then the main force would plow in at us, an open buffet too tempting to refuse.

Doc came running from the alley with Smitty and joined us at the wall. He had a LAW—Light Anti-tank Weapon—in his hands. He had an idea. He told Zulu and Mongol to keep engaging the enemy, but not to waste too many rounds. They fired intermittently on semi-auto whenever the shooters appeared. Doc said that they weren't changing their tactics and the zombies were coming our way, so it was time to shit or get off the pot. The two shooters on the second floor were either at the opposite ends of a large room or were next door to one another.

"Fuck this shit," Scales said, when rounds chewed into our wall.

They had us sighted perfectly and could keep us boxed in all day as long as their ammo held out or we didn't get a lucky hit. Doc pulled the pin on the LAW and it expanded to its full length. He aimed the green tube up at the second story window. When the shooters started firing again, he didn't even flinch or seek cover. He pulled the trigger and the rocket with its 66mm HEAT warhead zoomed right at the window. Not only zoomed at it, but right through it. There was a resounding explosion of smoke and fire as the room behind the window went up, debris shooting out into the air along with a funnel of black smoke. Several sections of brick broke free and dropped into the street below.

"All right," Doc said seconds after the detonation. "Get in there...let's go."

We dashed over to the building and waited there as Doc and Smitty joined us. The LAV-25 waited in the alley. Doc got on the Icom and told the crew to neutralize the zombies marching in our direction. The LAV rolled out of the alley and it had barely stopped moving when its 25mm chain gun opened up. The rounds—armor-piercing and incendiary—flew at the zombies, leaving bright green tracer trails in the dusk. They hit the zombies with one resounding explosion after another, lighting up the streets. The walking dead seemed to disintegrate as we watched, vaporizing in clouds of blood and meat. Flames erupted in rising white-hot clouds, smoke filling the air. The LAV crew didn't fuck around. The chain gun had barely stopped firing when they swept the area with their .50-cal machinegun.

The entire thing lasted maybe a minute and probably a lot less.

The smoke cleared some and we could see nothing was moving over there. In fact, one of the houses was burning. Another had collapsed.

"Night-night, maggotheads," Zulu said.

"All right," Doc told us. "I want this fucking place cleaned out, room by room by room. Maybe we got a couple of them with the LAW and maybe we didn't. Now we're going to find out.

This is what it always came down to.

No matter how much firepower you had, no matter how many helicopter gunships or fighter-bombers, armored vehicles or artillery, it still came down to soldiers doing what soldiers did: taking the ground inch by inch and mopping up, fighting the stragglers in the ruins.

"Let's do this," Doc said.

Big Bird kicked in the front door and he and Little Gun marched in. The rest of us followed, save Doc and Mad Mike who watched the streets. We marched into the mouth of hell.

THE HOUSE OF HORRORS

I'd been through it so many times by then I did it by rote, as did the others. We got inside and slipped our NVGs on so we could see what the hell we were doing in the gathering gloom. The place looked, as far as I could tell, like some sort of apartment building and we were in its lobby. There wasn't much in there. I imagine most everything was scavenged unless maybe the place had been condemned even before the Necrophage outbreak.

No matter.

Corridors led to the left, to the right, and another we discovered behind a door led towards the back of the building. We broke up into teams. Scales and Smitty took the left corridor, and I went with Zulu down the one leading towards the back. Mongol took the right passage. He had always been a lone, effective hunter and nobody argued with him even though we all knew things might get hairy. Little Gun and Big Bird found a door leading to the basement. They were shaking with excitement as they went down there.

Zulu and I checked it out room by room in a very orderly military fashion, calling out "clear" as each room was checked. We saw very little of interest. Several of the rooms were empty and smelled like cat piss. I found some rats that disappeared into a hole in the wall as I entered. They had been feeding on the corpse of some throwaway, an old dude whose face was chewed off but still sported a very luxurious Santa Claus beard. As far as corpses went, it was nothing exceptional. I checked the next room and found a dead woman in bed. She was little more than a mummy with a seamed face and long dark hair. Judging from the cobwebs, she'd been there a long time. Something about her intrigued me and I just wasn't sure why.

I clicked on the tactical light on my M4 and slid my NVGs up. I studied her. I pulled the coverlet away from her and it came free with a tearing sound. I suppose whatever had been growing on her had grown right into the coverlet, too. She was little but a rack of bones with a crucifix around her throat that was tangled in ancient webs.

But her hair…

As I studied it in the light, I was amazed by it. It was very black and shiny, the highlights sort of an indigo blue. The color of it reminded me of something I could not remember. Had I known a woman with shiny dark, dark hair like that before? A muddled image of a woman with such hair passed through my mind. She was beautiful, olive-skinned with a very sensual mouth and high cheekbones.

I felt a sudden pang of fear and loss…then it was gone.

One of those déjà vu sort of things I got all the time that were gone before I could properly analyze them. I stood there, trying to recapture it. But I started to get a headache, so I let it go.

"Dog," Zulu called out in the hallway. "Down here."

I clicked off my light and slid my NVGs back on. The world was green-hued and surreal again like I was playing a video game.

Zulu stood down at the end of the corridor. "Check it out," she said.

About that time, Doc came over the Icom and we all had to call out about our status. That dispensed with, I followed Zulu into a big room at the back that was long and carpeted. It reminded me of a meeting room or a boardroom. Something like that. There were even some watercolor prints on the walls. There was no table or furniture in there. Not a damn thing except for a dozen or so skeletons tangled up on the floor, all of them disarticulated. I couldn't see how they all could have died together like that unless it had been a mass suicide or something and scavengers had scattered the bones about.

"Mother ain't seeing no bullet holes on the bones," she said. "Not so much as a scrape or cut. Skulls are intact. Can't be zombies somebody mowed down."

By then, we were both on our knees in front of the pile, sorting through it. I don't know why it interested me so much, but it did. I had another of those déjà vu moments. *Bones. Bones scattered in a street.* I associated the image with terror. Then, like the other one, it was just…gone. We pulled our NVGs back and examined the ossuary in the beams of our tac lights. It was stupid. Real stupid. If a shooter came through the door, they would have capped both of us.

But we didn't seem to care.

I started seeing things about the bones I didn't like. "Teeth marks," I said, examining the indentations in a femur, then on another ribcage. "All adults, too. Those are human teeth marks…at least, I think they are."

But I wasn't sure.

I'd seen lots of bones by that point that zombies had been at. The spacing of human teeth and the blunt trauma they left on bone was characteristic. Once you saw it, it was easy to identify again. But these teeth…there was something off about them. The indentations and gnawing were not blunt, but looked more like the work of dogs, creatures with pronounced—and sharp—canines.

I shared this with Zulu.

She stared at me with huge dark eyes, licking her lips. "Funny…maybe zombies got 'em. Maybe dogs chewed on what was left."

"Yeah, I bet you're right."

But I didn't believe that and I didn't think she did either. It was like we were trying to fit the most rational explanation to something that didn't seem rational to us at all. *The sound in the closet is not the boogeyman, dear. It's just the pipes in the walls. That scraping outside your window at night is not claws but a tree branch. That cold patch in the attic is not a ghost but a draft from the eaves. Those weird lights in the sky are not invaders from another world come to snatch you out of your bed by moonlight, they're just satellites or meteors or planes.* That was how we adults rationalized things. It made our children sleep better and it made us sleep better. The tone of my voice and that of Zulu's carried that same sort of desperate rationalization.

"We got work to do," she finally said.

Agreed.

As we stood up, there was sporadic gunfire coming from below. Big Bird and Little Gun must have made contact. As we rushed out into the hallway, Big Bird came over the Icom and told us to cool it, as if he knew we were going to crash his party.

"Wasted a couple shitheads…throwaways. They were hiding behind the furnace down here," he said. *"Funny, though. They got*

some shit growing on their faces…looks like that stuff that grows on trees in rings…what do you call it?"

"Fungi?" Doc suggested.

"Sure. Something like that. Weird shit…hey, wait…" There was silence for another thirty, forty seconds in which we all got pretty tense. *"You ain't gonna believe this…got more of that shit growing up the walls…and bodies. Yeah, gotta be ten or twelve of 'em, all covered with the shit."*

The idea of some weird fungus growing on walls and on corpses made déjà vu light up in my head yet again. I was like some A-head tripping out on LSD flashbacks. Whatever it was, it was very brief.

"You're not in there for fungi," Doc told us. *"Clear that place out."*

He was right and we knew it.

Zulu and I took a doorway at the other end of the room and it led into a sort of back lobby. There was a set of stairs leading up. The back stairway, I suppose. We called it in and started up.

"Be real careful," Mongol said over the Icom. *"I've found three tripwires now. This place is hot. Somebody don't want to get taken by surprise."*

"You hear that?" Doc said. *"Watch yourselves."*

But we didn't need much prompting by that point. We climbed the stairs, Zulu in the lead. She examined the door above carefully in her tac light but saw no wires or anything suspicious. Carefully, she opened it and started shooting right away. When I got to her, I saw a couple of dead throwaways on the floor. They weren't armed. Whether they were trying to get the drop on her or just trying to escape was anyone's guess.

When I was certain our section of the hallway was secure, I went back over to the bodies which had bled out over the floor.

"Mother just saw 'em and opened up," Zulu said, as if I thought it was her fault.

I called it in and slid my NVGs up again, turning on my light. Again, there was something real weird going on here. The throwaways were a young couple, man and woman, and the crazy thing was that they were tethered together. Their wrists were bound with wire and connected. Fuck was that about?

"What do you make of it?" I said.

But Zulu just shook her head.

We heard some shooting and Scales said they'd found some deadheads, but took care of them. We had no more than turned from the bodies when a door was thrown open and a throwaway came charging in our direction. I shot him down without thinking. He took three rounds in the chest and hit the floor face-first. He was dead when I got to him. I rolled him over with my boot. I judged him to be about thirty. The disturbing part was that the top of his head straight back to the nape of his neck was raw. Somebody had peeled him.

"Scalped," Zulu said. "Mother thinks we got some hardcore players here."

Again, we called it in. There was never any thought on our part to conceal anything from Doc and the others. This was a military operation, a tactical situation, and everyone needed all the intelligence they could get.

I led the way to the room he had come out of.

It was an apartment of sorts. A small living room. A bathroom. A kitchen. A bedroom. Nothing much…except that the stink of death was so strong in there it stirred my guts. I had to swallow to keep the bile down in my stomach where it belonged. In the bathroom, we found a butchered corpse in the tub. It was nothing recent, but a man that had been hacked and sliced maybe four or five days before. The white porcelain of the tub itself was dyed red and pink. He had been eviscerated, all his guts yanked out. His ribs were caved-in and, in my light, I saw no sign of a heart. The top of his head was open, his brain gone…as were his eyes and genitals and all the flesh from his legs and belly and throat.

"No deadheads did that," Zulu said.

I rubbed a finger along the opening of his cranium. It was rough. "They used a saw," I said.

"Cannibals," she said, looking worried. "Maybe nightcrawlers."

That was the name we had given the berserkers, particularly the ones that were degenerated into something not exactly human. The zombies were one thing. We understood them and their simple drives. But when humans...even head cases like the berserkers...started eating other people, it was scary. Even as drugged-up and brainwashed as we were and as sick and violent as we sometimes got, even we understood that there were certain taboos you didn't violate. Cannibalism was one of them.

"Come on," I said.

Carefully, silently, we checked out the rest of the apartment.

The bedroom was interesting. There were ropes at all four bedposts. What remained of them were bloody. It looked to me as if they had been gnawed through. I started making associations at that point like you probably are right at this moment. The blood on the ropes was still fresh and wet. Not all of it, of course. Much of it was old. Just stains. My guess was that the guy I had just shot down had been imprisoned in here, tied to the bed and he had chewed his way free.

It was horrible.

Even to my twisted, sadistic mind, it was horrible.

We went into the kitchen next. By this point, we weren't using our NVGs because we needed to *really* see what we were looking at. Well, the first thing we saw in the kitchen were bones. Human bones. It wasn't exactly an image from *Better Homes and Gardens* or fucking *Architectural Digest*. This place, much like the rest of the apartment, was a real sty. The tile floor was dark with bloodstains. The table was hacked and cut, bits of meat and tissue stuck to it, flies buzzing in the air and maggots feasting on the carrion. The countertops were much the same, but piled with bones that were all stained red. There was more carrion on them and more maggots. The sink had about three or four inches of congealed blood in it. The window above it was black with flies. I saw what looked like a human heart pegged to a corkboard with a steak knife. Even the walls were stained with whorls of blood and bits of blackened meat.

It looked like a cannibal's kitchen, all right. And the slaughtering that went on there was neither neat nor practiced, but manic and savage.

Zulu checked a pantry in the back.

There was no one in there, but there was a sort of little door at the back. It looked about big enough for a kid to crawl through.

There were bloody handprints all over it. Sucking in a sharp, uneasy breath, I pushed it open with the barrel of my M4. I was expecting some deranged monster to come leaping out at me, red teeth bared…but there was nothing. The door led into a little room with a sloping ceiling. To one side was a narrow passage that led right between the walls.

I panned it with my light. I could smell a hot stink of putrefaction blowing out at me. I looked at Zulu and she looked at me.

"No fucking way," she said.

I agreed. Neither of us were going in there. We were tough and merciless, but the very idea of what we might see in there even frightened us. It led somewhere and I didn't want to know where.

We got back out in the corridor where the air was a little better. We shared a cigarette and called in the gist of what we had just seen. I had the feeling that Doc did not believe us, not completely.

"Hey, Dog," Zulu said. "You forgot to close that little door in the pantry."

"Well, I ain't going back to do it now."

She was just ribbing me, but I don't think either of us found the idea of going back in there particularly funny. When we were done fortifying ourselves with nicotine, we checked the next room and it was another apartment. The window looking out of the bedroom had been smashed out, but beyond that there was nothing of interest except a big knife stuck in the wall. From the stains on the handle, we decided it was nothing we wanted. The only thing odd in there was a smell of human shit. From the stains on the wall, it looked like somebody had taken a dump and then tried to write their name with it.

The next door led into yet another apartment.

The stench in there was like the cannibal apartment, though nowhere near as strong. We didn't find much until we got to the bedroom where we saw stains on the mattress…blood and what might have been piss and shit.

But that was hardly the worst of it.

"Look," Zulu said.

She had her light on the bedposts and there were chains hanging from them. The one on the left had a human hand hanging from it. The wrist was a bloody stump, a knob of bone protruding from it. The bone was broken, the wrist mangled.

"Somebody chewed themselves free," Zulu said.

I just stared at it. I had seen some wicked things, some seriously fucked-up things…but this? Was it possible for someone to chew off their own hand? Wouldn't they bleed to death? Judging from the bloodstains everywhere, maybe they had. But the idea of a mind that broken, that desperate, that twisted…it was shocking. I mean, we've all heard of animals doing it, leaving a paw in a trap…*but a human being?*

We stumbled out of there and after we'd caught our breath, we checked another doorway. Zulu went over there, not really expecting to find anything. Nothing alive, anyway. It was secured with a padlock. She blew the lock off with her M4, then kicked it in.

And it was at that moment that the zombies came out.

THE HOUSE OF HORRORS, PART 2

Zulu stumbled over her own feet trying to get away as the dead poured out through the doorway. I grabbed hold of her and we ran back down the corridor. I don't know how many zombies there were. In our panic and seen by the jumping lights of our rifles, it seemed like there were dozens and dozens.

There was little to do in the heat of the moment but fight.

"WE GOT CONTACT UP HERE!" I shouted over the Icom. "WE GOT DEADHEADS EVERYWHERE! WE NEED BACKUP! WE NEED FUCKING BACKUP!"

A sane person would have run and lived to fight another day, but we weren't exactly sane. So we stood there, Zulu and I, shoulder to shoulder, and started blasting away, dropping the dead as they moved in our direction. We aimed high and blew heads apart. Shell casings flew and magazines were emptied. Zombie heads were drilled with slugs and exploded in gouts of gore. Blood and brain matter were splashed against the walls and dripped from the ceiling. The corpses piled up and the dead surged ever forward.

Finally, we pulled back towards the stairs and both tossed frag grenades at the massing hungry zombies. We hit the floor and the explosions down the hallway were so damn loud in that enclosed space that it nearly punctured our eardrums. The beams of our tac lights cut like white swords through the murk of dust and smoke and mists of blood. I saw gutted corpses everywhere, limbs and punctured torsos and heads split open like melons. The floor down there was a sea of blood and rot set with islands of gangrenous tissue. Zombie anatomy was splattered against the walls and draped from the ruptured ceiling tiles in strings of glistening meat.

But the dead were far from done.

More poured forth and it occurred to me that they must have been forced into that room or rooms, whatever space was behind that door, and locked in there by someone, possibly militia members or shitheads. They were kept there in the event the building was raided by us. Then they would be released to cause panic and confusion.

That was my guess, anyway.

Not that I was doing much thinking or guessing by that point. Some of the zombies could not refuse the banquet of the remains of their brothers and sisters and they fell to their knees and started shoving smoking meat into their mouths, yanking on snakes of intestines, and scooping brains from cleaved skulls with grave-filthy fingers.

But the others came on.

And we started shooting. We dropped eight or ten of them and by then the mob was less than fifteen feet from us and we knew there was no way we could put them all down before they reached us. They would overwhelm us by sheer numbers.

I pulled another grenade, deciding I would toss it and we'd beat a hasty retreat down the stairs where, hopefully, we'd link up with others of our team.

Then I sensed motion behind me and I think I cried out.

More zombies were coming up the stairs, white eyes shining, lipless mouths opening and closing, teeth gnashing.

"FUCK!" I cried out.

I started shooting down the stairs, dropping several before my magazine puked out on me. Zulu kept firing into the hallway as the mob surged ever forward. In the precious few seconds it took me to eject a mag and slap a new one in place, the dead were nearly on top of me. I don't know how many there were, but it was enough to fill the stairwell and that's enough to give you the cold sweats. I started shooting again and gore was flying in the air at such close quarters, it sprayed in my face and spattered my hands and weapon, bits of meat sticking to my tac vest.

Zulu let out a cry that was half surprise and half terror.

I instantly saw why.

There were even more zombies in the hallway now. I saw her rip open the heads of three of them but a fourth and fifth closed in on her. She gave one of them the butt of her M4 in the face and cracked another in the mouth with it, driving them back, but while she did that another launched itself at her. It seized her arm with white bloated fingers and I saw its mouth driving in to bite. I stuck the muzzle of my M4 right in its wormy face and capped three rounds into it that made it jump back and fall into the others.

They didn't just shove this one out of the way.

No, not by that point. The zombies were swarming and in their swarm they had become a single ravenous entity, a voracious eating machine that took down anything that fell into its path. The headshot zombie stumbled into their clutching hands and was literally ripped into pieces in a matter of seconds. Arms were yanked from sockets, legs snapped off. Seven or eight hands gripped its head and tore it free from its shoulders with a sound like tree roots being yanked from the ground.

Meanwhile, the zombies on the stairs were nearly on me.

I emptied my clip and blew heads apart, splashing gore in every direction, but for everyone I dropped two more took its place. I slapped in a fresh magazine and I heard Big Bird on the Icom.

"WE'RE CLOSING ON YOU! GET YOUR HEADS DOWN!" he cried out. *"WE'RE COMING IN HOT!"*

Within seconds, I heard them shooting. He and Little Gun were coming down the opposite side of the hallway, blasting away as they came. I heard explosions right away and I knew what was happening. They both had M203 grenade launchers attached to their M4s and they were slinging rounds right into the zombies masses. Shrapnel was flying along with pieces of the dead.

We had no choice then.

We had to fight our way down the stairs.

Zulu and I started blazing away with everything we had, cutting a path through the throng of the dead that reached out to snare us. We fired and kicked and smashed zombie faces with our rifles, driving them down and away until we had killed enough to open a path and then we charged down the stairs, knocking them out of our way. By the time we reached the landing below, I could hear Scales and Smitty on the Icom. They had joined Big Bird and Little Gun in putting down the zombie force.

When we stepped down into the hallway, we gunned down three or four more maggot-heads and then made a quick escape into the room we had found the bones in.

And that was a real bad choice.

Because there were more deadheads in there and we were on the dinner menu.

We fought like hell, shooting them down and knocking them out of our way and then Zulu ejected her last magazine and was clean out of shot. I had the selector switch of my M4 set for three-round burst and I fired selectively, trying to be as economical as possible with my last 30-round magazine. Zulu capped away with her 9mm sidearm, but there were just too many. She pulled her Stihl chainsaw from its harness. She primed it, set the choke, and yanked on the starter rope, cranking it into action. As the zombies pushed in from all sides at her, she went at them like some Viking warrior swinging his battleaxe. There's simply no way to overwhelm somebody with a chainsaw, particularly when said person is fast and strong and can move the saw like a slashing sword.

Within the first few seconds, two heads came off and a face was sliced lengthwise. She blinded two more deadheads and took off three or four reaching arms. She went at it with crazed, screaming mania, cutting and sawing and slashing. Blood splattered into her face, literally soaking her, but she kept at it.

Meanwhile, I'd spent my last few rounds and I pulled my 9mm and started firing. The zombies were so close by then, I was firing inches away from their faces. I dropped seven or eight more and then one of them grabbed me from behind and another peeled the nine from my fingers and I knew I was about to be a dead man. But that didn't mean I would go down without a fight. I pulled my knife and slashed one of them across the eyes as I knocked the one behind me away. I turned and buried the knife in his right eye, slimy goo spurting over the back of my hand.

And then three of them were on me and I was knocked down.

They fell on me and I kicked one of them away, but another— a woman—straddled me. The tac light on my dropped M4 lit up the scene enough so I could see her just fine. Her face was a stringy, riven mass of worms, the entire thing in motion like it was trying to crawl off the skull beneath. Gouts of vile-smelling drool hung from her mouth. She had chewed her lips away as victims of Necrophage often did in the violent convulsions preceding death. Her teeth were stained pink, jutting from graying gums at crooked angles.

I could hear Zulu and her saw going at it and I called out for her, but I knew she didn't hear me with all the racket. I could hear more firing and explosions from upstairs as the boys mopped up. They would never get to me either.

Two other zombies had handfuls of my hair and they yanked my head back, exposing my throat. You rarely saw such cooperative behavior from them. As the woman's mouth lowered to bite me, I hit her in the face two, three times, snapping her head back with each blow. But all that got me was gouts of reeking fluid that dripped down on my face and tangles of writhing worms that struck my cheeks. I had a certain immunity from the Zombpox, but I had no memory of that either. So maybe I would have survived a small bite, but I wouldn't survive her tearing out my jugular.

I fought right to the last...and then I heard the chainsaw get very, very loud. Meat and fluids were spraying in every direction and the hands released my hair and then the bar, blade, of the saw came whirring right out between the zombie's woman's eyes, blood and tissue spraying in my face, bits of bone ripping into me like shrapnel.

The saw retreated and I knocked the zombie corpse off me, fighting to my feet and pawing grave waste from my face.

Zulu killed the saw. "She bite you?"

"No, you saved my bacon. Thanks."

There were no more living dead around us. They were broken and mutilated, gutted and dismembered. There was anatomy everywhere. We were covered in blood. Clots of meat dropped from the ceiling into our hair. Body parts were underfoot, entrails coiled about like bloody, sleeping snakes.

That's when Scales and Smitty came through the door, putting tac lights in our faces.

"Man," Scales said. "Now this is what I call a real fucking mess."

THE HOUSE OF HORRORS, PART 3

But it was hardly at an end.

We went outside for a breather and a smoke and fresh ammunition. Doc paced around like an irritated foreman whose men were slacking on the job. He didn't care what we saw in there or what had happened. He wanted us to go back in. Mongol was still in there, cleaning out the third floor, giving us a blow by blow description over the Icom. He sounded like he was really enjoying himself and I'll just bet that he was.

"All right," Doc Feelgood finally said. "Go in there and finish up."

We got our marching orders and back in we went, our BDU pants stiff with dried blood. We slid our NVGs on and then the six of us went up the stairs. It was our intention to link up with Mongol. Once we had done that, we figured, the building could be considered secure.

When we reached the second floor, Big Bird and Little Gun took the corridor off to the left that led towards the back of the building where we had been earlier. The rest of us moved off towards the right where the corridor split in two. Scales and Smitty took the left and Zulu and I took the right.

Back at it again, room by room.

We had gone through two rooms when we found some serious destruction. The door was blown off a room along with most of the wall around it. Inside, it was complete wreckage. The walls were stripped down to the lathing, the ceiling caved-in, a couch was still smoldering. We found a dead man who had been nearly cut in half by a falling beam. We also found a badly burnt AK-47. This had been one of the shooters that drew us into the building in the first place. This was the room that Doc hit with the LAW rocket. Even things still standing were peppered by shrapnel and blown with soot.

There was a great hole in the wall where we could look into the room next door. There was damage in there, too, but not like this room. Collateral damage. There had been three shooters. One was dead and accounted for. One still on the third story and the other had been in the room I was now looking into.

I saw no movement, no suspicious forms lurking about through the green filter of my NVGs, so I climbed through the hole into the room. Zulu followed me. We checked it all out, bedroom and kitchen and bathroom. Nothing.

By the time we got back out into the corridor, Mongol came over the Icom and told us he had found a couple throwaways hiding in a closet. He had been trying to get something from them, but it was no go.

"It's like they're in shock or something," he said. *"Eyes are funny...they been through a lot of abuse and I think they're about to go through some more."*

"They can't speak?" Doc asked.

"Can't or won't. I'm starting to think they can't." He laughed. *"Confucius say: If tongue don't work, cut it out."*

"Just wait," Doc told him.

"Why?"

"Because I said so."

There was an edge to his voice we could hear even over the Icom. It was his way of drawing a line in the sand that you didn't dare step over. Even Mongol who was a first-class psychopath didn't dare tread on that.

Doc said, *"Tell me about their condition. Any marks? Bite marks? That sort of thing?"*

"Don't see no bite marks, but they're both naked. Both have a lot of contusions and bruises. Their wrists...let me see, I won't fucking hurt you...are very purple, lot of dried blood. My guess is that they have both been bound up for a while." He was silent for a few moments and we could hear him saying things to his prisoners. *"The girl has lash marks on her back. I'm guessing she was whipped. The boy is missing his right index finger and thumb...pretty crude, looks like they were torn off. In fact...wait..."*

"What?" Doc asked.

He had to ask it three times before Mongol answered. *"Nothing...hearing sounds up here. Gone now."*

"What sort of sounds?"

"Don't know."

"You're imagining things maybe."

"Don't think so. The throwaways jumped when they heard 'em. There was something out there, but now it's gone."

Zulu and I went back to checking rooms.

We had just entered the third room when there was an explosion somewhere on the second floor, it sounded like, and we heard a man screaming.

"What's going on?" Doc wanted to know.

But we didn't know ourselves. We ran down the corridor and met Scales and Smitty, then the four of us went in search of Big Bird and Little Gun. I had a real bad feeling in my guts. The screaming rose to a fever pitch and then cut out like somebody had stuffed a rag in the screamer's mouth.

"All right," Doc said. *"Everyone sound off."*

Zulu and I did. Then we heard Mongol, who sounded a little shaken for some reason. Scales and Smitty came next, but no Big Bird or Little gun. Doc started demanding they sound off. His voice started getting loud and pissed off which was something that happened very, very rarely. I didn't like it. Things were getting tense and it felt like they were about to go out of control.

Then we all heard Little Gun rambling nearly incoherently: *"GOT HIM...GOT HIM...THEY FUCKING GOT HIM...OH DEAR CHRIST THEY FUCKING GOT HIM..."*

Doc kept trying to get a status out of him, but it was hopeless. He just rambled on and on or he didn't speak at all. Zulu and I made it around the corner down there and into the corridor and we saw Little Gun right away. He was on the floor, rocking back and forth on his knees. He had Big Bird clutched to him. I could smell the burnt ordinance in the air and I could see a door that had been blasted from its hinges. The wall around it was blackened and pitted from shrapnel.

It was easy to put together the rest.

"Fucking booby trap," Scales said.

"Grenade trap," Smitty said.

Big Bird must have been farther down the corridor than Little Gun. When he opened the door, he snagged the tripwire which pulled the pin out of a grenade and...well, this was the result. We had our NVGs off by then and our lights on. But we all knew Big Bird was beyond help. It was a pathetic scene, all right. Little Gun was rocking Big Bird's corpse in his arms. There was blood everywhere—on Little Gun, on the walls, on the floor. Big Bird's eyes were open and they were staring straight up, his mouth open as if he had died saying something and maybe he had at that. His right arm was blown off and he was open from his crotch to his chest. Like Little Gun, he hadn't worn a tac vest so he didn't have any Kevlar protection and had been blown right open. His intestines were curled all over the floor, over Little Gun's legs, and draped over the remains of the door.

By then, Scales had called it all into Doc so he didn't have a cow down there. Everyone just stood there, looking down at the mess of Big Bird.

Scales tried to pull the body away from Little Gun and he pushed him away. Something had to be done. I went over there and put my hands on Little Gun. I didn't dare touch Big Bird. Those two had been closer than brothers. "He's dead," I said. "You have to let him go now."

At that, Little Gun went ballistic. He jumped up and the body hit the floor. He stared at his bloody hands, whimpering. I tried to pull him away from it all and he turned and punched me right in the face. I hadn't expected that and down I went. It was like getting kicked by a bull.

Before anyone could stop him, he screamed and ran off down the hall.

"Okay," Doc said when we told him. *"Go get him."*

We ran after him and I saw him dart through a doorway. When we got there, we all saw there was a ladder in there that led straight up. It must have gone right through the third floor and to the roof itself. We told Doc and he ordered me and Smitty to go get him. Zulu and Scales were to rendezvous with Mongol on the third floor. Zulu and I didn't like being separated because we operated as a team, but an order was an order.

I went up the ladder, climbing those rungs one by one, up and up and up. I kept my light shining up there. I could see the trapdoor above getting closer and closer. What I didn't want to see was some insurgent pointing a rifle down at me. When I was almost to the top, I heard gunfire.

"Keep pushing," Smitty said. "We gotta fucking get up there, man."

I went up faster, knocking the trapdoor open and climbing up onto the roof. I saw the stars above the city, a perfect even blackness above the rooftops. I flipped my NVGs back on and just in time to see Little Gun climb up onto the ledge in the distance and jump.

"HEY!" I called out.

But he had just jumped onto another rooftop and was running off at top speed. I saw him go through a doorway and disappear. We soon found what he was shooting at. An insurgent who was bleeding out. Little Gun must have caught him sleeping.

"You...you better get away," he managed. "You don't know...you...don't...know..."

That's where he died.

What didn't we know?

We called into Doc what was going on and he told us to get Little Gun. He and Mad Mike would enter the building at street level and we'd sandwich Little Gun between us. It sounded like a plan and we gave chase. Doc sounded pretty calm over the Icom, but I knew he was pissed and I knew Little Gun was in deep shit. It was hard to say what Doc would do to him.

Smitty and I got to the doorway on the other roof. It was set in a little brick riser. Smitty yanked the door open and I went in. I moved down a set of steps until I got to a doorway. I waited there until he caught up with me. It gave me a chance to catch my breath and mellow down a bit.

"Ready?" I said, when he was there.

"Always."

We went through the doorway and found ourselves in yet another corridor. It was quiet. No motion. No activity. I called out to Little Gun on the Icom, but got no response. I wasn't about to start shouting his name. We moved down the corridor. Neither of us were saying a thing. I could hear Scales talking to Mongol on the third floor next door.

"*I'm just holding here,*" Mongol said. "*I think there's others up here.*"

"*Deadheads?*"

"*No.*" Pause. "*I don't think so. They're real quiet. Can't be deadheads.*"

"*Then what?*"

"*Nightcrawlers maybe.*" He was practically whispering. "*Whoever they are, they're real good in the dark. Watch yourself when you come up.*"

"*Will do.*"

Then Doc got on the line. "*Anything with your throwaways?*"

"*Nothing. Gave 'em to the dogs.*" That meant he had killed them. No surprise there. Killing unnecessarily was like a hobby to Mongol. "*Figured out why they wouldn't talk, though.*"

"*Yeah?*"

"*Somebody cut their tongues out.*"

I felt a chill go up my spine. Had to be nightcrawlers. They were very good in the dark and they liked tongues. They always cut them out. They must have liked to eat them.

Smitty and I kept moving.

I had a real bad feeling about this building. The same sense of crawling dread I had had in the cannibal's lair before or when I peered through that little door in the pantry. Something was wrong and I had the feeling we were being watched. I wasn't worried about zombies; they weren't much on stealth. If we were being hunted, it was by something else entirely. At a bend in the corridor, I stopped and Smitty stopped with me. I waited there, listening. It seemed like when we were moving I kept hearing things, but when I stopped there was nothing. Maybe it was our own sounds coming back at us. But I didn't believe it. There was danger here and I had been living so close to my bones for so many months by then, I didn't for a moment doubt my instincts or that internal alarm that was telling me we were in danger.

"*We're inside now,*" Doc said. "*We're taking it slow.*"

"Us, too," I said. "I don't think we're alone."

So far, there was no sign of Little Gun and I had the worst feeling about that. I was thinking that when and if we found him, we weren't going to like it at all.

"Listen," Smitty said.

But I'd already heard it and my muscles were tense from my neck to my feet. I heard a shuffling as of bare feet and then…I wasn't quite sure…but almost a hissing, slithery sort of sound. It came from farther down the corridor.

We moved down there slowly.

My skin felt tight.

My heart was so far up my throat I could have licked it.

Sweat was trickling from my scalp down my temples.

I smelled something coming from Smitty, something beyond the gore that was dried on his skin or his body odor…a sweet, yet metallic sort of smell that was very sharp almost like vinegar. I had smelled it before: it was the odor of fear. Some hormone secretion that came out of the human body during times of great stress and great terror.

I heard the shuffling again.

There was still nothing down there, nothing I could see in my NVGs at any rate.

Now I heard footsteps.

Running footsteps. I heard a gunshot. Small caliber, maybe a pistol and I saw muzzle flashes coming around the bend at the end of the corridor. A guy came running around the corner, looking behind him almost fearfully.

"FREEZE!" I said when he was maybe twenty feet from us. "YOU MOVE AND I'LL FUCKING PASTE YOU!"

He waited there and I could hear his labored breathing. He kept looking behind him. "They're coming," he said. "Get out of here! *They're coming!*"

What I could see of his clothes marked him as an insurgent. He wore camo fatigues. He had something on his belt and he held it up. I heard the shuffling of bare feet again. Many bare feet and that hissing sound.

"GO!" he said.

And I should have listened to him because he had an electronic detonator in his hand and he was about to fire it. Smitty fired before I did, drilling the guy in the chest milliseconds before my rounds punched into him. As he dropped, he fired the detonator and there was flash of bright light and a deafening booming. Then I was in the air and the walls came tumbling down.

THE HOUSE OF HORRORS, PART 4

When I woke up, I had no idea where I was. I lay there, coughing and coughing, trying to move and finding it impossible. By degrees it came back to me and I remembered the insurgent with the detonator and Smitty and all the rest. That's when I started to panic. I found I could move my legs and arms just fine so I figured I was still in one piece. The problem was that something was pressing down onto my forehead and I couldn't turn my head in either direction. Whatever it was, it wasn't crushing me, it was just pinning me.

Get out of here! They're coming!

The insurgent had tried to give us a chance that we would never have given him. Why? The answer to that was obvious. Whatever threat we presented was minimal in comparison to who or what was chasing him. He must have had an explosive charge wired in one of the rooms or under the floor. Maybe he had gone in there as bait to draw them into a trap so they could be destroyed.

My guess was nightcrawlers.

Everything Mongol said about the *others* on the third floor, from the stealthy figures being very good in the dark to the tongues being cut out of the throwaways, pointed at nightcrawlers. Add to that the cannibal's lair we found and those two we killed that had been bound together. They were here, all right. I was just hoping the explosion had killed them or sent them back into their holes.

Following the blast and the floor collapsing beneath me, I had managed to loose my NVGs and my rifle. I still had my sidearm and knife, but my Icom was damaged. I couldn't get anything on it.

So I was alone.

Maybe buried beneath a mountain of rubble for all I knew.

I dug around in my vest until I found the pocket with my lighter in it. I flicked it and found myself staring an immense wooden beam that was pressing against my forehead. I had to get myself free. Carefully, I worked my hands around the back of my head. There were bricks or rubble beneath it. Slowly, sweating rivers, I worked a piece of jagged stone free, then another. I could move my head maybe an inch in either direction by that point. How ironic it would have been if I dug myself free only to have my head crushed by the beam. I kept digging at the rubble behind my head, removing what felt like bricks or broken stone.

There was one last good piece under there that trapped me.

I began to dig it free with trembling hands, praying that shifting the rubble wouldn't make the beam shift, too. It didn't. I slid my head free of the beam, nearly tearing my nose off in the process.

I was free.

Or was I?

I lit the lighter again and saw heaped rubble all around me along with broken lathing and sections of walls, shattered plaster and split planks. I was in a little hollow scooped out of the debris. It was freakish luck. I crawled around looking for an escape route, anything, even a little worm hole I could widen…but there was nothing. Overhead was the broken remains of the ceiling from above that fit over my hollow like a cap. I moved the lighter around, clouds of dust settling around me.

I wondered about Smitty. Was he dead? How about Doc and Mad Mike? Had they been trapped or crushed in the cave-in?

My hollow was about twelve feet by twelve feet. I began circling around it, flicking the lighter from time to time to see if I could locate a draft. If I couldn't find even that then I was going to have to start digging blindly. My luck held. A slight draft made the lighter flame waver a bit. I tracked it down. It was coming through a tiny three-inch aperture in the rubble. Carefully again, I started removing bricks and sections of splintered wood. I dug out a floor lamp, then I unearthed the arm of a sofa. I kept working at it, removing the debris piece by piece until, suddenly, the entire wall shifted and rubble fell and I slid down farther into the hollow.

I waited for the whole thing to cave-in, but it didn't.

I climbed back up there and flicked the lighter. My tunneling paid off, I saw, because the wall had opened into another room. Maybe not a room exactly, but another chamber hemmed in by debris. I crawled in there and it was a bit bigger than the one I had just left. There was a small crawlspace that I widened. It led into darkness. It was big enough to creep through and I couldn't ask for much more. I started in, slinking forward like a worm until I came to a sort of pit that dropped down about four feet below me. But above, as I held the lighter up I could see an opening. I got down in there and climbed up the wall of rubble until I reached the opening. It was a corridor. The entire thing was shifted about twenty degrees or so, giving it a very weird, surreal sort of angle.

I moved down it, passing several rooms whose doors were buckled in their frames and would not budge. I followed it until it turned off to the right, more rubble and debris heaped around me. I was exhausted. I sat there, my back up against the wall and had a cigarette which didn't taste real good with my dry throat, but the nicotine did wonders in waking me up.

I heard a sort of scraping sound close by.

I flicked the lighter and there was nothing. I knew I couldn't let my imagination go running away on me. There were going to be sounds. Things would still be shifting and falling. It only stood to reason. I pulled off my cigarette, closing my eyes, wondering if the others were looking for me or if they had written me off as being dead. If Doc was alive, he would make the others look. Then again, it was night, so he might call it off until morning. I kept listening for the sound of voices or the rumble of the LAV, either of which would have told me if I was getting closer to freedom.

I heard nothing…save for that scraping sound again.

I flicked the lighter and, again, there was nothing.

I had a few drags left on my cigarette. I enjoyed each one. When I took the final and last drag, pulling hard off it, the cherry glowing orange and lighting up the corridor briefly…I saw a shape moving away in the darkness.

I saw it.

But it made no sound.

I reached down and pulled my 9mm Beretta from its holster. I knew I hadn't imagined the shape. It had been moving back the way I had come and I hoped like hell it would keep going. I listened for awhile, my senses acute, my heart pumping in my chest. But there was nothing more. I started off again, moving faster now, needing badly to put as much distance as I could between myself and what I had seen. I came to another wall of rubble that sealed off the corridor. That was bad. But what was good was a hole in the wall that I slid through and found myself in another tunnel cut through the debris.

It had to lead somewhere.

At least I hoped so.

But after following it for another twenty minutes or so, I wasn't so sure. I wasn't so sure of anything. The explosion had pretty much turned the building inside out and it was hard to know where anything was or to even begin orientating myself. But I had to keep going so I did…and then the floor fell away beneath me and I was sliding down a mountain of bricks into what had to be the cellar. Luckily, I hung onto my gun and lighter. My face was scraped, my arms laid raw, but I was still holding onto the two things that could keep me alive.

I was in what looked like a huge cavern.

I moved around piles of rubble and stepped through pools of standing water.

And that's when I found the bones.

Heaps of discarded animal bones and human bones. I saw jawless skulls whose craniums had been staved-in, femurs and tibias, a few ribcages, a section of vertebrae.

Jesus, what was this place?

Then I heard the scraping sound again that I had heard above. I flicked my lighter and I saw a ring of grotesque faces pressing in at me. I saw something like a child scraping together two sticks of bone. Nightcrawlers. They were naked and hunched over, their bodies white with plaster dust, their hair long and matted. Their faces were narrow, teeth jutting from pink gums. They hissed at me and I started shooting. I fired again and again and then something hit me from behind and I pitched face-first into a puddle.

When I came around again, I was being dragged off by the ankles. It was pitch black. My lighter and gun were gone. I reached down for my knife, but it was gone, too. I heard that reptilian hissing all around me. Then I blacked out again.

When I came to, I was suspended by my wrists.

It felt like wire cutting into me.

I couldn't see a damn thing, but I knew I wasn't alone. I didn't dare make a sound. The dread I felt was nearly incapacitating, an instinctive fear that was hanging above me, it seemed, like some immense spider waiting to drop down on me and suck out my blood.

There was an odor in the air, hot and revolting. It reminded me of gutted deer, marrow and blood.

I heard a sound.

And it was the worst sound imaginable.

The sound of a knife being worked on a stone by a practiced hand, its blade patiently being sharpened. There was a flash, followed by another and another and a fire was lit. It was small, but pale hands fed it until it blazed up high. And that's when I saw the sort of place I was in: a butcher shop. That's exactly what it was. The floor was scattered with bones and scraps of meat, the walls splashed with dark stains. I saw limbs hanging from them, arms and legs, stray hands and feet, a dozen or so heads with open bloody mouths and gouged-out eyes. That was all bad enough, but what I saw stretched over a table was the thing that took the heart out of me: a body. Two old women were poised over it. They each had meat cleavers and they began chopping on it, sectioning it, twisting bones from sockets and sawing through ligaments and tendons. Using a carving knife, they opened the abdomen and began yanking out organs and entrails, carefully sectioning them and dropping them into pots of water. All the pots were emptied into a kettle which boiled over the fire on a makeshift tripod.

I saw the face of the corpse.

It was Little Gun.

I had no true love for him, but he was still part of KIA-9 and I felt a burning hatred over what they had done to him and a burning terror of what they were soon going to do to me. Yes, these were nightcrawlers, the eaters of men, cannibals and ghouls and night-stalkers. I had read once that cannibalism, from a cultural viewpoint, was taboo because once men tasted the flesh of other men then they would be less than human. It was feared that they would regress into primeval flesh-eaters, descend into the dim past of their savage ancestry.

I have no doubt that in many ways that is true.

But at that moment, as I dangled there like a side of beef, I had no such memories of things I had read. I only knew simple animal fear and raging hatred. I wanted to get free. I wanted get a weapon in my hand so I could put these things down.

I saw their grotesque faces ringed in the darkness, the shining eyes and narrow faces, the overlapping teeth. Maybe they had been human once, but now they were only monsters. There were children there. I saw infants nursing at their mothers, toddlers playing with bones in the accumulated filth of the floor, and older children tearing at hunks of offered meat. A couple of them came over to me with blackened sticks in their hands. Making those hissing sounds, they began poking me with the sticks like a prize hog until one of the men shrieked at them. Then they disappeared back into the darkness.

If I was a rational man, I would have bided my time and tried to reason my way out of it, if such a thing was even possible. But I wasn't a reasonable man. I was a soldier. I was a killer. I was an exterminator. Dr. Cripps had seen to that. All I wanted was to get a weapon in my hand so I could kill.

Two of the women and one of the men came over.

The man lifted me up and one of the women cut my hands free. I still played dead, dropping limp into their arms. As they dragged me over to the fire I saw my chance and took it. One of the women had a knife stuck in the back of her pants and I seized it, knocking the man into the fire. I slashed one of the women across the face and grabbed the other by the hair when she tried to get away, slitting her throat ear to ear. And then they were all charging at me. I slashed and cut and hacked and then the knife was knocked out of my hands and three of them tackled me, pounding my head against the floor.

One of the women had her hands around my throat.

She was squeezing with incredible strength, strangling me while the others held me down. I was done for and I knew it, but still I shouted and screamed and raged...and then I heard an M4 firing and tactical lights speared through the darkness. The nightcrawlers were screeching, grabbing up simple weapons— knives and hatchets and clubs and spears—but it did them no good because I heard the sound of a SAW, the M249 Squad Automatic

Weapon, opening up, 5.56mm rounds ripping through the nightcrawlers. Bodies hit the floor and blood spattered the walls.

The three tormenting me got up and were cut nearly in half instantly. It happened very quickly. I saw Mad Mike come storming in, drilling anything that moved with the SAW. Doc was with him. He had his M4. He walked amongst the blood and bodies, capping nightcrawlers in the heads that still moved.

He reached down and pulled me to my feet.

"You wouldn't have tasted good anyhow, Dog," he said.

THE UNDEFEATED

The night didn't end there much as I might have liked it to. We went back outside and linked up with Scales and Mongol and Zulu. Little Gun and Big Bird were dead and they were never discussed again. We never did find Smitty. My guess was that he was crushed when the floor gave away, buried in the rubble.

I was given a new weapon and we moved through the streets for hours, mowing down zombies in great numbers and killing nightcrawlers and insurgents in the ruins.

When the sun finally came up, we were exhausted.

We leaned there against the LAV-25, covered in dust and old blood, soot and grit. We were worn out, nauseous, our ears ringing from the constant drumming of automatic rifles and machine guns throughout the night.

I remember Mongol blathering out how we were warriors, the best of the best, but nobody was really listening to his carefully-programmed propaganda. In retrospect, I'd heard shit like that in Iraq from officers who didn't know any better and soldiers who wanted, hell, *needed* to believe they were fighting for something tangible. But like in Iraq, we weren't warriors, we were just soldiers trying to survive to fight another day. And once the flag-waving and propaganda are dispensed with, that's all it ever is in any war. Leave the higher concepts to the people on the homefront. Like I was told in infantry school, *"You were hired from the neck down, leave the thinking to people with brains."*

We smoked and avoided looking at each other, each knowing there was something wrong with who we were and *what* we were, but our brains wouldn't let us remember just what and I think by the time the sun came up we were too tired to even contemplate such things.

Ultimately, we were wind-up toy soldiers.

We were mannequins.

We were puppets.

We pulled triggers because that's what we were told to do. We didn't know anything else and we weren't allowed to know anything else.

PSYCHO WARD

I woke up alone in a place I did not know, certain blood was running down my face. It wouldn't stop running. Terror that was huge and crushing weighed down on me. It was the instinctive fear of a trapped animal. I couldn't move my arms or legs. I couldn't move anything, it seemed, except my fingers and I could only wiggle them a bit.

I was strapped down.

You're dreaming. You've got to be dreaming.

A voice in my head kept telling me that, but I didn't believe it. Slowly, I was able to move my head and I saw I definitely wasn't alone. I was in some kind of hospital ward. There were others strapped down to beds like I was. I could see Zulu. She was convulsing, yellow foam coming out of her mouth. I could hear people moaning. I could hear someone else screaming.

Where the fuck am I?

My mind came out of the fog slowly, but it did come out. My memories were confused and overlapping. I saw faces—Mongol and Zulu, Doc Feelgood and Mad Mike, Scales and Smitty, Little Gun and Big Bird—and those were eclipsed by still other faces—Sabelia and Tuck and Diane and Jimmy and Paul. It was all scrambled in my head.

Make it stop. Dear God, make it stop!

But it wasn't stopping. If anything, it was getting worse, a riot of images and memories and faces and incidents and I wasn't sure what was dream and what was reality.

And a voice in my head said, *Remember.*

Yes, I had to get my thoughts organized. I had to sort out reality from fantasy. I knew who I was. My name was Dog. That's all. Dog. I was a soldier, an exterminator. I served the greater cause of...of...ARM. Yes, I served the cause and Dr. Cripps told me the only things I had to know. The rest was unimportant. The rest was trivial. It was marginalia and I didn't need to think about it.

Your name is not Dog.

No, no, no, that wasn't true. I had to shut all that out. I had to escape from it. I had to hide from it. Memories were returning to me, they were shining like a bright light in the darkness of my skull. I had to avoid the light. The light would undo what had been done. It would make me unhappy. It would take away the simplicity of being. I would question things and worry about things and fear things and maybe, yes, maybe I would even fear myself.

Your name is Steve Niles.

The memory caused pain and I didn't want pain. I was something that gave pain but I didn't want to receive it because it frightened me. Like all brutes and bullies and thugs, I was terrified of being hurt.

Steve Niles.

There was no hiding from it. The light found me and enveloped me and then I knew all those things maybe I would have been better off not knowing. I was a programmed killer with a synthetic life that had been engineered for me by Dr. Cripps. I went around with a group of savages, killing and killing, but that wasn't who I really was. That was an act and Baneberry was strictly theater.

Jesus, how long had this been going on?

Weeks? Months? How long had I been drugged up and conditioned and where was Sabelia? I had to get to Sabelia because…because, yes, I loved her and she loved me and together we would hook up with Tuck and the others and get back to the Silo and my son. That was the plan. That had always been the plan. Why in the hell did I let Cripps sidetrack me? Use me like a fucking vicious attack dog? Why did I let him control me?

"I see you're awake," a voice said and I saw Cripps standing there, that crooked grin on his face.

"Get these off me," I said to him, indicating the straps that held me down. "I need to get free. There's things I have to do."

"You're right," he said. "There *are* things you have to do and when the time is right, I will tell you what they are."

"You fucking asshole! Let me loose! *Let me goddamn loose!*"

I fought and strained and got red in the face but it all did me little good. I wasn't going anywhere and I wasn't going to do anything. Not until Dr. Cripps decided otherwise.

"Where's Sabelia?"

"She's upstairs living a peaceful, productive life with the others in the bunker. When KIA-9 finishes its appointed task, I'll let you go up and live with her. In fact, in the new Baneberry you and she will live together as man and wife."

"We have lives outside of here."

"You have nothing until I say otherwise."

God, how I wanted to beat his priggish, self-satisfied face to a bloody pulp. The satisfaction it would have brought me. But I wasn't going to be doing anything like that in the foreseeable future. I was a rat in a trap. I was a convict in a cage. I was an inmate in an insane asylum and I could fight and rage all I wanted but it would get me nowhere. I had to think. I didn't know exactly how he had accomplished turning us into killing machines. It had something to do with Agent 17 and other psychotropic drugs, behavior modification and post-hypnotic suggestion. Probably other techniques as well. All of them evil and inhumane. It was one thing to torture the body, but to scar the mind...the only true place of privacy that any of us really have. That was unforgivable.

He had a syringe in his hand. He drew some clear fluid from a tiny bottle. "Nearly time to go back to work," he said. "But have no fear, you're nearly done."

From what I understood of brainwashing and the like, which was very little, such things required a trigger to activate them. Once Cripps brought us out of our drugged-up fugues, he probably said some word to us, some trigger phrase, that would activate our programming. But I thought I had read somewhere that American POWs that underwent rigid political indoctrination and drug-induced brainwashing techniques at the hands of the North Koreans and Chinese had created something like a *counter*-trigger. This was just a word or phrase that when you encountered it, recognized it, and said it aloud, it would bring you back to reality and make you remember who you really were or at least question everything you were doing, seeing, and believing. It created a disassociation with reality, self-critical thinking. It was one of the few ways to undermine conditioning.

"You're going to go to sleep again," Cripps said as he wiped an alcohol swab on my arm. "When you wake, you'll go to work."

Think, think, think! I told myself.

A counter-trigger. I needed a counter-trigger. I knew it had to be specific. Not *floor* or *wall* or *tree.* It had to be very specific. Once I had it, I would keep repeating it to myself, creating a neural pathway and once I saw the object when I was out with KIA-9, it would confuse me. It would begin to erode the conditioning. It might make me remember or it might just scare me or panic me.

I thought of Ricki.

I thought of her beautiful blue eyes.

That was it.

Beautiful blue eyes, beautiful blue eyes, beautiful blue eyes. Remember! Remember! Beautiful blue eyes. When you see them, you have to run. When you see them you have to escape. Beautiful blue eyes, beautiful blue eyes...

The needle went in and I began to feel loose and limp right away. I could barely keep my eyes open.

"I'm going to count back from ten," Cripps said. "When I reach four, you'll be gone..."

Beautiful blue eyes.

"...eight, seven, six..."

Beautiful blue eyes.

"...five...four..."

I slipped away into the darkness, beautiful blue eyes watching over me.

BAIT

We were out in the streets again playing our games and having our fun. KIA-9 was actually KIA-6 now that Smitty was MIA and probably dead and Big Bird and Little Gun were most assuredly dead. Doc Feelgood said as far as he knew, there would be no replacements for them. Not in the near future anyway.

"So who gives us our orders?" Zulu said.

We all just looked at her. We were shocked and nearly confused by what she said. It was practically a revelation. *So who gives us our orders?* It had never occurred to me and I don't think it had ever occurred to the others either. Who *did* give us our orders? Funny, but when we marched out of the bunker it seemed like we'd already been given our orders and there was no question about what we had to do.

Doc swallowed, his eyes glazed. "We just...we just get them. What kind of question is that anyhow?"

Zulu shrugged. "Seems like when you're in the army or something, somebody has to give you orders. Maybe that person would know if we're getting replacements."

"They didn't tell me," Doc said.

"Who are *they?*" Scales asked.

Doc looked like a cornered animal. I thought he would bare his teeth and start slavering at any moment. He didn't, of course, but he was riled and we could all see that. "You don't have to worry about that. Those aren't questions you can ask."

"But you're in charge," Zulu said. "When we have questions, we're supposed to ask you."

We all nodded. Even Mad Mike who never said a word moved in a little closer, grunting in agreement.

Doc was shaking. "You better watch what you're doing," he said to Zulu, his hand slipping down to the 9mm Beretta in its holster. "You can't ask these things. It's dangerous. If you're a threat, then you have to go."

Zulu brought up her M4. "I'm not going."

Doc's hand shook. "Lower that weapon."

"Get your hand away from that gun," she told him. "If I go, I don't go alone."

His hand moved away from it. We learned at that moment the power of asking questions, of putting those in power on the spot. It confused us thinking that way, but I know it not only excited me but thrilled me. I think the others felt the same way. Here was a new kick. Something to beat back the boredom of constant fighting and killing that no longer were the sort of high they had once been. But the more the idea of asking questions occurred to me the more one of those headaches began to blossom in the back of my skull.

Doc didn't like the idea of us all turning on him.

What he liked even less was Zulu standing up to him.

Maybe Dr. Cripps had not programmed him on how to deal with open defiance and subversion. Maybe there were limits to his control. Of course, none of that occurred to me at the time. If it had, my conditioning and that of the others would have broken right open.

Diversion.

Doc Feelgood decided that's what we needed. Some good old diversion. Some fun and games to straighten our thinking out and blow off some of our steam.

Mongol and Scales grabbed a man, some throwaway who was wandering about with a paper bag of odds and ends. He kept saying, *"Mut-mut-mut-mut-mut."* No doubt he'd been emotionally disturbed long before Necrophage made the rounds. He was bound and gagged and shoved before us until Mongol, out on point, found a couple zombies out walking around.

We took the man and tied him to a STOP sign. As the rest us found a good place to watch the festivities from—the top of a bus that was nearly torn in half from machinegun fire—Mongol went and led the zombies in. The walking dead will follow you easier than a stray dog. He just showed himself to them and right away he had three new friends. He led them on in and then disappeared. The man tied to the STOP sign, his gag off, kept going, *"Mut-mut-mut-mut-mut."* That drew the zombies in and we sat there watching them as they approached our living bait pile.

There were three of them, two women and a man. One of the women was middle-aged and wore fuzzy bunny slippers and nothing else. Gaping black ulcers were eaten through her purple-green skin. A couple stray curlers bounced in her hair. Her nose was gone, decayed down into a grisly hollow, her eyes blank white. The other woman was younger, college-age maybe, wearing skinny jeans and a gore-encrusted red-and-black flannel shirt that was torn open to the waist. One pert, greening breast poked out. The man, naked and fat, had a section of his belly missing. He looked like stout, bulbous mushroom somebody had taken a bite out of.

"Mut-mut-mut-mut-mut," the throwaway said, unconcerned about the zombies. More interested at something in the sky the rest of us simply could not see.

The woman in the skinny jeans got there first.

She wasted no time. Presentation mattered little to her. Probably no more than taste did…and the throwaway couldn't have tasted so good. It looked like he hadn't had a bath in years. But it didn't bother her. She bit into his throat and blood squirted into her face. The throwaway made a high, keening sound like a locust as she chewed a flap free and stepped back, trying to shove the entire mass of meat into her mouth. She was a petite little thing, probably quite pretty and desirable in life. The sort of lady who probably ate a lot of salads, fruit, nuts, and tuna fish, hit the gym four times a week. She would have been a petite eater as well, little nibbles and bites, never enough to make a mess or get crumbs on her lap. A very precise little thing. Which made it all that much more amusing to watch her trying to shove all that meat in her mouth at once.

She gobbled and chomped and slobbered.

We laughed.

This was great comedy for us.

The man got to the throwaway next who was bleeding out pretty quickly. Skinny Jeans must have bitten out his carotid. Just as he was moving in for a little taste, the other woman—Bunny Slippers—shoved him out of the way. When she tried to go in for a bite, he clubbed her on the back of the head with one big fist and drove her to her knees. He was second after all. But as he tore a chunk of flesh from the throwaway's shoulder, Bunny Slippers bit his leg. He just kicked her aside. He was hungry and he was taking no shit.

Now Skinny Jeans came in.

She didn't bother fighting with the other two. As the throwaway stopped muttering and went limp, she ripped his shirt open and buried her teeth in his belly. Now Bunny Slippers wanted some of that, too. Instead of fighting Skinny Jeans, she worked in tandem with her as they chewed on his belly, ripping out great shanks of bloody meat. Then they tore him open. From our vantage point, it looked like they unzipped him. His bowels fell from his abdomen and they greedily went after them which attracted the fat guy—Mushroom Man—and the three of them had a real feast. The sound of them chewing and slobbering was enough to make your guts roll over.

Skinny Jeans got bored, though.

She ripped the guys pants open and filled her mouth with what was between his legs, tearing it out by the roots.

"Damn," Scales said. "That's gonna leave a mark."

It was rare that we sat around and watched the festivities like that. Usually, we just blew the deadheads away, but this time we got to see it all in graphic, clinical detail and I'm pretty sure that as hard and ruthless as we were, none of us were craving any lunch by the time it was over.

And it took time.

The zombies were absolutely gluttonous. They ate and ate and ate, tearing and clawing and biting. They couldn't shove meat in their mouths fast enough. They were such mindless slobs that half of what they chewed on fell out, but there was always more, plenty more. I think by the time they tore the throwaway's arms and legs off we were getting kind of bored with it all. The remains of their meal were scattered all over the ground and all over them. They kept at it until there was nothing but a set of bloody bones tied to the STOP sign.

"I'm gonna have some fun," Mongol said.

Before Doc could say anything, he climbed off the bus and went tearing after the zombies. Gore dropped from their blood-smeared mouths when they saw him coming. Mushroom Man shambled in his direction and Mongol whipped out his two machetes. As Mushroom Man reached for him, Mongol did some of his famous chop sockey moves and sliced one of the guy's arms off with an overhand arc of a blade. Mushroom Man was inconvenienced by the loss of his limb, but he was hardly done in.

"'Tis but a scratch," Scales said and we all laughed.

Mushroom man went after Mongol with a vengeance and Mongol barely got out of his way. He ducked under his clutching hand, nearly tripped over his own feet, and when Mushroom Man reached for him, he chopped his other arm off. The move was nice. We all had to admit that. Taking an arm off with a single blow takes practice.

Mongol kept circling around Mushroom Man to keep him off balance. Without arms, the zombie's bite was the only real danger.

"Shit, man," Scales said. "Ain't nothing but a flesh wound."

We laughed again.

Mongol wasted no more time. He slashed open Mushroom Man's belly and his guts seemed to explode from the wound, slopping to his feet in green and black loops of rot. At the same moment, he projectile vomited out a gushing stream of gore that struck Mongol right in the chest. We couldn't help laughing at that.

Mongol was pissed, pawing stringy bits of tissue from his tac vest. "YOU MOTHERFUCKER!" he cried out and went at Mushroom Man full steam, chopping and slashing him until he hit the ground. Even then, Mongol kept hacking until there was nothing but a lot of blood and meat and bones scattered about.

"Guess we're gonna have to call this a draw," Scales said.

By then, the other two were bearing down on Mongol. He took off the head of Bunny Slippers with one devastating arc of the blade in his right hand and split Skinny Jeans' noggin right down to the chin with an overhand chop. So much for that. They both hit the ground, flopping a bit but going still eventually.

Then our fun was at an end and Doc ordered us down off the bus. Break time was over. He broke us up into two-person teams— me and Zulu, himself and Mad Mike, Scales and Mongol. We went up the street and started going house to house looking for someone to kill. We saw few zombies and those we did see we put down right away.

We came to an ordinary little two-story house. There was nothing special about it. Nothing special at all. But as we started looking around on the main floor, we found empty cans of food—pork-and-beans, Franco-American spaghetti—on the kitchen counter.

"Somebody's been living here," Zulu said. "Mother thinks we better find out who."

"Agreed."

We checked out all the rooms down there. We found a bedroom at the back that looked like it had been occupied recently. There was a sleeping bag unzipped on the bed and some clothes on the dresser. We found nothing in the closet, so up the stairs we went. Maybe we should have been more careful, but we had been through so much action by that point and came away again and again with nothing but a few cuts and bruises, that we were cocky. Maybe not even cocky so much as complacent.

Zulu started up the stairs and I was right behind her.

I don't think either of us expected anything. So when she got to the landing and turned a right into the hallway up there, nobody was as surprised as we were when two rounds hit her point-blank. The Kevlar of her vest stopped one, but the second went right through her throat and she made a sort of gasping sound and hit the floor, blood pooling around her.

I dashed up there, diving low because I knew the shooter was waiting for me.

I heard the gun crack off a few more rounds that chewed into the wall above me. I squeezed the trigger of my M4 before I had even hit the floor, drilling some teenage kid with a three-round burst that threw him off his feet like he'd been kicked. By the time I got to him and kicked the .30-06 away from him, he was already dead. One of the slugs must have clipped his heart.

I went back to Zulu.

She was dead, too. I saw that right away. The round that went through her throat had taken out her jugular. The .30-06 is a good weapon at long range, but close in like that it's devastating. Most of Zulu's neck was blasted away and sprayed against the wall. The slug went right through her without even slowing down, it seemed. There wasn't a damn thing I could do for her. I kissed her bloody lips, knowing, if nothing else, that she had not suffered. My guess is she had maybe lived a few seconds after she hit the floor, but certainly no more than that.

I crouched there by her, lighting a cigarette and thinking about her. I liked her. If I'd had a friend in KIA-9 it was probably her. My emotions fought with themselves. I think I needed to cry over a fallen comrade, but at the same time I was unable to. My programming wouldn't allow it. So I smoked and looked down at her beautiful ebony face and huge dark eyes and was unable to feel anything but confusion.

Doc called in over the Icom, but I ignored him.

Fuck him.

Fuck them all.

And, most assuredly, fuck us.

I finished my cigarette and crushed it out on the floor. It was then that I had the feeling that I was not alone. I don't recall hearing anything. It was just a feeling, a stirring of that vague sixth sense we all feel now and again. Someone was up there with me. I looked down at Zulu and I knew that whoever was there was going to die. Only I wasn't going to use my rifle. I was going to use my knife on them.

I pulled my K-Bar and death was all over me.

It owned me.

I wanted to kill like I had never wanted to kill before. I checked the bathroom, one of the bedrooms. Nothing. I was tense, frustrated, angry. If whoever was hiding up there had slipped away from me, then I was never going to forgive myself. There was one more bedroom at the end of the hall and I went there, breathing hard with rage, the knife in my hand. I kicked open the door and I don't think even a hail of bullets could have stopped me.

There was no one in there.

Then I yanked open the closet door and there was a girl hiding in there. She couldn't have been more than seven or eight. She cried out and I grabbed her by the hair and pulled her out into the light coming in through the window. She squealed and fought and I slapped her across the face. I jerked her head back by the hair and brought my knife in to slit her throat.

Her face was wet with tears, snot coming from her nose.

She looked up at me with big, crystal blue eyes.

Lovely eyes.

And something in my head snapped.

The blue eyes.

Beautiful blue eyes.

Something was going on, only I didn't know what. My knife hand trembled, a sort of whining sound came from deep in my throat. I felt dizzy, lightheaded. My stomach was roiling.

"You...you little...bitch," I managed through clenched teeth as sweat rolled down my face.

Beautiful blue eyes.

I couldn't make myself slit her throat. I released her hair and not because I wanted to but because there was no strength left in my hand. The knife dropped from my other hand and I fell to my knees. The girl jumped off the bed and pressed herself into the corner.

Beautiful blue eyes.

My head felt like it was going to blow apart. There was an agony up there I could not think through. It was like a war was being fought in my skull and all I could do was sit there, shaking and sweating, drool running from my mouth.

Beautiful blue eyes.

Beautiful blue eyes.

"What? What? What...?" I muttered.

Beautiful blue eyes. When you see them, you have to run. When you see them you have to escape.

Yes, escape. Despite the pain and confusion, there was a very real, very strong desire in me to run away as fast as I could until I could get my head straight again. It was sort of a fear response, a flight response.

Beautiful blue eyes.

The words wouldn't stop. I stood up and the pain faded a bit. I looked over at the girl. "You...you better hide," I told her. "They'll be coming...coming for you."

And she ran out the door.

A few seconds later, I picked up my knife, sheathed it and grabbed my M4 off the bed. I still didn't know what any of it was about or why it was so strong, but I had to get away. I had to get somewhere safe and I needed to do that right now.

Beautiful blue eyes.

I stumbled down the stairs and out of the house. I could hear traffic over my Icom, but I could not be sure who the people were speaking on it. I snatched it off my head and threw it. I didn't want to hear anymore voices. I needed to be free. I needed to run. I needed to get away before they—and I didn't really know who they were—found me.

I stood out in the relatively fresh air.

The Icom, you dummy. You need it.

For some reason, I knew that I did. I picked it up and stuffed it into my ammo bag where I wouldn't have to hear it. Maybe later, much later, I would put it back on.

I heard voices shouting to me. Two men down the street. I took one look at them and I ran, I ran the other away as fast as I could with them in hot pursuit.

They wouldn't get me.

I couldn't let them get me…because…because of the…

Beautiful blue eyes.

BEAUTIFUL BLUE EYES

I ran and ran until I could no longer hear them shouting or coming after me. I crawled through the wreckage of houses and over heaps of rubble. Dirty, dusty, sweating and scared, I found a set of steps leading down into a basement and went down there. The house above had been blown to kindling. I waited there in the semi-gloom, studying the shafts of dust-speckled light coming down the stairway. I sipped from my canteen. I took a piss. I smoked. I ate some crackers from an MRE pouch and spread jelly and peanut butter on them.

Still, that fucking voice would not stop saying, *beautiful blue eyes,* and I thought I was going to scream if it didn't stop tormenting me. It seemed to lessen after an hour or two. I took out the Icom and put it on, trying to get an idea of what KIA-*4* was doing now. Were they hunting me or had they given up and returned to their original mission profile?

But I knew Doc Feelgood.

He wouldn't just shrug his shoulders and say, *Oh well, scratch another one.* It wasn't in his makeup. He'd want to know what went wrong just as I wanted to know what had gone wrong and what was still going wrong. I smoked and sipped from my canteen and wondered just what the hell I was doing or what I was going to do.

I must have nodded off because when I woke a couple hours later the shadows were long. I stood up and stretched, ducking my head beneath pipes that were hanging from the ceiling like tree roots. I was starting to remember things that made no sense. If I thought about them too hard, I started getting a headache. But if I dismissed them outright, it started again: *Beautiful blue eyes.*

Darkness found me still sitting there with no better idea of what the hell it was that I was supposed to do. There was nothing on the Icom so either Doc and the others were out of range or they had simply given up for the night.

They'll be back, I told myself. *You know they'll be back and you'll be a hot target for them until they decide you're dead or lost.*

I had never spent a night alone in the Main Street sector of Baneberry and I wasn't too happy about it. Crazy ideas kept occurring to me. I could go out there and try and make my way back to the bunker…and Doc would probably shoot me for freaking out and breaking with unit discipline. I could go out there and try and escape the city. Just run until my head cleared and I was out in the country. Then I'd be out of harm's way—KIA-4's way—and I could sort things out. But I didn't care for the idea. It was already heating up out there as it did most nights. I could hear people screaming or shouting from time to time. Lots of sporadic gunfire.

It was deadly out there and I knew it.

I had already decided I wasn't going to risk linking back up with KIA-4. No fucking way. I didn't know what was going on in my head, but I knew, somehow, that I was through with all that. The bottom line was I didn't really like those people—something that had never really occurred to me before. I kept thinking about Zulu. She was the only one I would have called a friend and she was dead. Maybe, had we survived, the both of us would have been here in the cellar. I had a feeling she was ready to break with Doc, too.

There was nothing to do, I figured, but wait for dawn.

That was the safest course of action.

Wait for dawn and listen to that voice saying, *Beautiful blue eyes* in my head and try to make sense out of all the strange questions that had never occurred to me before and wonder about all the faces I was seeing in my head that had no names. There were so many after a time that they crowded out my own thoughts.

Using my ammo bag as a pillow, I stretched out holding onto my M4 and hoping I wouldn't have to use it tonight. I was exhausted and I nodded off. I must have slept for hours. When I woke it was still dark and I heard my voice say, *"Where do you think Sabelia is?"*

Then I went out again.

THE HUNT

When I finally came awake, it was full light. I was sore from sleeping on the concrete and it took awhile to work the chill and stiffness from my body. I ate some MREs and drank some water, repeating that name again and again under my breath, "Sabelia."

There was power in that name.

It was a key to something.

I would not let it go.

Whatever it meant, it was getting stronger, it was getting closer. I could even concentrate on it without getting a headache. I was making progress…but to what, I just didn't know.

As I packed up my stuff and made ready to leave, the Icom crackled into life and I received a broken transmission: *"Dog…Dog, you out there? We're…a sweep for you, man. If you're…just call out…just call out…"*

That was Scales' voice. I realized then that I liked him in a way. Not the way I had liked Zulu, but he wasn't too bad. He had his moments and we'd shared a lot of laughs together. I nearly hailed him…but, no, I wasn't about to do that. KIA-4 had its marching orders and I was almost certain it would be to either bring me in as a corpse or as a prisoner.

The broadcasts began to get clearer and I was almost certain they were moving in my direction. I got my gear together and my weapon in my hands and I crawled up the steps until my eyes were at ground level and I could see what was going on out there. I saw a couple zombies shambling down the street, moving away from me. A couple of dogs hunted through the rubble of a row of houses across the way that had fallen into themselves.

Then I heard the sound of running feet.

I saw two guys dressed in jungle camo fatigues come running through a partially-blocked alley. They were carrying M-16s and what looked like an RPG. They came so close that I could see the blood on their fatigues and the streaked filth on their faces. Their eyes were huge with fear.

Then—

WAAA-RUMP!

There was a huge explosion a few streets over and the ground shook. Clouds of smoke and debris rose into the air. I could hear the fragments raining down like hailstones. Both of the men, well down the street by then, let out cheers and I heard no more of them. Insurgents. Guerrilla fighters. The thorn in the side of the bunker and the primary target of the KIA teams.

Terrorists.

And as I thought that, I heard a voice in my head say, *"Terrorists? Well...only if you're the target of their terror. To their friends they're not terrorists, they're freedom fighters."* I heard a peal of laughter coming from an audience. Some old TV show I had forgotten about? A stand-up comedian? So many things were activating in my brain my head practically hurt.

"We got 'em on the run," Scales said over the Icom. *"We'll keep pushing."*

Then Doc: *"IED...the LAV took a good hit. Get those SOBs. I want 'em."*

There was some gunfire exchanged in the distance.

"That's three," Mongol said. *"Got two more trapped."*

"Go at 'em easy," Doc Feelgood said.

"Burn 'em out," a voice I didn't recognize said which meant that there were new bodies in KIA-9.

I heard another voice I didn't recognize.

I heard a chopper pass close by. I couldn't see it, but I definitely heard it. This was a major mop-up operation. They were putting the squeeze on the insurgents and I was caught in the middle of the action. Not good. I had a feeling that I was now a *freedom fighter* whether I liked it or not. The new guys would kill me on sight. And I couldn't be sure the old boys wouldn't either.

I slipped up the stairs and moved in the direction the insurgents had gone. I would stay on their trail as KIA stayed on mine, then I would cut back towards the west and get around them and out of the city. I hadn't gone more than half a block when a few rounds tore up the real estate around me. I was being targeted. I ran in a zig-zagging pattern, more bullets following me, and dove through a hole in the wall of a crumbling brick building. A few more slugs hit the outer wall.

Shit.

Now I was in the fight whether I liked it or not.

I clambered up a mountain of broken bricks and debris and I could hear more gunfire. Not the shooter who had targeted me, but KIA-9 out cleaning up. I could hear Mad Mike cracking away with his SAW. Zombies, insurgents, throwaways...hell, it could have been anything. I had to put some distance between me and them. The back wall of the building was blown apart like the front. I slid down the brick pile until I reached the aperture and slid through it into a little grassy courtyard and stopped dead there on my knees.

A pair of zombies were busy dismembering a corpse that looked like it had been dead for days. The stench was horrible. They both looked over at me with those dead-white eyes, clots of gore dropping from their mouths. They instantly abandoned the body for fresher pickings.

Damn things.

Now I didn't have a choice. I had to shoot and in doing so, I was pretty much going to telegraph my position. Fuck it. I didn't have a choice. I drilled both of them and, right away, I heard the KIA boys calling in that they were in pursuit. Shit. I moved through the courtyard. The only way out was back the way I came unless I took an iron utility ladder that led up to the roof. It was about twelve feet off the ground but a pile of rubble solved that for me. I climbed up it and went up the ladder as fast as I could. If any shooters showed up, I was going to be a real easy target.

I was almost to the top when I saw the chopper go zooming overhead. I saw its profile just fine—a fucking Kiowa Warrior—just as I saw its armament: a .50-cal machine gun and twin Hydra 70 rocket tubes. These were the sort that were used for close air support, pulverizing the enemy.

And I was now the fucking enemy.

The Kiowa made me think of LAV-25s and people on a road. I saw some of those same people in my mind in connection with a Kiowa scout chopper and an AT4 missile. What the hell was that about?

No matter and no time.

I reached the top of the ladder and was in for more disappointment. There was no roof to crawl on up there. There was nothing. There was only the wall. The rest of the building had collapsed into rubble. It was either back down or I took a chance and crept over the wall to the next building which looked intact. The top of the wall was about two feet wide and I had no way of knowing if my added weight would make the thing fall or not. I'd have to take the chance.

More gunfire from the direction of the KIA boys got me moving. I got on top of the wall, telling myself not to look down. On my knees, I crept over the top. Now and again, bits of it crumbled away and once a section fell and I nearly went down. I kept moving. I went as carefully as I could, but I didn't have much time. If that chopper passed overhead again, they were going to see me and a volley of .50-cal rounds would end my pain right there. I kept going until I reached the next building. Now the tricky part. The building was about six or seven feet above the height of the wall. Pressing my hands against it, I stood uneasily, fighting the vertigo that I felt.

I heard the chopper.

Jesus, it was coming in my direction.

I jumped up and got my hands atop the ledge of the other building and scrambled up and over. Soon as I made it, I dropped to the flat roof on the other side and lay there, squeezed up against the ledge. The chopper came and passed. I didn't hear it coming back and there was no chatter on the Icom about sighting an insurgent, so I was safe.

I got up and ran across the rooftop.

The bad news was that the next building over was down much lower. It would be a drop of twenty feet onto an inclined roof. Even I wasn't that crazy in my desperation. There was a hatch leading down into the building, but it was locked which meant I'd have to blast it open and, again, telegraph my position.

Bullshit.

I had another plan.

A fire escape. It was a drop of about ten feet from the rooftop. I made a quick scan to see if anyone was watching me or drawing a bead on me, then I climbed over the ledge and dropped. I hit the fire escape just fine, but the whole thing clanged and shook. I thought for a moment it would come right off the side of the building. I climbed down it to the next landing and then took the ladder down into an alley.

I heard more explosions in the distance.

The KIA boys were running into masses of zombies now and the Kiowa went into action, blasting away with its Hydra 70s. *BOOM, BOOM, BOOM!*The ground shook with each impact. I saw black smoke rising above the rooftops behind me. Mongol was shrieking with excitement over the Icom. The zombie menace had been eradicated, according to Doc, and they were pushing ahead again. In my direction. I had to get somewhere where I could hide out as they passed and then double back. It was my only chance.

I cut down the alley, climbing up and over a couple rusted cars that blocked the street, and darting to the next street of ruined buildings. I was being watched. I was almost certain of it. I climbed over a gutter and pushed through a doorway and something went *thunk, thunk, thunk* and I saw a grenade not three feet from me. I heard it sizzling. I jumped back through the doorway and dove for the gutter as it went off. *BOOM!* Dust and debris fell over me.

I laid there with my M4 in my hands.

I did not move.

I did not do anything.

Somebody was going to come and check on me and I had to be ready to cap them when they did. No soldier in the world threw a grenade and just left it at that. They would come for a quick BDA, Battle Damage Assessment, to see if their target was dead. I waited and soon enough, I heard footsteps coming…slow, careful. One of us was going to die and if I made so much as a sound, it was going to be me. All it would take was another tossed grenade.

I waited, tense and sweating.

My adversary crept forward very carefully.

That's when I heard another sound. It was coming from farther down the gutter. I craned my head and looked. Christ, a zombie. About thirty feet from me, a little zombie boy was crawling in my direction on his hands and knees. He wasn't moving fast, but he *was* moving and I was his target. There was so much fungus growing on him he almost looked like a small furry ape. It looked like he had been in some sort of a blast because most of his hair was burned away and his face was burnt nearly down to the skull. He had no eyes, but that didn't seem to matter because he knew right where I was.

If my adversary didn't show soon, I was going to have to show my hand and cap the little deadhead.

This was what they meant by being in-between a rock and a hard place.

The zombie crawled closer.

He was twenty feet away and closing.

My adversary had paused as if he sensed something was amiss. Maybe he heard the zombie boy even though he was being very silent.

C'mon, c'mon.

The zombie boy was fifteen feet away. I could hear his teeth chattering, wanting to bite.

My adversary was within feet of the gutter now.

The zombie was ten feet from me now and I could see the drool hanging from his mouth.

My adversary accidentally kicked a rock and that made the zombie boy turn his head in interest. My adversary saw him. He fired in panic, capping a few rounds into the air that completely missed his target. Then he zeroed in, blowing the zombie boy away. His head flew apart in a Technicolor eruption of brains and skull matter.

My adversary, breathing hard, looked over the edge of the gutter and I saw the terror widen in his eyes right as my round punched into his forehead and he fell backwards.

I climbed out and he was dead.

Jesus, he looked like he was about fourteen.

He was dressed in camo fatigue pants and work boots, a black Nike shirt. He carried an M4 like me. He had two extra mags and I tossed them in my ammo bag.

I heard the chopper again and knew I had to keep going.

What happened next was pure luck, absolutely pure luck. You sometimes run across it in combat and, later, when you think about it, it scares the shit out of you because you realize how easily it could have gone wrong. I moved into the doorway of the building my adversary had been waiting in. I didn't know if there were more fighters waiting in there, but I didn't have a choice. I had to get off the streets before the KIA team arrived or some guerrillas drew a bead on me.

"We got shitheads hiding in those ruins," I heard Mongol say over the Icom. *"Deadheads massing beyond. We ain't got no choice but to go right through."*

"Roger that," Doc said.

Hiding in the gutter had cost me. The KIA boys were on the opposite side of the street and they were going to come right at me once Doc cut the order. And from what they said, zombies were massing on the other side.

"No bullshit now," Doc said. *"We go right through those motherfuckers. Anybody gets hit, leave 'em and keep pushing forward. Move!"*

I heard boots running in the street.

I had to find a place to hide because I was about to get in a shootout with my old friends. I was in the remains of a store of some type, I saw. I ducked behind a counter, trying to get out of harm's way and I tripped over a man crouched there, waiting for me. He was an insurgent and he stabbed out at me with a knife and he would have had me except that in his excitement to kill, he smashed his hand against the counter and lost his knife. I brought my weapon around and cracked him in the face with it. He fell back, grabbing the counter and trying to bring his boot around to kick me.

A volley of bullets ripped through him.

KIA had arrived. I heard one of them charge in and I saw it was Scales. He didn't see me. Not until it was too late and I had him in my sights.

"Joined the other side, did you?" he said, smiling, real cool and easy.

It probably would have won over just about anyone, that smile of his. But I knew better. I knew how Scales operated. I knew how fast he could move and, true to form, he threw himself back and tried to bring his M4 around and I pumped three rounds right into his face. He made a weird screaming sort of sound and crashed into the wall, leaving most of his face smeared there and hit the floor a corpse. I was up and shooting when another guy—I didn't recognize him—came through the doorway. I dropped him before he made it two feet. He hit the floor, moaning, making a gurgling sound from his ripped-open throat.

I got out while the getting was good.

I went through an archway in the back and out a door which I thought must lead into an alley. I was right it did.

But it also led into the clutches of a dozen zombies bearing right down on me.

DOG FIGHT

Two of them were on me before I could even raise my weapon. I bashed one of them in the face with the butt of my M4 and gave the other a good kick that drove him back. I brought up my rifle to fire.

It jammed.

I tried to clear it.

No time.

The one I had kicked pushed in and I pulled my Beretta 9mm and shot him in the head. I punched and kicked and shot but there were so damn many, I was fighting a losing battle. What I thought was a dozen was quickly becoming four times that many. They pulled at me, pushed at me, grabbed me from behind and from the front. Again and again, I slipped from their clutches only to be faced with a new swarm. I used all my usually tactics—shoving them into each other, using my body as a human battering ram, shooting with my 9mm and slashing with my knife. But they kept coming and when the Beretta clicked on an empty chamber, I knew it was all over with.

And it was at that moment—as dozens of hands reached for me and moldering faces pressed in—that something went in my head with a dizzying, almost popping sort of sound and I thought I had been shot. But it was nothing physical. It was something bigger. All the questions and confusion, the taunting voices and mysterious faces suddenly just exploded and...*I remembered.* It came in a frenetic rush: Yonkers and Ricki, Tuck and Jimmy, Paul and Diane, Tuck and Sabelia and Robin and who I was and what I was and how I had been turned into a mindless zombie by Dr. Cripps at the bunker.

Oh God...oh my God...

And with the return of my mind, my faculties and my memories, I screamed full out and I was filled with a fighting rage like I'd never, ever experienced before. All I had were some grenades and my knife. Splattered with zombie remains and being pushed up against the alley wall by dozens of them, I just lost it and went hog fucking wild. Crying out, I ran at them with everything I had, bringing my strength and weight and sheer mental intensity to bear. I crashed through them, knocking them aside and underfoot, tripping over them, jumping and crawling and kicking until I was free from the mob. One of them clung to my back and I flipped him into the brick wall with such velocity I heard something crack inside of him. A blonde girl with maggots in her eye sockets seized my arm and I slashed her face to ribbons. A big biker dude still wearing his colors took hold of me and hoisted me into the air and I buried my knife in his throat, sawing frantically until his head dropped off to the side, hanging from a knob of bone. He dropped me and I shoved him right into a hungry mass of the dead.

Then, I pulled a thermite grenade and let it fly at them as I ran and dove for cover. There was a blinding flash behind me and a wave of heat that singed the hair on the back of my neck. Behind me was a firestorm of burning zombies. Some staggered forward like human torches only to drop from the blazing heat that burned like a welding arc. The flaming thermite not only engulfed them, but it was melting them right down to the bones beneath.

But there were more.

Many more.

Some were only singed. Some had holes burned through them. Some shambled from the conflagration with their hair on fire or flames licking up their clothes. And dozens and dozens more were fighting right through the flaming remains of their brothers and sisters to get at me.

That's when I heard the chopper.

It was coming in fast.

I saw it coming out of the sky like a hunting wasp.

Shit.

I ran towards the end of the alley, then sighted a missing wall and dove through the chasm seconds before the .50-cal on the Kiowa opened up and strafed the alley, slugs blowing chunks of concrete into the air, punching right through brick walls, and blowing zombies into fragments. The chopper passed and right away I heard it circling and coming in again. It would be rockets this time and I knew it.

Practically out of my mind with fear, feeling much as my enemies on the battlefield must have felt when I called a fire mission down on them, I crawled through the rubble of the building, over a broken wall, and slid down into a flooded cellar. As I hit the standing water, I heard the Hydra 70 rockets hit. *WHUMP! WHUMP! WHUMP-WHUMP-WHUMP!* The building I was in, or the broken shell of it, shook with each impact, bricks falling and dust raining down, scraps and fragments dropping into the water around me.

I knew there would be no more zombies out there.

I moved through the water in the gloom until I found the steps leading up and out. As I reached for them, I must have stepped in a hole and I went under into the black depths, fighting my way back to the surface of the chill water and brushing wet leaves from my face. I dog-paddled over to the stairs, breathing hard from exertion, fear, and the shock of the icy water.

Drenched, feeling like I weighed three-hundred pounds, I began to pull myself up the steps. I made it maybe four or five of them when I heard something come up out of the water behind me.

I turned in time to see an absolute monster coming for me.

It was a nightcrawler.

It had to be a nightcrawler, one that had mutated into some hulking thing with a face that reminded me of Ghostface from the *Scream* movies. But if Ghostface was in the middle ground between being scary and comical, this thing was completely in the former category. Like the movie villain, its face was unnaturally long and drawn out like it was made of putty, the eye sockets immense ellipses with bulging yellow eyes, the mouth a cavern of rodentlike teeth jutting from purple-black gums. As it breathed, water ran from its nostrils and trickled from the corners of its mouth.

It clawed out at me with a scaly hand and I kicked it, driving it back into the water.

I climbed up the steps and kept moving through the rubble until I was free of it, my heart hammering in my chest. I only had my knife and a few grenades as I squatted there next to a dumpster. I could see a few stray zombies.

Then something else.

I saw Doc, Mongol, and Mad Mike. I wasn't picking up any chatter from them so I assumed they had lost their Icoms or they weren't working anymore. I was looking out at them from a narrow aperture between two buildings. I crawled closer until I could get a good view of the street and see where they were going.

They started shooting.

I heard it before I saw it: Doc and Mongol with their M4s on full auto and Mad Mike's SAW blazing away, spent cartridges bouncing off the pavement. Then I could see what was going on. They were caught in the pincers between two zombie armies pushing in from either direction. And it only got worse because more zombies came out of the ruins of the buildings to either side of the street.

They were trapped.

It looked like a classic military encirclement, only, of course, it was purely accidental. Regardless, it was going to have the same ending and there wasn't a damn thing I could do about it. Even though I hated what Doc, Mongol, and Mad Mike were and what I had been, I knew it was not their fault anymore than it was mine. They were to be pitied, despite their savagery and genocidal tactics. They were nothing but pawns. Hell, I would have fought with them if I had anything to fight with.

The way things were, I could only watch them die.

They fought to the bitter end, let their tombstones record that, but they never had a chance. They threw grenades and blew away dozens of zombies, but the mob pressed in ever closer.

Doc went down first. A pack of them took hold of him and he screamed as they tore him apart and fed on him.

Mongol kept firing, dropping the dead very methodically, emptying magazine after magazine. There were so many maggot-eaters out there that they absorbed everything he threw at them. Their bodies piled up, but the others steamrolled right over the top of them in their maniacal lust to feed. By that point, of course, Mongol knew he was going to die so he planned on going out in a blaze of glory. He drew his machetes and brought the fight right to the zombies like some demented, kill-happy samurai. He slashed and hacked and cut. His moves were lethal and impressive as the dead dropped around him, but he was simply outnumbered by a hundred to one and he disappeared in the thrashing sea of the undead with a last cry of rage.

Mad Mike was the last man standing.

Even when he was out of shot for the SAW, he used it like a club, casting aside one zombie after the other. And when he lost that, he used his fists. That's something I'll always see, a testament to human ferocity and survivability—Mad Mike going under as a wave of them attacked him and still fighting, still knocking them aside and throwing them and lifting them up into the air with his powerful arms and smashing them down on their brethren.

It was amazing.

Simply amazing.

But, eventually, he was inundated and all was silent save for the sound of the wind skirting broken rooftops and the sound of the zombies eating, stuffing themselves in the streets. I had to get away or I'd be next. I looked down the street and there were none down there. I slipped from my hide, turned a corner, and tripped over a corpse in the street. He was a KIA member. The top of his head was blown off. I helped myself to his M4, ammo bag, and everything else I could lay my hands on.

Then I ran.

I had to put some distance between myself and the hordes of the dead, then maybe I could figure my bearings. I spent the next thirty minutes picking my way through the wreckage of Baneberry. By then, I was free of the Main Street sector and things began to look familiar. I realized I was in the same part of town we had originally entered from, Tuck and I and the others. It took some careful navigating but I finally found the brick house we had hid out in. It looked real quiet over there, but at least it was still standing. That was something.

I was hoping against hope my friends were still there.

I lowered my weapon and walked over there. I saw no signs of life. The door was open, not a good sign, and I went in, looking around. I went from room to room and found nothing. The game room we had camped out in was empty. I remembered that night when Sabelia, Jimmy, and I went out in search of Seppy, Scott, and Sandy. How long ago was that? I thought about Jimmy and had to choke back a tear because he had been such a good friend.

Then I thought about Zulu. I wondered about her. Who had she been before Cripps initiated her into his killing squad? How about Doc and Scales and Mongol? Who the hell were these people before?

That was something I'd never, ever know.

I left the house and sat on the steps. Autumn leaves were blowing up the street and I could feel the chill of winter coming. Just a suggestion of it, but I knew it was there.

I dug through the stuff I had taken from the dead KIA guy, who I realized now were just part of ARM in the first place. Some MREs, cigarettes, a half-eaten Snickers bar, a deck of cards, and a well-worn photograph of a woman standing beneath a tree in the summertime with her arm around a little boy in a baseball uniform. Jesus. He hung onto that, the last fragment of a life he no longer remembered thanks to Dr. Cripps. My guess was that it was a picture of him and his mother taken on some warm, wonderful green day in July when he was heading off to Little League. Cripps must never have known about the picture or he would have confiscated it. I could just imagine the poor guy with no memories, clutching the photo like some talisman, knowing it was important but not remembering why. Like I said, it was pretty worn and I bet he looked at it a lot.

I put it back in the bag.

I smoked one of his cigarettes and looked out into the empty street. No zombies, no insurgents or KIA killers to be found. There was nothing but the shattered corpse of an empty town blown by wind and memory.

I felt remarkably calm.

I knew who I was now and there was no longer the odd questions or headaches or sense of confusion. My original aim had been reestablished: I had to get to the Silo and see my son. But before I made the journey, I was going to find Sabelia and Tuck and the others if that was even possible.

I crushed out my cigarette, knowing I had to start somewhere.

It was time to go back to the bunker.

THE BUNKER

I waited at the perimeter of the razorwire entanglements.

I had to be careful now.

I had to remember where the landmines were. One false step...I had come too far and through too much shit to die that foolishly. I had thought for sure as I climbed over the crash barriers and concrete berms that somebody would take a shot at me, but it didn't happen. All was silent over at the firing ports of the bunker. A flock of blackbirds were picking in the grass over there. Other than that, there was no life.

When I was with KIA-9, we used to call over our Icoms that we were coming in, give the password, and enter without any fear of being gunned down. I knew there was no way in hell that I hadn't been seen coming in. If there was anyone behind the firing ports then I had been spotted long ago. I didn't have my Icom. I think I lost it in my plunge into the flooded cellar, so I was going to have to take my chances.

I knew the path through the razorwire.

It was like a maze.

I picked through it carefully, amongst the bird-picked corpses of zombies and sets of white gleaming bones that were tangled in the wire. When I was almost clear of it, I paused. I crouched down and watched the bunker. Cat and mouse. Was somebody drawing me in for a kill? But why? They had M107 sniper rifles with scopes. They could have easily popped me when I first climbed over the crash barriers or at any moment since.

I stepped free of the razorwire, waiting for the impact of the round that would toss me into eternal blackness.

None came.

The inner perimeter was mined. I had to think now. The mines were laid out in a very precise way and I had reverse that because I was facing it in the other direction. Okay. I think I had it. One step, two, then three. So far, so good. A few more careful steps as sweat boiled from my pores. Another fifteen feet and I was free.

Still no activity from the firing ports.

Curious.

I was still trying to see the barrels of rifles, but there was nothing. As if to show me how safe it was, a blackbird landed in one of the ports and waited there casually a moment or two before flying off. Either it was scared away by someone inside or it had other matters to attend to. It hadn't looked like it was spooked.

Fuck it.

I strolled right over to the nearest gun port. I brought up my rifle and poked it through the slot and capped off a few rounds. Nothing. No scrambling. No return fire. The ports were big enough to squeeze through with my equipment. I tossed my ammo bags in there and worked my way in. There was no one in there. When I stepped out into the corridor, the lights were off which meant the generator was probably down. I went from one firing port room to the next, but they were all empty.

What the hell was this all about?

Had the bunker been abandoned? It seemed unlikely, but there was no other reason the power would be out and the firing ports left unmanned. I took the stairway to the next level. This was where most everyone lived and worked and ate.

But there was no one.

Rooms were empty. There was no one in the kitchen or cafeteria, supply rooms or armory. The machine shops were empty as was the greenhouse. I checked every inch of it and there was not a soul to be found.

I went to the lower level.

Same and same.

No people. Where had they all gone? Had they evacuated? Had there been some exodus in my absence? What had Cripps done to them? I didn't know...at least until I reached the iron blast door that Pratt had told me led down to a subterranean passage that had once linked the bunker to Baneberry, but was now flooded.

The door was open a few inches.

I swung it open.

Lights.

There were lights on down there.

I went down the metal steps, moving as quietly as I could. When I reached the bottom, I saw a long corridor stretched out before me. Lots of the doors had biohazard symbols on them. But the most interesting thing was the video cameras. Everything was being monitored. There were little red lights on top of them and they were lit which made me think they were in operation.

I had no doubt I had just entered Dr. Cripps' playhouse.

Down here, somewhere, must have been the medical wards where I and the others were drugged-up and conditioned. I approached the first door, adrenaline rising in me. I was dearly hoping I would find Cripps behind it because I was going to kill him.

I opened the door and threw it in.

I was expecting zombies to rush out at me, teeth bared, but there was nothing there to greet me. It was black inside and I couldn't see a thing. I clicked on the tac light on my M4 and saw what looked like some kind of lab. There were tables with straps. They were gleaming and stainless steel and had drains set into them. I panned the light around and saw…wreckage. Drug cabinets had been tipped over, equipment smashed on the floor. It looked like a bomb had gone off in there.

I scanned the wall for a light, but I couldn't find one.

The room was pretty big and there were shadows everywhere that jumped and pranced as I moved my light around. Something was telling me I wasn't alone in there. I felt tense. The back of my neck was crawling with gooseflesh.

You're here and I know it, so why don't we quit playing games? If you want to kill me, then why don't you get to it already?

But there was no movement.

The heavy, breathing darkness was like a pall.

I stepped carefully forward, glass crunching under my boots. I moved around an IV stand and a table set with shattered glassware. I moved my light slowly from side to side, trying to find anything that didn't belong, trying to find a target to spend my anxiety on.

Something like a bottle crashed to the floor off to my left and I turned, firing three rounds which harmlessly drilled into the wall and knocked a digital clock from its bracket.

"I know you're here," I said. "So why don't you cut the shit already?"

I thought I heard a low, sibilant laughter.

I turned to the right and saw a low, slinking shadow slide along the wall. A form disappeared behind a tipped-over metal cabinet that was leaning against one of the tables.

I heard a sound right in front of me and brought my weapon around. I saw someone standing there and right away I recognized it as Pratt.

"What the hell's going on here?" I asked.

He just stared at me with blank, dark eyes set in red-rimmed sockets. He was grinning, drool running from his mouth. I knew right then he wasn't normal. He had been dosed with Agent 17...or maybe something even worse.

His mouth opened and closed, more saliva coming out along with something that looked like yellow foam. In my light, his eyes were shining glass balls, his face pale and set with shadows. Whatever he had been given, it had twisted his mind and turned him into some kind of raging beast far beyond anything KIA-9 had known.

I stepped back two, three, then four steps.

Pratt let me. He was watching me, giggling.

I heard movement behind me and turned quickly, just in time to see something like a shrieking demon with long black hair come jumping out of the shadows at me. It was a woman; I saw that much, but little more. Hair was plastered to her face with snot and blood, her teeth bared and stained pink as if she had been chewing on raw meat.

Her fingers were talons that reached for me.

Her mouth was hooked in a bestial snarl.

I pulled the trigger and put three rounds into her that knocked her back and away. She struck the wall, then slipped on something and went down, howling and throwing gouts of blood in the air.

I turned back around quickly and Pratt was reaching for me.

I busted a few more into him and then backed from the room. I slammed the door shut and waited out there for them to come for me, but they never did. I didn't know what Cripps had done to them. I only knew they were no longer human.

I had the worst feeling that by coming down here I had descended into the lower labyrinth of hell itself.

parNECROPHOBIA 4

LAB RATS

I tried two more doors and they were both locked, both set with security keypads and I wasn't about to waste time trying to blow them open.

I moved down the corridor and found another door.

It was open.

Inside, the lights were out, but it was lit by various security monitors set into the walls and a laptop with which to manipulate them. I closed the door behind me. It had a lock and I set it. This was some sort of security station. That wasn't surprising. When it was a CDC facility back in the good old days it must have been a high security installation.

There was a high-backed, leather chair and I sat in it.

The monitors showed various corridors. Some were lit, others were the green fields of night vision. There were six monitors and I watched them for a few minutes as I pulled on a cigarette. It looked like a real maze out there. It wasn't going to be easy finding my way around and, worse, it was going to be damn dangerous if I ran into anymore crazies like Pratt and the woman.

The laptop had a mouse and I moved it around until I got a feel for how it worked. The screen was fairly simple. It read:

A CORRIDOR
B CORRIDOR
C CORRIDOR
D CORRIDOR

I clicked on A and found it was the one I had entered through. I saw the corridor outside and it was empty. That was good. There was a submenu with hyperlinked settings that read BIOCHEM, PHARM, MICROSCOPY, ISOLATION. I checked out several of then and saw nothing of interest. BIOCHEM was the room Pratt and the woman had been in. In the green night vision, I saw nothing moving in there. The two locked rooms were more labs, untouched and sterile-looking. There was no one in them. I went to ISOLATION which led me to a sub-submenu for ISOLATION A and ISOLATION B.

195

There was movement in A.

Not crazies, but zombies. I saw five or six strapped to tables. They thrashed their heads back and forth and chattered their teeth, but they weren't going anywhere. I saw two that weren't strapped down and they were feeding on another that was.

I had to remember to steer clear of ISOLATION A.

The lights were off in ISOLATION B, but I could see more forms strapped to tables in the green field. I could see that they weren't zombies, but that's all I could see. The other rooms held nothing of interest save MICROSCOPY where the lights were on and I could see two corpses on the floor, a lot of blood around them.

ISOLATION B was my target.

I got back out into the corridor and moved slowly down it past a door marked ELECTRON MICROSCOPY and another marked PHARMACY. The corridor ended there. I went through a swinging door and found that the corridor split to the left and the right. A sign on the wall told me that B Corridor was to the left and Isolation was to the right. I went down there, giving the door to Isolation A a wide berth.

The silence of the place is what was really bothering me.

It got under my skin. It made me nervous. Regardless, I went over to the door marked ISOLATION B. It was locked. There was a key pad there and I blew it free with a few rounds. The door still remained locked. I pulled out a frag grenade, wedged it on the bracket that had held the keypad and pulled the pin, dashing down the corridor and hitting the floor. It went with a tremendous, rocketing explosion that echoed from one end of the labyrinth to the other, coming right back at me.

But it worked.

The door was blown open.

I waited for a few minutes, ready to kill anything or anyone that came to investigate, but no one or nothing did. I was alone. That feeling of being watched persisted, but I put it down to the cameras spying on me.

Sucking in a breath, I pushed the door open the rest of the way with the barrel of my M4. The tac light showed a row of switches on the wall and I flicked a few until the lights came on. I scanned with my weapon quickly, but saw no danger in there. Beds lined the walls like a hospital ward in an old Warner Brothers movie. Most of the beds were empty. The light was dim, but it was enough to see by. Some of the people I saw in the beds were ones that I had seen in the bunker when Pratt had given me the grand tour. One of them was Jeggs, one of the snipers from the firing rooms above.

He was alive.

His breathing was shallow, but he was alive.

"Jeggs," I said. *"Jeggs...can you hear me?"*

There was no response. He was hooked up to an IV and I didn't know if what was in there was giving him life or zombifying him. I took a chance and removed the IV needle from his arm. I found a Band-Aid and stuck it over the bleeding pinprick.

"Jeggs," I said. "Wake up."

After a minute or two, his eyes opened. He looked up at me, but his eyes were glazed and unfocused. It was like he was seeing me through two panes of glass. He tried to speak, but no words came out. He was really out of it and I imagined the others were, too. I left him strapped down just in case he might come to and act like Pratt, though I doubted it. There were eight more people in the room and I pulled their IVs and put Band-Aids on them. I spoke to each and everyone, giving a couple a few light slaps in the face to shock them out of it. They were all stirring by then.

It was a start.

Still, I wondered about all this. Had Cripps been creating another group of brain dead killers to fill out the ranks of the KIA teams? Or was it possibly something worse? Was he turning these people into nightcrawlers or berserkers as Pratt had called them? Dosing them slowly and continually with Agent 17 or fear gas until they were no longer human exactly?

Questions.

Too many damn questions.

I noticed there was a door at the other end of the room. It was off to the side, partially hidden by a drawn privacy curtain. I pulled the curtain aside and went to it. It was open. I clicked on the light and saw another ward. Three beds were occupied. The one nearest me was the one that drew my attention.

"Sabelia," I said under my breath.

I rushed over there. She was breathing, but her pulse was slow. I unhooked her from the IV. I shook her gently, saying her name again and again until her eyes flickered. Chances were, she might not even consciously recognize her name if she was drugged like I was, but apparently something in her did because a slight smile touched her mouth. I found that I couldn't swallow. I pursed my lips tight. There were tears that wanted to come but I could not let them. This was not the time to become an emotional wreck.

When she started slipping back into her fugue, I gently slapped her face until her eyes opened. She looked at me blankly. She looked confused. Probably from the drugs but also partially from the fact that even though she didn't recognize me, something told her that she should. I wished I had some of the adrenaline we had in the Army. It was pre-measured. You just injected it into somebody and, *bam,* they were wide awake. That stuff could have brought the dead back to life...a very unfunny exaggeration under the circumstances.

"Sabelia," I said. "It's me, it's Steve. Try and stay awake. Try and concentrate on my voice."

I kept blabbering on as she fought to keep her eyes open.

There was probably adrenaline in this place somewhere, but I wasn't about to use it even if I knew where it was. A pre-measured, pre-loaded syringe was one thing, but to fool around with unknown dosages was quite another.

I undid the straps that held her and made her sit up. There was a water cooler nearby and I got her some to drink and some more that I rubbed her face with. She didn't care for that. She groaned and moaned, but I knew she was nearing full consciousness.

"...then I went there," she said. "I told them...no more houses..."

She was making no sense, but that was okay. I knew she was slowly connecting to reality.

"Stay awake," I told her. "You have to fight it."

"...no more ribbons in the box," she said, her lower lip jutting out in a little girl pout.

I went to the others and unhooked their IVs, shook and slapped them awake and gave them each a sip of water. When I got back to Sabelia, her eyes were beginning to focus and she watched me distrustfully.

"You, everyone here, was doped up by Dr. Cripps," I said.

"He wouldn't do that," she said.

"Yes, he would."

She shook her head. "Thank God for him," she said.

I tried not to smile. I went into the other rooms and the people in there were coming around. I brought them water and undid their straps. None of them seemed to be dangerous. I helped them to sit up, telling them that they had been drugged, just not by who.

When I went back in the other room, Sabelia still eyed me warily. "Did we go to school together?" she asked.

I told her I didn't think so.

She stood up, swaying from side to side but holding her hand up, palm out, to keep me away when I tried to help. Her hospital johnnie was undone in the back and it slid from her shoulders, exposing her breasts. I saw the rose tattoo on one, the 182 on the other. She didn't seem to be aware that she was showing her charms for a moment, but when she did she covered herself and gave me a fierce look. "What are you looking at, perv?"

She turned away from me, cinching up her johnnie in the back, but giving the guy in the next bed a good view.

"Hey," he said. "Nice tits."

"Fuck you, man!" she said, the venom I knew so well rising in her. *"Chinga usted! Hijo de tu puta madre! Pinche idiota!"*

I thought that her Latin temper rising to the surface was a good thing. She went up one side of the guy in the bed and down the other, holding her johnnie closed as she shook a finger at him. When she was sure it was cinched properly, she flipped him off, telling him his mother was a whore in Spanish. I recognized that one. It was a common insult amongst Hispanics.

"Okay," I finally told her. "Just take it easy. No one will touch you."

She turned on me then, her eyes molten and black. *"No me jodas! Beso mi culo!"*

I didn't know what she was saying, but I'm sure it wasn't good.

She stormed past me, almost daring me to open my mouth. I knew better. She started searching around through closets until she found her clothes which she promptly took behind the security curtain, still bitching in Spanish and what I thought might be some Portuguese thrown into the mix. That didn't surprise me because she was born in Brazil and lived there until she was five or six years old.

"That's a hot tamale there," the guy on the bed said.

I smiled and unstrapped him and the other woman three beds down. After that, there was little to do but let them come out of it. There was no black coffee available so it was pretty much a waiting game. Sabelia was keeping her distance from everyone. She watched me with hating eyes.

About an hour later, I was still wondering what to do with them. Some of them were slow coming out of it, but most were okay by then. They were still bunker people, though. Some of them wanted to go to the kitchen and make coffee and eat and I figured that was probably the best idea...as long as the water up there wasn't treated with anything. I knew it was getting late in the day and it would be getting dark out soon. I wanted to get them out of there, but I had a feeling most wouldn't go, at least until their memories returned.

Sabelia came over to me. "Why do I think I know you?"

"Because you do. When the drugs wear off, you'll remember."

"Maybe you're just full of shit," she said.

"If I'm full of shit, how do I know about the One-Eight-Two Posse?"

"Because you saw it on my tit."

"Then how do I know it was a posse?"

She shrugged. "Ah, man, you probably heard of us. We don't take no shit."

"Give it some time. You'll remember."

"When I knew you before, were you a sonofabitch, too?"

"No, you liked me."

"You better hope so. I remember I didn't and maybe I stick a knife in you."

Yeah, she was coming around, but the Sabelia I was seeing was the tough-talking girl gangster she'd been as a teenager.

About thirty minutes later, the natives were getting pretty restless, so I suggested we go up and get food.

The guy who'd ogled Sabelia said, "There's others. They're in C."

"We better get them," I said.

One of the men opened the door and some of the people moved out into the corridor. Zombies were waiting for them. I heard them cry out as they were attacked. Some of them were too dopey to do anything but fold up, others fought, but it did them no good. The dead grabbed them and bit them.

"OUT OF THE WAY!" I cried out, elbowing my way to the door and shoving people aside. "LOOK OUT!"

I charged out there with my M4 and opened up on the dead and, unfortunately, their victims. I blasted heads open and shot down stragglers, victims caught in my volley of bullets. When I was done, there was blood and body parts all over the corridor.

"We're going to C now," I said and nobody argued with me.

KILLSHOT

They lined-up behind me, keeping their distance, all except Sabelia who stayed real close. I had the feeling that her respect for me had gone up after I wasted the zombies. Some of the others were still pissing about the fact that I'd killed *people* back there, too, but once you had been bitten, you were no longer a person in my book. Nothing could save you unless it was some completely bizarre and still poorly understood series of events that had give me supposed immunity.

Sabelia kept telling them to shut up in English and directed a series of pretty unflattering remarks at them in Spanish.

I could feel her behind me, I could feel her strength.

"Be careful," she said as we cut down B Corridor, following the signs to where it connected with C.

Towards the end of B, the dead were waiting.

They had been feeding on a couple of corpses and now they turned to face us. I heard a few of the bunker people call out that they knew them. It didn't matter. Maybe they'd known them before, but they didn't know them now. There were three deadheads and I pasted them without a second thought, spraying their brains against the walls.

Another zombie showed.

I heard a guy scream that it was his wife.

It was a woman and she carried a severed human arm in one hand that she'd been gnawing on like a chicken bone. She was pale and white-eyed, her mouth smeared with gore. As I brought up my weapon to put her out of her misery, the guy who'd screamed out knocked me aside and went over to the zombie woman.

"Get away from her!" I called out to him.

"Yeah, seu cazao!" Sabelia said.

But the guy, like many of the bunker people, just could not be certain whether I was to be trusted or despised at that point. He held up his hands so I would not shoot and said, "You just can't keep killing people! You can't go around acting like that!"

It had to be one of the most idiotic things I'd ever heard. It was like telling a doctor he couldn't go around exterminating disease germs with antibiotics.

"What do you want him to do?" Sabelia said. "Have a fucking tea party with that brain-eater?" She shook her head, looking at me. *"Fudeu caralho!"*

Meanwhile, of course, as our stalwart young hero tried to protect his wife, she took complete advantage of the situation, getting in close and taking hold of him. *"No, no, no, Carolyn, don't!"* he said, but she did and we all saw it. She sank her teeth right into his throat and yanked out a strip of meat while he screamed and blood ran down his shirt. He went down and Carolyn went down with him, tearing into him ravenously.

"STOP IT!" one of the bunker people cried. "SOMEBODY STOP IT!"

I shot Carolyn and then I shot her husband.

By then, nobody interfered and nobody said a word.

In about ten minutes, we made it to C Corridor. I was shown where the isolation wards were and we found a new batch of people. Among them were Diane and Robin, Ginny and Carrie. I was so glad to see them after so long. We brought them around and it was going to be some time before they came out of it, but the way I was seeing it, I was making great gains.

Still…where the hell was Tuck?

I handed my Beretta 9mm to Sabelia and said, "Keep them safe until I get back."

"And where do you think you're going?"

"I'm going to find a friend," I told her.

She locked the door behind me and out I went. I searched all the rooms in C Corridor, but there was no sign of Tuck. I found a few more crazies and I put them down. It seemed that's all I was anymore, just a man with a gun, a killer that seemed to know nothing else. I was starting to wonder just who I was in the first place.

But I had to keep my mind focused.

I didn't have time for shit like that.

I had to find Tuck. I had already lost Jimmy and the idea of losing another friend was unthinkable. I followed the signs to D

Corridor and searched over there, but I couldn't find him. When I got back, I went over it all with Sabelia and Jeggs. I told them everywhere I had looked and, as far as they knew, there was nowhere else.

Nowhere, save the locked rooms in A Corridor.

That's where I went next. The first of those rooms had a square pane of security glass set up at eye-level. Using the tac light of my M4, I shined it around in there, but I couldn't see much. There had to be a better way to target my search. I went over to the security station and keyed up the monitors. The room I had been looking in was apparently something of a file room. It no doubt held highly classified stuff that these days was absolutely worthless. The next room, I saw on the monitor, was another ward of sorts.

I sat there, smoking, thinking, just staring at the green night vision field, clicking on the mouse and panning the camera back and forth. After about ten minutes of that, I was certain I'd seen something move in there.

I went over there and blew the keypad off the door and inserted a grenade in its place as I had before. Again, it did the trick. After the smoke cleared and my nerves stopped jangling, I moved towards the door, absolutely terrified of what I might find in there.

Go back, go back, a voice kept telling me and, God knows, I wanted to obey. *Get out of here before you see something you might never forget.*

My gut feeling was that Tuck was dead.

I might as well admit that flat out. Knowing who he was and what he was, he would have been the perfect candidate for one of the KIA teams. It was very possible he had died in combat. Maybe, down deep, part of me was hoping for that. I wanted him to die with honor, with glory. I wanted him to go down with blood in his mouth and smoking pistols in his hands like some old time desperado. He deserved that.

Drawing in a slow breath, I went in the room carefully, feeling around for a light switch and finding nothing. There were switches somewhere, but I didn't have time to search for them. Once again, I brought up my M4 and clicked on my tac light. Yes, it was sort of a ward like the others, but it was more of a research room with steel tables and lab stations, computers and electronic equipment of the sort I had never seen before. There were cabinets of drugs and corpses strapped down on tables.

Some of them were moving.

As I put my light on them, they craned their heads in my direction, their jaws opening and closing.

But I wasn't interested in them.

They weren't going anywhere.

The figure at the end of the room was another case entirely. It was hunched over one of the tables, tearing at what was there, chewing and slurping.

I waved flies away, swallowing, ignoring the putrid stink that was like a charnel mist in the air.

The shadowy figure was unconcerned with me.

It was feeding and that was all it cared about. It was a man, a large man. He was naked, bent somewhat at the waist, his flesh shiny and yellow-tinged. I could see purple patches of lividity where his blood had settled after death. His head was bald and he was making a snorting, guttural sort of sound like a wild boar or a hog tearing into its slop.

Oh Jesus, I thought, *not like this, please...not like this...*

I had watched Jimmy die infected with Necrophage. I didn't need to see another friend done in by it, reduced to some primeval horror that crawled through the slime of graves.

I moved closer and closer, the living dead on the tables getting very excited at my proximity. I was breathing hard. My hands were shaking on the M4. I thought of Ricki, my dead wife, and hoped she was not out there, turned into something like this.

When I was twenty feet away, daring not to get any closer, the hulking shape turned towards me. It turned with a stiff, shuffling sort of gait. In the glaring illumination of my tac light, it looked degenerate and subhuman, a grinning simian nightmare. Its head cocked, it showed me its loose yellow visage, the lips chewed away from blackened gums, the seams of mold like branching lightning up its cheeks and chin, the juicy white eyes that reminded me of the swollen backs of grubs pushing from garden soil.

"Oh shit," I said. *"Oh, Jesus H. Christ..."*

It was Tuck.

I knew somehow that it must be, but the realization was like every ounce of blood had been drained from me. My head with was filled with a noise like static. I felt tears run from my eyes. My lips quivered. I tried to contain the whimpering in my throat.

All I could think was that Dr. Cripps had done this to him. Maybe I wanted to believe that because he was Dr. Frankenstein in my book, the architect of nightmares and pain. There was always the possibility that Tuck just picked up the bug like so many others...but I just couldn't accept that.

Tuck, I believed, had been purposely infected.

Infected and turned loose where we would find him sooner later.

Cripps, you motherfucker.

He was gone from the bunker, but I would see him again. I knew it. And when that happened I would make his death an ugly business.

Tuck came for me, reaching out gnarled hands.

I brought up the M4.

I heard a broken sobbing coming from my own throat.

I thought of how he had kept us all alive. How our survival was his absolute obsession and everything else was secondary to it. He was like a father and a brother to me. I'd never be on the receiving end of his intolerant, salty humor or hear him play his fiddle again. And, worst of all, I'd never feel his strong, sure hand on my shoulder guiding me ever forward in times of trouble.

"Oh, Sixty-Five," I sobbed. "Please forgive me."

The M4 shook in my hands as I aimed it at his head. He made a growling sound as if something from the tortured core of his being was telling me to do the right thing, to get it over with already, to put him out of his misery if I was truly the friend I claimed to be.

When he was five feet away I squeezed the trigger and ended it for him. I heard him hit the floor and I turned away, shutting the door behind me. I made it about ten feet down the corridor and I folded right up. I went to my knees, my face wet with tears. I clutched my rifle and held tightly to it for dear strength.

"You be good to him, God," I said under my breath, "or you'll fucking answer to me."

I leaned against the wall for a long time. I smoked and I remembered, I cried and I laughed and finally, I accepted. And as I did so, everything within and without became gray and meaningless. I didn't think I'd ever be the same again.

After a time, I heard footsteps and I saw Sabelia standing there with my Beretta. "We were worried," she said. "Are you all right?"

"No, I'm very far from being all right."

She blinked a couple times and I could see she was close to becoming herself again. She kneeled down by me. "Did you find your friend?"

"Yes. I found him. Then I killed him."

She understood without me saying anymore. "I'm sorry," she said.

"Me, too."

COMING DOWN

It was another twenty-four hours or so until everyone came to their senses and when they did, they started pelting me and each other with questions. I had very few answers. The hardest part was when Sabelia and then Diane came out of their drug fugue, followed by Robin, Ginny, and Carrie. Each time it was pretty much the same. They were happy to see me, then confused and angry and disoriented when I told them exactly what had happened...or what I guessed had happened. Eventually, they all wanted to know where Tuck was and I had to tell them.

I had questions, too.

Lots of them.

Diane said that Tuck refused to pull out of Baneberry until he knew whether I was alive or dead. Eventually, Pratt made contact with them. He seemed very friendly, very helpful. Tuck didn't trust him, of course, and that made me smile slightly. They went back to the bunker with him and, after that, things got blurry. Their food was no doubt drugged like everyone else's. It stood to reason. What had come of Tuck after that, only the dead and Dr. Cripps knew. And, some day, when I found him, he was going to tell me before I killed him.

Here's what it comes down to.

The bunker and everyone there were part of a feasibility study, an experimental drug trial. That's what it was all about. Yes, I blamed Cripps for it all, but I also blamed myself. If I hadn't gone out in search of Sandy that night, then none of this would have happened and Tuck would still be alive.

Was I playing hero that night?

Partly, I suppose. And in war—and we were definitely at war—there's very little difference between a fool and a hero.

Most of the bunker people wanted to stay where they were because everything they needed to survive was there. After Sabelia and the others had a good rest, we packed up what we could and got ready for our trip to the Silo. I was going to get there this time.

That was my first and primary responsibility. My second would come later when I tracked down Dr. Cripps.

But for now, getting to the Silo was enough.

When everyone was ready to go, Sabelia found me outside the door of Tuck's tomb, smoking and brooding.

"They're ready, Steve." She put an arm around me and kissed my cheek. Her lips were very warm. "Are you?"

I nodded, holding her hand and walking away from the door. "Yeah, let's get the fuck out of here."

THE END

www.ingramcontent.com/pod-product-compliance
Lightning Source LLC
Chambersburg PA
CBHW060436180626
46817CB00007B/2843